Magical Realism and the Postcolonial Novel

Magical Realism and the Postcolonial Novel

Between Faith and Irreverence

Christopher Warnes

First published 2009 by
PALGRAVE MACMILLAN

Palgrave Macmillan in the UK is an imprint of Macmillan Publishers Limited, registered in England, company number 785998, of Houndmills, Basingstoke, Hampshire RG21 6XS.

Palgrave Macmillan in the US is a division of St Martin's Press LLC, 175 Fifth Avenue, New York, NY 10010.

Palgrave Macmillan is the global academic imprint of the above companies and has companies and representatives throughout the world.

Palgrave® and Macmillan® are registered trademarks in the United States, the United Kingdom, Europe and other countries.

ISBN-13: 978–0–230–54528–1 hardback
ISBN-10: 0–230–54528–9 hardback

This book is printed on paper suitable for recycling and made from fully managed and sustained forest sources. Logging, pulping and manufacturing processes are expected to conform to the environmental regulations of the country of origin.

A catalogue record for this book is available from the British Library.

A catalog record for this book is available from the Library of Congress.

10 9 8 7 6 5 4 3 2 1
18 17 16 15 14 13 12 11 10 09

Printed and bound in Great Britain by
CPI Antony Rowe, Chippenham and Eastbourne

Contents

Preface

The term magical realism is an oxymoron, an appropriate condition given that it designates a narrative strategy that stretches or ruptures altogether the boundaries of reality. By contrast, literary criticism, in its institutional forms, is tasked with rational interpretation, explanation and clarification. The language of magical realist fiction and the language of traditional criticism part company over the former's decision to take seriously the claims of unreason. This makes magical realism an intriguing, exasperating, sometimes terrifying topic about which to write a work of serious literary analysis.

Fortunately, I have had a great deal of help from family, teachers, colleagues, friends and students on the road to getting this book, finally, to the point at which I have resolved to leave it alone. Without the support and encouragement of my parents this book would never have materialised. Many years ago Jill Arnott, David Attwell, Barbara Harlow, Don Beale, Anton van der Hoven, Bill Bizley and Liz Gunner put me in touch with ideas and contexts which surface from time to time in this study. Ato Quayson and Tim Cribb supervised my first steps with grace and good humour. Benjamin Cornford made me aware of how fitting a place Cambridge is for the study of magical realism. Kevin Durheim, Georgina Evans, Gudrun Freese, Jana Giles, Priya Gopal, Lucy Graham, Christian Holler, Doug McCabe, Elizabeth Vlossak, and Astrid Swenson provided friendship, advice, proofreading, conversation, and translation assistance. Colleagues in Stellenbosch, in Cambridge and in the Postcolonial Studies Association offered encouragement and helpful feedback. For financial support, I am grateful to the Cambridge Trusts and to St John's College. In the course of writing this book I spent several happy months in Spain and Cuba and I am grateful to the friends and teachers there who generously and enthusiastically discussed these texts with me. Several anonymous reviewers made suggestions that proved extremely useful. I also owe a huge debt of gratitude to the students from three continents on whom, at various points, I have tested many of the ideas in this book.

Translations in this book are taken where possible from published sources. For their commitment to making these texts available to a wider audience I am grateful to, among others, Donald A. Yates and James E. Irby (Borges), Harriet de Onís, Tanya Huntington and Lois Parkinson Zamora (Carpentier), Gerald Martin (Asturias) and Gregory Rabassa (García Márquez). Where no published translations exist, or where modification was required, I have provided my own translations.

Parts of what follows have appeared in print in different forms as: "Magical Realism and the Legacy of German Idealism." *Modern Language Review* 101.2 (2006): 488–98; "Avatars of Amadis: Magical Realism as Postcolonial Romance," *Journal of Commonwealth Literature* 40.3 (2005): 7–20; "Naturalizing the Supernatural: Faith, Irreverence and Magical Realism." *Literature Compass* 2.1 (2005): 1–16; "The Hermeneutics of Vagueness: Magical Realism in Current Literary Critical Discourse" *Journal of Postcolonial Writing* 41.1 (2005): 1–13. I am grateful to these journals for permission to reprint.

1
Introduction: Re-thinking Magical Realism

The term magical realism has appeared in print with increasing frequency over the last few decades. It can be found in a vast number of university course descriptions, dissertations, academic articles, in the popular press, and it is now familiar to millions through the appearance on Oprah Winfrey's Book Club of Gabriel García Márquez's *One Hundred Years of Solitude*. Even the advertising industry has begun to take an interest in the term, though it long ago learned how to capitalise on magical realist visual techniques in its quest for ever more novel ways of marketing products.[1] But in the domain of literary studies this popularity has, until recently, not been matched by any certainty over what magical realism actually is and what it does.

Scholars new to the field are thus likely to be confronted by a number of contradictory attitudes. Thus, we find Homi Bhabha referring to magical realism as "the literary language of the emergent postcolonial world" (*Nation* 6), while for Jean Franco it is "little more than a brand name for exoticism" (204). According to Matei Calinescu, it can be "a major, perhaps *the* major, component of postmodernist fiction" (Zamora and Faris, dustcover). But Fredric Jameson sees it as "a possible alternative to the narrative logic of contemporary postmodernism" ("Film" 302). Magical realism has by turns been praised for founding "a new multicultural artistic reality" (Durix 162) and it has been denigrated as "dangerous and shallow" (Barker 14). It has even been accused of being underpinned by "pernicious – even racist – ideologies" (Martin "Magical" 104). At the heart of the critical uncertainty about magical realism are the meanings that the term is assumed to signify: ideas clustered around notions of narrative and representation, culture, history, identity, what is natural and what is supernatural. There are, in the final analysis, very few realms of modern thought not undergirded by assumptions about the nature of what is real and what is not, and it is to these very assumptions that serious magical realist literature claims to speak. With such an enormous scope of reference, it is not difficult to understand why disagreement and confusion proliferate.

A fundamental question concerns the type of category that is constituted by magical realism. Is magical realism simply a mode of narration that may be sporadically engaged by an author; is it a literary movement with a specific agenda and defined geographical and cultural boundaries; or is it a genre of fiction that can be compared across continents and languages? Before these questions can be addressed, we must acknowledge that magical realism's problems are rooted yet more deeply in the fact that both magical and realism are terms fraught with a complex history of contradictory usage.[2] And, of course, central to critical discourse's problems with magical realism is that the term is an oxymoron: magic is thought of as that which lies outside of the realm of the real; realism excludes the magical. Magical realism, in its very name, flouts philosophical conventions of non-contradiction. How should one begin to pick a path through such cluttered terrain?

Some critics have suggested that we ought to do away with the term altogether (González Echevarría *Carpentier* 108; Connell 95–110). The problem with such a suggestion, even if it were possible to implement, is that it ignores the fact that the tenacity of the term is due in large measure to its explanatory value. There is a growing corpus of literary works that draws upon the conventions of both realism and fantasy or folktale, yet does so in such a way that neither of these two realms is able to assert a greater claim to truth than the other. This capacity to resolve the tension between two discursive systems usually thought of as mutually exclusive must constitute the starting point for any inquiry into magical realism. A brief survey of canonical magical realist texts – Gabriel García Márquez's *One Hundred Years of Solitude*, Isabel Allende's *The House of the Spirits*, Laura Esquivel's *Like Water for Chocolate*, Salman Rushdie's *Midnight's Children* and *The Satanic Verses*, Toni Morrison's *Beloved*, Angela Carter's *Nights at the Circus*, and Ben Okri's *The Famished Road*, among others – will reveal that what these otherwise different texts all have in common is that each treats the supernatural as if it were a perfectly acceptable and understandable aspect of everyday life. As Rushdie says, talking of García Márquez, "impossible things happen constantly and quite plausibly, out in the open under the midday sun" ("García Márquez" 301–302). A basic definition of magical realism, then, sees it as a mode of narration that naturalises or normalises the supernatural;[3] that is to say, a mode in which real and fantastic, natural and supernatural, are coherently represented in a state of equivalence. On the level of the text neither has a greater claim to truth or referentiality.

Notwithstanding the confusion that the oxymoronic nature of the term continues to attract in some circles, the literary boundaries of magical realism are in fact clearly delimited, and have been for some time. As Erik Camayd-Freixas points out, Todorov's identification in the 1970s of the structure of the fantastic provided the impetus for formal definitions of magical realism to be developed. The most important of these early structural approaches, Irlemar Chiampi's 1980 book, *O Realismo Maravilhoso: Forma e Ideologia no Romance Hispano-Americano* (a Spanish translation appeared in 1983), was, ironically, an attempt to supplant the term magical realism with the Carpentier-derived term marvellous realism. Nevertheless, Chiampi's approach made it possible for her to describe in detail the operations of a literary mode in which natural and supernatural were presented in a non-disjunctive manner, facilitating "the denaturalisation of the real and the naturalisation of the marvellous" (205). In 1985 Amaryll Chanady continued in the structuralist vein. Her book, *Magical Realism and the Fantastic: Resolved Versus Unresolved Antinomy* identifies a three-part taxonomy of magical realism: the text must display coherently developed codes of the natural and supernatural, the antinomy between these codes must be resolved, and a measure of authorial reticence must facilitate the co-existence and legitimacy of both codes (3–6).

As her title suggests, Chanady is concerned with distinguishing magical realism from fantastic literature, and in this regard her theory is useful both in understanding the formal dimensions of the mode and in distinguishing magical realism from its neighbouring genres. One can show, for example, how fantasy, fairy-tales and science fiction de-privilege codes of the real by taking as settings realms removed from our recognisable, empirical world. Or one might show how the Gothic novel, the uncanny and some examples of horror make coherent use of codes of the natural and of the supernatural, yet present them in such a way that their co-existence is rendered a source of unease or anxiety – thus leaving the antinomy unresolved. Finally, with regard to Chanady's third criterion, it needs to be emphasised that if the supernatural is in any way explicable – such as when Lewis Carroll's Alice awakes to find that her adventures were all a dream, or when the fantastic bats swooping down on one of Hunter S. Thompson's characters are revealed to be the result of drug-induced hallucination – then the code of the real is effectively privileged over that of the fantastic, and magical realism is therefore not the best category within which to consider the text.

The landmark publication in English-language critical discourse on magical realism is Lois Parkinson Zamora and Wendy B. Faris's 1995 anthology, *Magical Realism: Theory, History, Community*. The volume treats magical realism for the first time as an international phenomenon, bringing together literary contexts as diverse as Europe, Asia, North and South America, the Caribbean, Africa and Australia. One of the main strengths of the anthology is that it presents alongside one another founding texts of magical realist discourse by Roh, Carpentier, Flores and Leal. A useful history of the term – straddling literary and art historical contexts – is provided by Irene Guenther, and Chanady contextualises the Latin American debate helpfully by interpreting it as a "territorialisation of the imaginary." Also noteworthy is Faris's attempt at constructing a coherent set of generic defining features for the mode, an effort she has renewed and extended in her 2004 monograph.

The Zamora and Faris anthology suffers, however, from an inability to sustain consistency of definition across the range of essays. A similar charge must be levelled at the two critical anthologies that have followed it, edited by Linguanti, Casotti and Concilio (1999) and by Hart and Ouyang (2005), respectively. The result is often a vague and arbitrary approach which allows vastly different texts to be grouped under the same rubric with no measure of caution as to the distorting consequences this generates.[4] Second, essays in edited volumes are seldom able to pursue in any great detail comparative approaches based on close and contextualised readings of magical realist texts. Monographs are better positioned to do this, and indeed recent works of criticism by Erik Camayd-Freixas (1998), Brenda Cooper (1998), Shannin Schroeder (2004), Maggie Ann Bowers

(2004) Wendy B. Faris (2004) and Anne C. Hegerfeldt (2005), could be said to be in broad agreement about the crucial issue of definition. Vastly different though they are in their choices of materials, methodologies and in the conclusions they reach, on the question of definition none of these critics could be said to diverge substantially from Chanady's 1985 account of the key attributes of magical realism.

In Camayd-Freixas's account, magical realism is understood to be a sophisticated aesthetic expression of primitivism that served the yearnings of Latin American writers for identity and cultural emancipation. The magical realism of Carpentier, Asturias, Rulfo and García Márquez is shown to develop from an urge to reclaim a space of otherness by appealing to myths of difference (49). Importantly, Camayd-Freixas's approach differs from that of the early formalists in that he treats magical realism as a historical style deriving from an "'ethnological version' based on the presence of myth, legend, the syncretism of Indian, black and peasant from the most isolated and remote regions of the Americas" (320). His attempts to ground the mode in the literary and cultural contexts from which it emerges, while productive in terms of the texts he studies, does not, however, attempt to account for the ways magical realism has become an international phenomenon, nor how his ethnological version would apply to non-Latin American texts.

Faris adopts exactly the global perspective lacking in Camayd-Freixas's account, asserting that magical realism is "perhaps the most important contemporary trend in international fiction" (1). She is at pains to define her understanding of magical realism in the clearest fashion possible. Thus, for her magical realism is a mode of narration primarily characterised by five features.

First, the text contains an "irreducible element" of magic; second, the descriptions in magical realism detail a strong presence of the phenomenal world; third, the reader may experience some unsettling doubts in the effort to reconcile two contradictory understandings of events; fourth, the narrative merges different realms; and, finally, magical realism disturbs received ideas about time, space and identity. (7). Of these five elements, I would argue that only the first two are crucial, but the point is that Faris's approach shows a full appreciation of the necessity of starting with a clear and unambiguous definition of magical realism.

The books by Camayd-Freixas and Faris represent two different critical approaches to magical realism. The former is anthropological (in the broad sense of the term) and seeks to interpret the magic in magical realism culturally, as an expression of particular belief systems or ways of seeing the world. The latter perspective sees magical realism as akin to a form of epistemological scepticism, a productive fictional mode of critique. The two books differ in scope, too, with the former confining itself to the study of just four writers, while the latter incorporates a dizzying range of texts from around the world. The consequences are predictable: Camayd-Freixas has been criticised as having too restrictive an approach (Shaw 578). Faris is to be faulted for showing too little interest in the specific cultural contexts from which her texts emerge, and for being content to assign a single paragraph, or in some cases even less, to the discussion of individual works of magical realism.

I have attempted, in this book, to incorporate Camayd-Freixas's depth of analysis with Faris's international range by treating magical realism as a global phenomenon, while at the same time respecting the local currents – cultural, literary, political, historical – that always run through any fictional text. I have preferred to run the risk of being criticised for adopting too limited an approach to definition and text selection than the opposite. Generalising accounts abound describing the ways magical realism represents the "writing back" of the margins to the centre, how it blurs the binaries of modern thought, how it critiques the assumptions of the Enlightenment, how it shows up the limitations of European rationalism, how it reveals the ethical failings of realism. Neil Lazarus has pointed to the ways that the "politics of postcolonial modernism" have constrained current approaches in postcolonial literary studies, and I believe that many of his criticisms are applicable to the study of magical realism. Lazarus argues that "the tendentiousness and partiality of the theoretical assumptions that have structured postcolonial studies hitherto" have resulted in a "leadenly reductive" approach to the few texts that are read. "To read across postcolonial literary studies," he asserts, "is to find, to an extraordinary degree, the same questions asked, the same methods, techniques, and conventions used, the same concepts mobilized, the same conclusions drawn" (424). For too long a similar case has prevailed in the study of magical realism, with the term being simply a drudge for a postmodernist postcolonialism obsessed with hybridity, liminality, and what Peter Hallward calls "the facile denunciation of binaries" (xv). By limiting the range of texts to be discussed I am attempting to provide the space for specific texts to be considered in the detail required to shift thinking about magical realism from programmatic responses to more nuanced conceptions of the origins, nature, and functions of the mode.

While Lazarus singles out several of the authors studied in this book as being part of the "woefully restricted and attenuated corpus of works" dominant in postcolonial studies, he also concedes that the problem lies not so much in the fact that these authors are so much read, as in the ways in which they are read. To various degrees the opportunism, narrowness and inappropriateness decried by Lazarus can be seen in much of the criticism on magical realism: the endlessly repeated potted histories of the term; the vague and inde-terminate ways questions of definition have been treated; the assumption that there is a single kind of magical realism – usually that of García Márquez or Rushdie; the distorting comparisons that result from this normative approach; the ways magical realism is so often automatically seen to deconstruct notions of subjectivity, history, nationhood, reality, without any sense of how it can also construct these notions; a general inability to relate magical realism to its specific cultural contexts. It is only by returning to the key novels of magical realism, and by affording them the time and atten-tion they require, that a theory of magical realism can progress beyond these critical dead ends. Importantly, this theory needs to emerge from the novels rather than imposing itself on them.

The kind of formalism I am recommending, which requires lucid and consistent definition and a close attention to the semantics of structure, faces immediate epistemological and political objections. First, the definition of magical realism being used here makes possible a focus on the interplay between certain key concepts while avoiding the very significant question of what cultural reference points and assumptions are being invoked. In other words, this definition dodges the fact that the signifiers, *natural* and *supernatural*, *real* and *fantastic*, depend for their meanings on a stable point of comparison – a shared notion of reality – that is undermined by the relativising effects of magical realism. This crucial issue, discussed below, demands careful contextualisation in terms of questions about culture, relativism and referentiality. Second, close attention to questions of form and structure is to be conceived of as an antidote to inappropriate generalisation, not as a substitute for engagement with the cultural, political and historical fields with which any novel is inevitably in dialogue. The challenge is, as always, to reconcile these two levels throughout the analysis.

In its concern with a dialectic between natural and supernatural, literary criticism overlaps with the disciplines of anthropology, religious studies and sociology. In particular, the revisions made to anthropology over the past half a century allow us to rescue the term magic from its relegation to the domain of the illusionary, the primitive and the childish. Ever since the armchair intellectualism of Victorians like Spencer, Tylor and Frazer yielded to phenomenological and participant-based approaches, anthropology has had to confront its use of rationalist approaches to understand the beliefs and actions of others. A very important consequence of this confrontation has been the development of models of understanding based on a contrast between two different modes of thought and being, one "sacred," the other "profane," to use the terms introduced by Durkheim and developed by Eliade. It is possible to trace this distinction, or related versions of it, in the work of a great number of thinkers, from the structuralist-functionalism of Radcliffe-Brown and Evans-Pritchard to the more symbolic approaches of Lévy-Bruhl, Mary Douglas, Clifford Geertz and others.[5] This distinction is one of the most dominant preoccupations of anthropology and religious studies and provides a significant – and as yet largely unexplored – point of intersection with magical realism's treatment of the relationships between natural and supernatural.

A useful anthropological intertext for the study of magical realism is Stanley Tambiah's *Magic, Science, Religion and the Scope of Rationality.* Tambiah returns, rather unfashionably, to the work of Lucien Lévy-Bruhl in order to develop the notion of "world view" as an indicator of a collective, cultural, pattern of thought and outlook, and in order to account for cultural differences in the perceptions of reality. Collective patterns of thought, indicated by other concepts like "mentality" or "ordering of reality," are ways of demarcating the scope and limits of knowledge construction at different times and within different societies and depend on a very different model of understanding from that utilised by the Victorian intellectualists, still common in some quarters today. Spencer, Tylor and Frazer developed an approach that was predominantly psychological, and which tended towards a unifying theory of culture that did not have to accommodate difficult questions about difference. Magic, religion and science were all considered to be rational attempts to make sense of the world, and were therefore arranged according to their efficacy. When the Victorians related magic, religion and science to their cultural contexts, they came up with an evolutionary sequence that took the shape of a single line from barbarism to civilisation. Tambiah returns to Lévy-Bruhl because of his early attempts to contest such social evolutionism. For all their faults, Lévy-Bruhl's theories offer a pluralist attempt to account for belief and action, paving the way for later theorists to grapple with the dynamics of cultural difference – dynamics which also often underlie the practice of magical realist writing.

Contemplating examples like that of the Bororo of the Amazon, whose claims to be parakeets he refused to see as metaphorical, but as expressions of belief in an inexplicable union, Lévy-Bruhl proposed the possibility of a "mystic" mentality, quite different from modern causal logic. For Lévy-Bruhl, mystic "implies a belief in forces and influences and actions which, though imperceptible to sense, are nevertheless real" (38). This belief is pervasive, and implies that there is no distinction between natural and supernatural: "The primitive's mentality does not recognise two distinct worlds in contact with one another and more or less penetrating. To him there is but one" (68). The organisation of this type of thought was determined by what Lévy-Bruhl called the "law of participation," the characteristic quality of which was spatial and temporal fusion. "Logical mentality," by contrast, is characterised by a law of causality that seeks to identify and eliminate contradictions, and is conceptual, empirical and scientifically rational in nature.

In response to criticisms from colleagues, and especially from Evans-Pritchard, Lévy-Bruhl modified his ideas in ways that move them away from a simple dichotomy. Evans-Pritchard pointed out that it was a mistake to describe "primitive" culture only in terms of its mystical qualities, or Western cultures as exclusively scientific and rational, since both mentalities could be identified in each culture, and to different levels of complexity (Tambiah 92). Lévy-Bruhl came to conceive of these two mentalities as co-existing, rather than in a relationship of succession, and he named them "participation" and "causality."

Tambiah shows how Lévy-Bruhl's ideas about participation have been useful to anthropologists like Maurice Leenhardt, who formulated ideas about "mythic landscape" and "sacred geography" to understand Melanesian village life (87, 106–108). But Tambiah also takes Lévy-Bruhl's ideas about the co-existence of mentalities, which he prefers to call "orientations to reality" or "orderings of reality," outside of the domain of anthropology by comparing them with Freud's primary and secondary thought processes, and by relating them to common threads in aesthetic theory, phenomenology, feminism, contemporary psychoanalysis and Nelson Goodman's theories of "worldmaking" (93–105). Importantly, Tambiah, following Lévy-Bruhl, refuses to dichotomise: causality and participation become, in his account, expressions of "two modes of ordering the world that are simultaneously available to human beings as complementary cognitive and affective interests" (108). Some of the concepts and characteristics that Tambiah attaches to causality are:

> Ego against the world. Egocentricity. Atomistic individualism. The language of distancing and neutrality of action and reaction. The paradigm of evolution in space and time. Instrumental action that changes matter and the causal efficacy of technical acts. The successive fragmentation of phenomena, and their atomization, in the construction of scientific knowledge.

Participation, in contrast, is characterised by:

> Ego/person with the world, a product of the world. Sociocentrism. The language of solidarity, unity, holism and continuity in space and time. Expressive action that is manifest through conventional intersubjective understandings, the telling of myths and the enactment of rituals. The performative efficacy of communicative acts. Pattern recognition, and the totalisation of phenomena. The sense of encompassing cosmic oneness. (109)

Participation and causality, then, are "contrasting and complementary and coexisting orientations to the world, perhaps best illustrated by complexes labelled 'religion' and 'science'" (110). These labels are used for convenience, rather than precision, and "religion" here can be assumed to include "magic" in its ambit.[6] What is notable about

Tambiah's account is that, drawing on a history of attempts to grapple with the dynamics of difference, he is able to utilise a language of analysis and explanation without resorting to or explicitly rejecting the "either/or" dichotomies that have been such a thorn in the side of literary criticism's attempts to get to grips with magical realism. Considering magical realism in terms of the connections between form and underlying cultural dynamics, then, one way of understanding magical realism would be to see what Chanady calls codes of the natural and of the supernatural as being parts of discursive chains that are bi-directionally linked to collective world views where either participation or causality is dominant.

This proposition is complicated by several factors. First, magical realist novels are deliberate, carefully contrived and manipulated works of art rather than unmediated conduits of cultural values and perspectives. A level of hermeneutic flexibility is required to appreciate the fluid relationships between the aesthetic, the narratological and the cultural in such texts. Second, the specific generic and formal qualities that these works draw on – the novel and realism – are far more heavily indebted to what Tambiah calls causality than they are to participation. As the next chapter will show with reference to *Don Quixote*, the break between realism and romance, or between modernity and tradition is one predicated on an epistemological rupture in which inherited or sacred conceptions of the world are forced into the margins by a notion of reality which is sceptical in its attitude to received knowledge, and empirical in its approach to developing new versions of reality. Modernity, at least in the influential Weberian narrative, could be said to be defined by the triumph of causality over participation. Because it utilises realism, even as it strives to extend or subvert it, and because its preferred mode of expression is the novel, magical realism, however much it may try to make the situation appear different, finds itself always already answering to the terms of causality.

This book proposes that magical realism organises its response to causality in two ways. First, as I shall argue in my readings of Asturias, Okri and, in a more qualified way, the early Carpentier, magical realism may represent an attempt to supplement, extend or overwhelm causality with the terms of participation. The causal paradigm is seen as flawed because it has been too limited by preconceptions and prejudices born of the circumstances of its development from the early modern period. For these postcolonial writers, it is tainted by its association with colonialism and neo-colonialism. As a postcolonial response to colonialism's often brutal enforcing of a selectively-conceived modernity, magical realism of this kind seeks to reclaim what has been lost: knowledge, values, traditions, ways of seeing, beliefs. In this model, the horizons of the causal paradigm are extended to include events and possibilities that would ordinarily be circumscribed.

From within the causal paradigm, such attempts are resisted on rational-empirical grounds, giving rise to an impasse in which the language of causality forecloses on the legitimacy that is being sought. The apparent solution, as will become clear in the next chapter, is to develop a notion that has long been offered by apologists of monotheistic belief, especially Christianity: faith. Often regarded as "a special faculty" to be distinguished from the intellectual, faith is "the spiritual apprehension of divine truths, or of realities beyond the reach of sensible experience or logical proof" (OED). In New Testament teaching, faith is very often associated with that which cannot be seen but which is nonetheless real.[7] It requires an acceptance of an order which is revealed and not derived from empirical observation, reason or proof. In the hands of the early Alejo Carpentier, no longer concerned with the theological but with the literary and the mythico-cultural, faith is what grants access to an appreciation of the participatory realities of the Afro-Caribbean and beyond into Latin America as a whole. It is the mechanism by which participation can be reconciled with the causal paradigm of the realist novel. Faith-based[8] magical realism often assumes a vatic function, calling upon the reader to suspend rational-empirical judgements about the way things are in favour of an expanded order of reality. Frequently, though not always, it does this in order to recuperate a non-western cultural world view. As will become clear in my discussions of Asturias, Carpentier, and Okri, implied in this process is also a different kind of faith: faith in the capacity of literature, and especially the novel, to convey this expanded sense of reality.

Magical realism's second mode of engaging with causality is focussed more on the assumptions of the causal paradigm itself than it is on legitimising alternative, participatory realities. Though it may draw on features like myth, legend, miracle, the marvellous, ritual or superstition, this second mode does this not to further Tambiah's "sociocentrism," "intersubjective understanding" or "the sense of encompassing cosmic oneness," for example. Rather, this strand of magical realism seeks to critique the claims to truth and coherence of the modern, western world view by showing them up as culturally and historically contingent. The truth claims of causality are seen as contingent on consensus, founded in language, and driven by discourse about reality rather than reality itself. Here, as chapter three of this book will show, the key figure is Jorge Luis Borges, who developed in literary directions the implications of scepticism and philosophical idealism. Responding to his own position on the margins of world letters, Borges claimed that the Argentine writer should adopt a position of irreverence with regards to questions of literary tradition. The term irreverence can productively be extended to include in its ambit the processes by which Borges engaged with realism, which he felt was ethically and epistemologically flawed as a project, and from there it radiates outwards to general questions about the nature of reality and how we claim to understand it. Irreverence, in Borges, generates a laughter capable of shattering, as it did for Michel Foucault – inspiring him to write *The Order of Things* – "all the familiar landmarks of my thought – our thought, the thought that bears the stamp of our age and our geography" (xv). Irreverent magical realism seeks to do something similar.

The idea that there might be different types of magical realism is one that has been around for some time – at least since Roberto Gonzalez Echevarría's study of Alejo Carpentier, published in 1974 – but never fully developed. Gonzalez Echevarría distinguishes between the ontological and the epistemological. This distinction overlaps somewhat with that which I am making between faith and irreverence. By "ontology" I mean something different from the way this term is used by Brian McHale in his well-known study of postmodern fiction. McHale's use of the term is based on a western and individualistic tradition of thinking about being. The ontologies I will be discussing in my comments on faith-based magical realism are collective – they are ways of understanding *cultural* being-in-the-world. Second, "epistemological" does not quite capture the nature of irreverent magical realism, because the concern of the latter is not only with knowledge itself, but also with what is done with that knowledge – how it replicates itself and the values that accompany it, how it is used in the perpetuation of privilege and oppression, how it takes on the status of truth. Irreverence frequently attaches itself to specific cultural, historical and literary discourses that are asserted, negotiated and critiqued. The core difference between the approaches I am labelling as irreverence and faith is that the former treats discourse as discourse; the latter frequently translates it into being. Where faith-based approaches utilise the magical in order to expand and enrich already-existing conceptions of the real, discursive magical realism deliberately elevates the non-real to the status of the real in order to cast the epistemological status of both into doubt.

The distinction between faith and irreverence can be refined by locating it in relation to the semantic models of metonymy and metaphor developed by Roman Jakobson. Metonymy depends on contiguity, that is to say that words are combined according to the logic of proximity, when the part stands in for the whole or vice versa, or when a quality or effect of a thing stands in for the thing. Metaphor depends on similarity: words are selected not on the basis of proximity, but because a quality of one is transferred (carried over) to another word or quality. Jakobson claims this dichotomy to be "of primal significance and consequence for all verbal behaviour in general" and provides examples of its relevance from the study of painting, folktales, novels, dreams and magic, where Frazer's division between contagious and homeopathic magic is similarly based on a division between contiguity and similarity. Significantly, Jakobson avers that the scholarship of his time is biased towards metaphor over metonymy: "The actual bipolarity has been artificially replaced [...] by an amputated, unipolar scheme which, strikingly enough coincides with one of the two aphasic patterns, namely with the contiguity disorder" (61).

I would like to contend that the supernatural in faith-based magical realism operates metonymically, while that of irreverent magical realism operates metaphorically. Furthermore, it seems to me that much current literary criticism displays signs of Jakobson's "contiguity disorder" in that it is biased towards the irreverent, discursive potential of magical realism over its realistic, faith-based sides. In faith-based magical realism, the supernatural event or presence may stand synecdochically or metonymically for an alternative way of conceiving of reality usually derived from a non-Western belief system or world view. By contrast, in the irreverent strands of magical realism such an event or presence, which is not rationalised or explained away, nonetheless stands in place of an idea or a set of ideas, say, about the ways language constructs reality, or about the incapacities of binaristic thinking. The supernatural event or occurrence may be the same in each of these approaches. To give a brief example: in the novels to be studied here, Asturias and Rushdie both include instances of human beings metamorphosing to animal form (as do Carpentier and Okri, but I shall leave them aside for the time being). But the meanings of these metamorphoses differ: Asturias's representation concurs with the belief in nahualism held by his characters. Rushdie, by contrast, literalises the metaphor of dehumanisation by turning Saladin Chamcha into a goat/devil because he wants to demonstrate the violence that racist language can perpetrate. In the case of Asturias, the metamorphosis stands as one part of a culturally-specific, non-Western way of relating to the world in which categories like natural and supernatural do not hold. In the latter example, Rushdie's reference points are literary rather than anthropological: metamorphosis becomes a figure of metaphor itself, showing how meanings are carried over from text to text, from language to the world and to the body, and back again.

Where a text displays fidelity to a set of cultural modalities – where it puts its faith in the cultural verities excluded from western ways of seeing – it may, metonymically, use magical realism to generate an effect of granting access to the modes of perception that characterise that culture's world view. While this process might appear to be phenomenological, rather than ontological, the line between the two is often deliberately blurred in order to enable the assertion of a specific cultural identity. In other words, certain ways of seeing the world become the basis for assertions about the way that part of the world, othered by the metropolitan powers, really is. The ontological impulse coincides in certain important respects with models of understanding, explaining or asserting cultural identity that lean towards essentialism and the positing of absolutes. An example of the danger of this approach will be discussed in detail in the next chapter: Ernst Jünger's appropriation of the term magical realism in order to further a reactionary and militant notion of German cultural identity. But not all ontological magical realism is guilty of this kind of reactionary politics. Examples of the extent to which ontological magical realism is capable of deploying its essentialism strategically will be seen in the ways Okri and Asturias both develop ecological dimensions in their novels. From these brief examples, it becomes apparent that generalisations will not do: examples need to be assessed on a case-by-case basis before more abstract levels of interpretation are pursued.

Where a text utilises the supernatural as a tool for the defamiliarisation of discourse, a process which is usually accompanied by other metaphorical and metafictional devices, we are in the presence of what I refer to as an irreverent, discursive impulse behind magical realism. The supernatural elements of this brand of magical realism do not typically emerge as a coherent feature of any particular world view. Indeed the more extreme forms of this approach actively work to disqualify the basis on which such representation depends through the metafictional foregrounding of the constitutive, performative aspects of language, and an insistence on the contingency of all representation. This does not mean that discursive magical realism is not similarly concerned with using the space opened out by its questioning of the rationalist project to assert new forms of cultural identity. Migrancy in *The Satanic Verses* becomes a cultural identity in itself; it operates similarly to an ontological category, but is, in fact performatively constituted.

Jakobson's criticism of the "amputated, unipolar scheme" of his times, in which metaphor dominates metonymy, is relevant to the study of magical realism in more than a simply illuminative way. Irreverent or discourse-oriented magical realism is better understood than its faith or ontology-oriented relative because it seems to coincide more readily with post-structuralist and postmodern approaches to art and the world. These approaches, as Neil Lazarus argues, continue to prevail in postcolonial literary studies. So closely aligned with a postmodernist perspective has been so much literary criticism of magical realism, that its recuperative, realist aspects have been neglected. This book seeks in some respects to redress this balance by arguing, without denying the ludic, metafictional power of irreverent magical realism, for the *realism* of some works of magical realism.

The distinction between ontological and discursive approaches to magical realism, between faith and irreverence, is not neat and each of the novels to be discussed here incorporates both dimensions, although one usually dominates. As I shall show in my discussion of García Márquez's *One Hundred Years of Solitude* it is possible that both elements can be equally present on the same page. This is not a reason for concern, however, for tracing the different strands through the same work is in itself a critically productive exercise, both exegetically and in broader terms. The presence of a split between magical realism's ontological and discursive orientations ultimately requires a revision of the relationship between critical discourse about magical realism and the magical realist text itself. In practical terms, the distinction facilitates interpretation because it necessitates a self-consciousness about definition and forestalls distorting comparisons. The distinction will also prove useful in returning literary critical discourse to the contextual circumstances of the magical realist text, insisting as it does on an awareness of the reasons and motivations behind each writer's deployment of the mode. This book is an attempt to grasp these critical nettles.

2
Magical Realism as Postcolonial Romance

In the previous chapter it was noted that magical realism has recently benefited from several critical works that have sharpened our ability to describe more accurately the fictional operations of the mode. Increased awareness of magical realism's distinctive characteristics and qualities has generated a clarity that will hinder the efforts of both those who would rather the term disappeared from use, and those who are tempted to celebrate it as the answer to all the aesthetic and literary problems of the postcolonial world. Welcome as these developments are in rehabilitating magical realism as a critical term, it was pointed out that they often tend to separate out form and narrative structure from context, history and ideology. The desire to affirm the category of magical realism often takes place at the expense of developing an understanding of the particular ways in which each work of magical realism uses the mode for its own ends: texts are used to understand magical realism, rather than magical realism being used as a tool to unpack and interpret texts. Literary critical category construction of this nature is a synchronic activity, depending as it does on the decontextualisation and comparison of textual features rather than a diachronic location of them within their social, literary and cultural trajectories.

Magical realism's greatest claim to usefulness is that it enables comparison of texts across periods, languages and regions, but when this comparison forgoes engagement with the specifics of history, the critical context is impoverished accordingly.

As discussed in the previous chapter, my decision to limit my focus in this book to just five writers is response to this concern. But it is not only magical realist texts that need to be placed in their contexts: it is also the term and the mode itself. Though many critics incorporate a potted history of the term into their analyses, the historical dimensions of magical realism remain improperly understood. Critical work in the field has typically failed to take a long enough view of both the history of the concept of magical realism, which has its roots in Romanticism, and of the ways the literature itself relates back to the romance tradition. The first person to write of a magical realist was not, as is commonly thought, the German art historian, Franz Roh, in 1925, but the Romantic poet and philosopher, Novalis, around 1798.[1] This chapter aims, firstly, to show how an awareness of the legacy of German idealism can prove productive for critics trying to understand the philosophical implications of literary magical realism. The chapter will then, in its second part, consider different, more literary senses in which magical realism is "romantic," showing how and why it often reaches backwards in time towards modes of narration rendered archaic by realism.

In attempting to historicise the term and the mode, it will be necessary to distinguish between related notions closely bound up with the concept of romance. Typically this term signals a set of structures common to the popular literature of the middle ages which often, though not always, involves idealised quests for honour, love and spiritual succour. A related concept is the historical romance, a genre which emerges in the nineteenth century and which uses history as the basis for narrative excursions that often resembles the adventures of chivalric romance. The most famous exponent of the historical romance in English, Sir Walter Scott, provides a useful link between the term "romance" and "Romanticism" because, as Mark Girouard shows in *The Return to Camelot*, Scott demonstrates better than anyone the ways Romantic aesthetics are linked to deeply-felt nostalgia about the pre-industrial values and modes of life depicted in the chivalric romance itself. Finally, the term "imperial romance" has become well-accepted to denote adventure stories in which colonial otherness takes the place of or supplements the interest in lost times that typifies the historical romance.

The points of connection and contrast between these concepts will help place magical realism in dialogue with romance, signalling the importance of magical realism's writing back to the paradigm of realism, and hence also to a perceived historical alliance between reason, realism and colonialism. From a postcolonial point of view, this alliance has served – indeed, continues to serve – to negate important questions about identity and difference, and it is to these questions, this book argues, that serious magical realism strives to speak.

I   Genealogies of the term: magical realism and romantic idealism

In 1798 Friedrich Freiherr von Hardenberg, the German Romantic poet and philosopher better known by his pen-name of Novalis, envisaged in his notebooks two kinds of prophet who might live outside the boundaries of enlightened discourse without losing touch with the real. He suggested that such prophets should be called a *"magischer Idealist"* and a *"magischer Realist"* – a magical idealist and a magical realist (*Schriften* III 384). He never developed the idea of magical realism, preferring the related concept, magical idealism. In the 1920s the term magical realism re-appeared in Germany in the art-historical criticism of Franz Roh, and in the political philosophy of Ernst Jünger, and also in Italy in the work of the critic and writer, Massimo Bontempelli. And from the 1940s it came to designate a mode of narrative fiction, originally Latin American but now global, in which magical and realistic elements co-exist with equal ontological status. While these second and third phases are frequently identified as key elements of magical realism's conceptual history, their relations to Novalis's formulation of the term have never been explored in any detail. Is the recurrence of the term merely coincidental, or does it suggest a conceptual continuity of any meaningful kind between German idealism and modern magical realism?

Novalis was part of the Jena group mentored by Fichte, whose other members included Tieck, Schelling and the Schlegels. In reaction to Kant's careful separation between the phenomenal and the noumenal, Fichte in his 1794 *Grundlage der gesamten Wissenschaftslehre* developed a philosophical idealism based on what John Neubauer calls "the simultaneous positing of subject and object." This position holds that "the world is the (unconditional) product of an absolute self; the task of the empirical self is to overcome the seeming objectivity of the 'not-self' and recapture it by means of reflection as a form of self" ("Novalis" 380). This idealism of the absolute subject constitutes a useful starting point for understanding the conceptual motivation behind Novalis's magical idealism.

Frederick Beiser has, however, recently criticised the "seductively simple" perception of German idealism as "the doctrine that the subject has an immediate knowledge only of its own ideas, so that it has no knowledge beyond its circle of consciousness." Beiser sees in the development of German idealism "more the story about the growing reaction against subjectivism, about the increasingly intense effort to break out of that circle" (2). He goes on to trace in convincing detail a growing realism and naturalism in the development of idealism from Kant and Fichte through Hölderlin, Novalis, Schlegel, and Schelling. At a certain point in this trajectory, the task of the young Romantics becomes not to capture the world as a form of self, but rather "deriving the transcendental subject from its place in nature" (4). The absolute could not, therefore, be seen as a form of ego, as it was by Fichte, for this would involve anthropomorphizing; nor could it be defined as either objective or subjective for such terms would "limit what is meant to be unlimited" (6). Beiser sees Hegel's famous dictum about the task of philosophy being to seek the "identity of identity and nonidentity" as expressing the central task of German idealism: "to explain the possibility of knowledge according to idealist principles, and yet to account for the reality of the external world" (14). Following this reading, finding ways of understanding self-as-world was, for Novalis, a task at least as important as the Fichtean approach to world-as-self.

Novalis's central aesthetic and critical project was Romanticising – the poeticising of the world and of life itself. A specific conception of magic lies close to the heart of this philosophical project. Novalis insists on inwardness and intuition; consequently, he draws a distinction between natural truth – that which requires validity in terms of objective reality – and magical truth, a subjective, self-referential truth that depends on an inward-looking mystical intuition. For Novalis, "All certitude is independent of natural truth [*Naturwahrheit*] – it refers to marvellous truth [*Wunderwahrheit*]. Therefore all natural truths rest equally on marvellous truth" (*Schriften* II 556). This *Wunderwahrheit* can thus be sought by practitioners of rational branches of learning, facilitating a "magical chemistry, mechanics and physics" and even a "magical astronomy, grammar, philosophy, religion etc" (*Schriften* III 247, 266). It is not surprising then, that

Novalis would also have conceived of a "magical idealist" and a "magical realist."

A magical idealist is one who participates in the project of apprehending truth not through correspondence with external reality, but by undoing the antinomies between language and the world and between subject and object. The fragment from the *Allgemeine Brouillon* in which Novalis alludes to a magical realist is characteristically brief and abstruse, yet the implication is that he is closely related to this magical idealist:

> Pathological philosophy. An absolute drive after finitude and completeness is disease, as soon as it destroys itself and rejects the *unfinished* and incomplete. If one wishes to undertake and attain anything precise, then one must also set oneself provisional limits. However, he who does not do this is perfect, like he who does not want to swim before he can – he is a magical idealist, in the same way that we have magical realists. The former seeks miraculous movement – a miraculous subject – the latter a miraculous object – a miraculous form. Both are *logical illnesses* – madnesses – in which, however, the ideal reveals or reflects itself on two levels – sacred – isolated beings – who wondrously diffract the higher light – true prophets. The dream is thus also prophetic – sketch of a wonderful future. (*Schriften III* 384–385)[2]

Magical idealists and magical realists are grouped together as "true prophets" because, as Novalis makes clear in the previous fragment, "The proof of realism is idealism – and vice versa" (383). Magical idealism became Novalis's form of absolute idealism – a synthesis of realism and idealism. Importantly, this synthesis did not involve simply subsuming realism into idealism. For Terry Pinkard, the refusal of the subject/object binary was a result of Novalis's "explicitly relational" notion of consciousness, a notion that lead directly to a conception of self-consciousness as "forever out of our reach" (145). This interpretation helps explain why "an absolute drive after finitude and completeness" becomes for Novalis a disease when it rejects the unfinished and incomplete. Beiser, at pains to observe the objective or realistic side of Novalis's thinking, points out that the reference to illness derives from his interest in John Brown's physiological theorising in which balance was held to be vital for the state of health of an organism (424). Beiser's epistemological focus emphasises the extent to which "sickness" derives from a failure to recognise the limits are that are imposed by the physical world. In Novalis's thought, these limits temper the subjectivist tendencies of Fichtean idealism.

Novalis never developed the concept of magical realism. He succumbed to tuberculosis at the age of 29, and his fragmentary and aphoristic mode of philosophising, well-suited, as Pinkard observes, to the poetic task of romanticising the "incompleteness of human existence as it is lived out," meant that some of his philosophical concepts were destined to remain under explored (145). But this fact should not distract from the extent to which magical realism expresses an important facet of Novalis's thinking. In the refusal to privilege either subject or object, and in the overt criticism of the drive towards knowledge, Novalis reveals the outlines of a committed anti-foundationalism. Along with his emphasis on enchantment and on seeing beyond the physical while still maintaining a place for the real world, this anti-foundationalism resonates strongly with the post-structuralist and postmodern turn in modern literary criticism. Most importantly, as is signalled in his use of the term magical realist itself, Novalis shows himself to be preoccupied with resolving the tension between two realms usually thought of as mutually exclusive: in his case real and ideal. In the case of literary magical realism a similar reconciliation will be sought between congruent concepts: natural and supernatural, realist and fantastic.

The second phase of magical realism's conceptual history begins in 1925 with a book by the German art historian and photographer, Franz Roh, published to coincide with an exhibition of paintings in Mannheim.[3] Two years earlier the director of the Kunsthalle in Mannheim, Gustav Hartlaub, had announced his intention to mount the exhibition, using the term *Neue Sachlichkeit* to describe the new developments in painting that he hoped to demonstrate. Roh's book and his label were directed towards understanding the same movement. Magical realism came to be eclipsed by Hartlaub's term, though sporadic usage of the term continues in art-historical criticism. Roh's book was translated into Spanish in 1927 by the influential publishing enterprise, *Revista de Occidente*, the major conduit through which the ideas of European modernism were disseminated in the Spanish-speaking world.

What did Roh see in the *Neue Sachlichkeit* paintings that prompted his use of the label, and what was he therefore trying to designate through its use? Roh was a major figure in critical and artistic circles in Germany for more than forty years. He studied art and art history at universities in Leipzig, Berlin and Basel before taking up residence in Munich under the influential critic, Heinrich Wölfflin, whose systems of classifications he used and adapted (Fernández 112). His academic training ensured that he was familiar with the traditions of German philosophy, and the influence of Romantic ideas is clear in his dialectical mode of analysis and in the language of freshness and novelty that characterises his commentary on *Neue Sachlichkeit* painting. Is it possible, then, that he inherited the term magical realism from Novalis?

In Roh's account, magical realism is the synthesis of Impressionism and Expressionism. Impressionism was, Roh argues, a form of nineteenth-century realism, focussing on reproducing the object in (relatively) naturalistic ways. Expressionism found this specific objectivity to be lacking in spirituality, but in its reaction against Impressionism it became for Roh a "roughshod and frenetic tran-scendentalism," a "devilish detour," and a "flight from the world." In the new painting that Roh is championing, "it seems to us that this fantastic dreamscape [of Expressionism] has completely vanished and that our real world re-emerges before our eyes, bathed in the clarity of a new day" (17). Thus, the new painting draws from Impressionism its focus on palpable, tangible reality, and from Expressionism a sense of the vital spirituality underlying the world of objects. As Fernández has noted, the influence of Wölfflin's systems of artistic classification can be identified here, as can that of Viktor Shklovsky, the Russian Formalist whose work had appeared in German translation throughout the 1920s. It is particularly Shklovsky's theories of defamiliarisation that Roh drew on in his assertions about what he saw as the purpose of the new art. But to understand more clearly the conceptual motivation behind Roh's specific choice of term, we must return briefly to Novalis.

Neubauer shows how Novalis took from Kant the definition of mathematics as the "construction of nonempirical intuitions" and extended it, arguing that concepts could be constructed for all kinds of intuitions, and vice versa. This approach allowed him to develop a "performative aesthetics" aimed at the production of non-mimetic art forms. Novalis was in fact violently opposed to mimesis, arguing that poetry should be "artificial – invented – fantastic!" and complained that "in the theatre the principle of the imitation of nature tyrannises" (*Schriften III* 691). On the other hand, he rejected exclusively subjective expression in art, for his notion of art "involves the projection of concepts rather than emotions and it anticipates therefore formalist, symbolist and conceptual rather than affective art" (Neubauer, "Novalis" 380). This wariness about viewing art as the representation of feeling and emotion was based on a reaction against *Sturm und Drang* (the "Storm and Stress" movement). In its struggle against neo-classicism and rationalism, *Sturm und Drang* was perceived as having gone too far towards rejecting reason. After all, as Kathleen Wheeler points out, "Kant had taught the young Romantics [that] it was a postulate of reason itself to seek for the eternal, the infinite, the final cause." Wheeler concludes that German Romanticism was, in the broadest terms, an attempt to integrate neo-classicism with *Sturm und Drang* (2).

Certain parallels can thus be drawn between the contexts that conditioned both Novalis and Roh in their conceptualisations of magical realism. Just as later German Romanticism developed away from the irrationalism of *Sturm und Drang*, so does magical realist painting break with the subjective bias of Expressionism. On the other hand, just as for the Romantics there could be no return to dogmatic neo-classicism, or to the tyranny of the mimetic principle referred to by Novalis, so too could the magical realist painters of the 1920s hardly return to painting Impressionistic landscapes and still-lifes. Novalis, as we have seen, operates from an attempt to posit the object in terms of the subject without descending into subjectivism: magical truth is self-referential, inward. Roh focuses his attention on objects themselves, but insists that the problem with Impressionism and Expressionism alike is that they "steal the seductive integrity of objective phenomena from the viewer" (19). What Novalis and Roh have in common, then, is a concern with the limits of mimesis and a reliance on dialectics of inwardness and outwardness, subject and object, spirit and the world in their formulations of this concern. While each responded to the circumstances of his own times, and these dialectics are pronounced features of the post-Kantian tradition in general, the striking point of overlap lies in the two thinkers' attempts to synthesise such dialectical opposites through their uses of the term, magical realism.

In the ideologically volatile milieu of the Weimar Republic it was unlikely that ideas such as those with which Roh grappled would be found only in the lecture room or the art gallery. Roh's art criticism was not overtly political, but his sympathies, along with those of his friends, Grosz and Maholy-Nagy, were on the left, and he, like many of his contemporaries, fell victim to Nazi purges. In 1933, he was interned at Dachau for several months. On his release, Roh was sentenced to silence for his support of "degenerate art" and published nothing between 1933 and 1946. The *Neue Sachlichkeit* movement itself contained a notably radical component, as is clear in the work of Grosz and Dix, but its apparently realistic qualities also appealed to more conservative tastes, as in the landscapes of Georg Schrimpf, for example, which were bought by Rudolf Hess (Guenther 54). The term magical realism, unable to distinguish between these tendencies, was, like the paintings, open to appropriation by the German right-wing. Here the work of Ernst Jünger is crucial in demonstrating the pliancy of the term and its role in reconciling antinomial aspects of a German identity in militant pursuit of cultural definition.

Though he never joined the Nazi party, Jünger was one of several reactionary intellectuals whose ideas facilitated, in imaginative and practical ways, the conservative climate that caused the downfall of the Weimar Republic and allowed the Nazis to come to power. Caught between the expansive aspirations of liberal capitalism and Marxist-Leninism, humiliated by military defeat and the terms imposed by the Treaty of Versailles, confronted with rapid industrialisation, and paranoid about cultural decay, Jünger and others developed an influential brand of cultural politics to support the nationalism that they saw as Germany's only salvation. Jeffrey Herf has studied Jünger and others like Oswald Spengler and Martin Heidegger under the label "reactionary modernism" because they rescued German nationalism from a backward-looking, pastoral, *völkisch* antimodernism and facilitated the process by which technology could be embraced within an essentialist, absolutist and anti-rationalist paradigm of cultural identity. From the hundreds of books and essays Jünger published during the Weimar years, Herf singles out "Nationalismus und modernes Leben" (Nationalism and Modern Life), the article in which Jünger develops his ideas about magical realism, to be the most significant aspect of his attempt at reconciling technology with the traditionalist tendencies in German nationalism (82).

Though Herf fails to make a connection between Jünger and the works of the *Neue Sachlichkeit* painters, it is probable that Jünger derived the term magical realism, and indeed many of his ideas about what it might mean, from Franz Roh. Jünger's interest in the paintings extended far beyond the art-historical, and the reasons why they would have interested him are not difficult to identify in the light of Herf's analysis. Jünger discussed, for example, "paintings of magic realism [in which] each of the lines of the external world is conjured up with the exactness of a mathematical formula, the coldness of which is illuminated and re-heated in an inexplicable manner, as if by transparency, by a magical background" (qtd Guenther 58). Herf locates Jünger's political Romanticism in his claims "to discern hidden, magical, yet real forces at work behind surface appearances" (71), claims which underpinned his linking of technology to "primordial forces of the will" and his presentation of a heroic acceptance of the body as machine (78). The "apparent sobriety" of the painterly style doubtless appealed to Jünger's conception of the "icy will" that was distinctively Prussian and which could be conjoined with the potential of technology. Above all, the appeal of magical realism to Jünger was that in what Roh called "that radiation of magic, that spirituality, that lugubrious quality throbbing in the best works of the new mode" (Roh, "Magic" 20), he would have seen those natural, elemental, suprahistorical forces that he believed animate human life.

Jünger was not the only reactionary to be attracted by the term magical realism. As Erik Camayd-Freixas makes clear, in terms of both concept (the reconciliation of the everyday and the miraculous; but also "conscious primitivism"), and terminology (the specific use of the phrase itself), the Italian writer and critic, Massimo Bontempelli, has always been a more relevant figure than Roh to magical realism's genealogy. In 1926 Bontempelli started the journal *900* in which he expressed his desire to further a new mythography that, unlike the fabrications of the avant-garde, would respect the continuities between past and present. The kind of art he proposed was one that would find miracles in the midst of ordinary and everyday life, and he specifically – and, it seems, independently of Roh or Novalis – named this art magical realism (Camayd-Freixas 351). Bontempelli exerted an influence over both Alejo Carpentier and Miguel Ángel Asturias, the two authors credited with the earliest works of Latin American magical realism, through the agency of Arturo Uslar-Pietri. A friend of Bontempelli, Uslar-Pietri collaborated with both Carpentier and Asturias during the time they spent in Paris in the 1920s, and renewed his acquaintance with Carpentier when the latter moved to Venezuela in the 1940s (60–61). Bontempelli, though he was later to regret it, was a fascist sympathiser.

It is tempting simply to dismiss the relevance of these right-wing intellectuals to contemporary literary-criticism's use of the magical realism. Jünger and Bontempelli use the term to designate something different from what is intended by today's critics, and clearly most late twentieth-century writers of magical realism are not inclined towards fascist ideas. I believe, however, that the question of the extent to which the term magical realism is marked by its history is one that should not be dismissed too easily. An analogy can perhaps be suggested with the case of the genealogy of the term hybridity, which, as Robert Young has shown in *Colonial Desire*, is ignored by contemporary cultural theory at its own peril. In Herf's argument, Nazism stands as an extreme example of the dangers of the political institutionalisation of syntheses of myth and history, the magical and the real.[4] There is no reason why the literary manifestations of these syntheses should *automatically* be considered innocent of such dangers. Just as the term magical realism can be used for a number of different purposes, so the mode of narration might also be harnessed to the cause of any of a range of possible agendas.[5] Claims about the politics of magical realism should be evaluated on a case by case basis, making every effort to read the texts in their contexts, rather than by grand generalisation.

For similar reasons, if magical realism as a literary mode is defined in a narrow fashion, it becomes impossible to limit it to any particular region, language, literary tradition or movement.[6] Writers like Kafka, Bulgakov, Grass, Suskind, D.M. Thomas, Angela Carter, Toni Morrison, Robert Nye, Jeannette Winterson, André P. Brink, and many others show clearly that a range of cultural trajectories can be established for the existence of magical realism in different contexts. But, while magical realist techniques have been utilised by writers from around the world, this book claims that it is in its postcolonial incarnations that magical realism fulfils its creative and critical potential to the fullest. Erik Camayd-Freixas, for example, outlines contiguities between Asturias, Carpentier, Rulfo and García Márquez, suggesting that magical realism in Latin American might in fact be thought of as something approaching a movement. These writers, especially García Márquez, have, in turn, provided powerful illustrations of magical realism's capacity to negotiate issues of identity, influence, and cultural difference, and these lessons have been well-learned by later Anglophone postcolonial writers like Rushdie and Okri. It will be the task of chapters three to six to prove this claim. First, it is necessary to turn to more specifically literary topics, and to ask why, in general terms, a moderated idealism of the kind suggested by the term magical realism should have appealed to the twentieth-century writers who pioneered the mode.

II Genealogies of the mode: magical realism and the return to romance

In each of the cases of Novalis, Roh, Jünger and Bontempelli, the term magical realism carries the burden of resolving the antinomy between two realms that usually exclude one another. For Novalis the issue is philosophical; for Roh, painterly; for Jünger, cultural/political; and for Bontempelli, artistic. In this study, as was made clear in the previous chapter, the oxymoron magical realism is directed towards understanding the technique of naturalising the supernatural in certain modern literary texts. Other, older narrative genres have operated in similar ways. Most notable among these is the popular literature of the Middle Ages. What is the nature of common ground between these genres or styles? And if similarities can be shown, what exactly did writers from the postcolonial world, distanced from the centres of political and cultural power, see in such European literary historical precedents?

Several critics have noted the similarities between magical realism and older narrative forms. Lois Parkinson Zamora, for example, asserts that "twentieth-century magical realism is a recent flowering of the more venerable romance tradition that [Northrop] Frye describes" (520). In *Anatomy of Criticism* Frye writes:

> In a true myth there can obviously be no consistent distinction between ghosts and living beings. In romance we have real human

beings, and consequently ghosts are in a separate category, but in a romance a ghost as a rule is merely one more character: he causes little surprise because his appearance is no more marvellous than many other events. In high mimetic [epic/tragedy], where we are within the order of nature, a ghost is relatively easy to introduce because the plane of experience is above our own, but when he appears he is an awful and mysterious being from what is perceptibly another world. In low mimetic [the novel], ghosts have been, ever since Defoe, almost entirely confined to a separate category of "ghost stories". In ordinary low mimetic fiction they are inadmissible, "in complaisance to the scepticism of a reader," as Fielding puts it, a scepticism which extends only to low mimetic conventions. The few exceptions, such as *Wuthering Heights*, go a long way to prove the rule – that is, we recognise a strong influence of romance in *Wuthering Heights*. In some forms of ironic fiction, such as the later works of Henry James, the ghost comes back as a fragment of a disintegrating personality. (50)

Ghosts are probably the most common otherworldly presence in all of literature, and, as Zamora shows, Frye's distinctions provide a useful means of understanding the formal overlap between magical realism and romance: both presume textual equivalence between the domains of natural and supernatural. It should also be noted that Frye's "low mimetic conventions" are those that inform the realist novel, and are thus both relied upon and subverted in magical realism. What is especially noteworthy about Frye's analysis is the distinction he establishes between reader belief and narrative convention. Frye asserts that the scepticism about ghosts held by Fielding's hypothetical reader *extends only to low mimetic traditions*. Unwilling to shift his focus from form and genre to the conditions under which literature is produced and received, Frye does not explore this distinction. The apparent caveat can, in fact, be re-phrased to suggest that such scepticism is actually a product of the low mimetic tradition itself rather than a reflection of an attitude held by Fielding's reader.

This type of critical reversal is characteristic of the mode of argumentation in Fredric Jameson's *The Political Unconscious*, which begins from a desire to historicise the kinds of generic and formal discourse encountered in Frye. Jameson's work is useful in periodising Frye's genres, and thereby illuminating patterns of relation between romance and realism that go beyond the formal.[7] He draws on Frye's discussion to tell an "old-fashioned linear history" of romance, one which assigns romance the role of "recognisable protagonist," and treats genre as if it were a natural, rather than an experimental construct. In this account

> some "full" romance form realised, say, in the *romans* of Chrétien de Troyes – evolves into the elaborate Italian and Spenserian poems and knows its brief moment on the stage in the twilight of Shakespearean spectacle before being revived in Romanticism, where under the guise of the novel it leads a new existence in the art-romances of Stendhal and Manzoni of Scott and Emily Brontë, only to outlive itself in modern times under the unexpected formal mutations of the fantastic on the one hand (Cortázar, Kafka) and of fantasy (Alain-Fournier, Julien Gracq) on the other. (*Political* 123)

Jameson uses this history as something of a case study for the relationship between the rise of capitalism and that of the novel, and, on a different level of abstraction, for a detailed evaluation of the nature of diachronic narrative in general. Under different conditions and at different times, particular literary-discursive formations have arranged themselves into patterns we now recognise as romance. Jameson's account, while deliberately artificial, nevertheless provides a useful point of departure for a genealogical enquiry into how and why, in historical, cultural and geopolitical terms, magical realism can be said to be an elaboration or revisioning of the romance tradition.

Michael Valdez Moses has approached the task of relating magical realism to romance by arguing that "despite its differences from the historical romance, the magical realist novel exemplifies the same cultural logic that structures and undergirds the historical romances of Sir Walter Scott" (104). Valdez Moses, unlike the critics mentioned in the previous chapter, plays down the importance of formal analysis, readily conceding that "Scott's best known historical romances do not depend upon the supernatural or gothic conventions that characterise the work of his contemporaries such as James Hogg" (120). He nonetheless chooses Scott because he sees both magical realism and historical romance as characterised by "nostalgic longing for and an imaginary return to a world that is past or passing away." Valdez Moses is aiming his argument at the assumption that magical realism is capable of subverting or providing alternatives to "an emergent world order" (103). His targets are thus both naïve or sentimental readings of magical realism and the common critical belief that magical realism is a means by which, in a literary and cultural sense, the "margins" are able to "invade" the "centre." The most important point of similarity between magical realism and the historical romance is thus that

> [f]ar from offering real, that is politically engaged, resistance to modernization, these fictional genres depend for their success on the fact that their readers (at least implicitly) accept that the pre-modern world is a historical anachronism. Both literary forms offer purely symbolic or token resistance to the inexorable triumph of modernity. (104)

If we insist on the formal distinctions that Valdez Moses dismisses – that is, the differences between the ways in which the two literary genres treat the supernatural – important differences between the historical romance of Scott and, say, the magical realism of the early Alejo Carpentier become apparent. These formal distinctions can be shown to open out onto wider questions of identity and difference, terms absent from Valdez Moses's analysis. These in turn can be abstracted into a consideration of, not how magical realism provides alternatives to or subverts modernity, but, when its implications are pushed to their extremes, how it calls into question the culturally selective terms on which the discursive category of modernity itself is constructed. This is, perhaps, not political engagement, but it does mean that the cultural logic of magical realism cannot be that of merely confirming the global horizons of modern culture, as Valdez Moses would have us believe.

The differences between historical romance and magical realism can be identified by considering more closely the disjunctures between medieval and nineteenth-century historical romance. As Umberto Eco puts it, "the universe of the early middle ages was a universe of hallucination, the world was a symbolic forest peopled with mysterious presences" (261). Amadís of Gaul in the romance of the same name, which probably dates back to the late thirteenth century, makes no distinction between the "reality" of damsels and knights on the one hand, and, on the other hand, the evil wizards, giants and supernatural beasts he encounters on his adventures. Considered in its context, medieval romance of this kind represents magic, in Frye's words, as "no more marvellous than many other events" because the categories of natural and supernatural, real and fantastic, simply did not exist in the ways they do in the modern world. Scott's writing, on the other hand, however much it may be tinged with nostalgia, quite clearly displays the marks of post-Enlightenment modernity. Jameson is again useful here in understanding the paradigm shift that resulted in the principle of realism so important to Scott's narrative projects:

> as any number of "definitions" of realism assert, and as the totemic ancestor of the novel, *Don Quixote*, emblematic²¹¹, demonstrates, that processing operation variously called narrative mimesis or realistic representation has as its historic function the systematic undermining and demystification, the secular "decoding," of those pre-existing inherited traditional or sacred narrative paradigms which are its initial givens. In this sense, the novel plays a significant role in what can be called a properly bourgeois cultural revolution – that immense process of transformation whereby populations whose life habits were formed by other, now archaic, modes of production are effectively reprogrammed for life and work in the new world of market capitalism. The "objective" function of the novel is thereby also implied: to its subjective and critical, analytic, corrosive mission must now be added the task of producing as though for the first time that very life world, that very "referent" – the newly quantifiable space of extension and market equivalence, the new rhythms of measurable time, the new secular and "disenchanted" object world of the commodity system, with its post-traditional daily life and its bewilderingly empirical, "meaningless," and contingent *Umwelt* – of which this new narrative discourse will then claim to be the "realistic" reflection. (*Political* 91)

Jameson makes clear that realism is not only a reflection or product of historical processes; it contributes to the development of those processes. Secularisation, rationalisation and the disenchantment of the world are integrally connected to capitalism, and realism in this account serves as an ally in eradicating non-productive beliefs and behaviours. In the literary domain this implies that realism does not merely follow romance chronologically: it actively works to render romance archaic.[8]

As Jameson notes, more than any other text it is *Don Quixote* that makes this process clear. Generalisations about this complex novel are difficult, not least because Cervantes' sympathy for his protagonist's idealism grows so compellingly over the course of the novel. But on the whole, by means of the distance it establishes between its implied author and its protagonist, *Don Quixote* effectively parodies the chivalric romance, and the medieval world view that underpins it. And so successful was *Don Quixote* that a writer like Scott could not create a romance of his own without registering the epistemological impact of Cervantes' novel. Thus, early in *Waverley*, Scott's first novel, we find the following comparison between Scott's eponymous hero and Alonso Quexana/Don Quixote:

> From the minuteness with which I have traced Waverley's pursuits, and the bias which these unavoidably communicated to his imagination, the reader may perhaps anticipate, in the following tale, an imitation of the romance of Cervantes. But he will do my prudence injustice in the supposition. My intention is not to follow the steps of that inimitable author, in describing such total perversion of the intellect as misconstrues the objects actually presented to the senses, but that more common aberration from sound judgement, which apprehends occurrences indeed in their reality, but communicates to them a tincture of its own romantic tone and colouring. (55)

Don Quixote is, of course, more anti-romance than romance, but Scott underplays this fact because he is more sympathetic to Waverley's romantic aspirations than Cervantes was, initially, to Alonso Quexana and his fondness for chivalry. If *Don Quixote* sounded the death knell of the medieval romance, *Waverley* signals a careful awareness of the terms required to resurrect it, terms self-consciously aligned with Cervantes's Renaissance world view, rather than Don Quixote's medieval orientation to reality. Don Quixote's failing, as Scott is well aware, is that his intellect has been "perverted" by romance. Crucially, this perversion is evident in the deviation his view of the world shows from one governed by empirical validations of reality (such as that of Sancho Panza, for example).

Scott's borrowings from medieval romance have been documented by Jerome Mitchell, and (though this is not part of Mitchell's project) it is possible to trace Scott's secularisation and sanitisation of the supernatural in medieval romance in a number of his works. To name just one example, Mitchell points to the ways Scott's *The Bride of Lammermoor* draws from the romances, *Bevis of Hampton* and *The Seven Champions* the theme of the undesired marriage. However, in the romances this theme is resolved through magic (magical charms to protect Josian's virginity; the intervention of St. George to rescue Sabra), whereas no such recourse to the supernatural is made by Scott (120–121). With a few minor exceptions, Scott, a product of what Jameson calls the secular and disenchanted, "bewilderingly empirical" world, chooses fidelity to "objects actually presented to the senses" rather than to Don Quixote's "universe of hallucination."

It is with Alejo Carpentier's 1949 introduction of a postcolonial point of view that the terms of this narratorial debate shift dramatically. Where Cervantes parodied, with growing affection, his protagonist's tendency to see giants where consensus dictated there were only windmills, and where Scott could only communicate to occurrences a "tincture" of "romantic tone and colouring," Carpentier, for reasons that will be explored shortly, makes clear that his position is one of sympathy with Don Quixote (and hence with that character's unwillingness to limit himself to empirical validations of reality) rather than with his creator, Cervantes: "Those who do not believe in saints cannot cure themselves with the miracles of saints, nor can those who are not Don Quixotes enter body, soul and possessions into the world of Amadís of Gaul" ("Marvellous Real" 86). Crystallised in the differences between Scott's and Carpentier's attitudes to the character of Don Quixote, I would like to propose, are the conceptual relationships between realism and magical realism.

Marking the paths that run between the very different contexts of medieval and historical romance are great movements of ideas – Renaissance humanism, the Protestant Reformation, the Enlightenment. Though Jameson's analysis alerts us to the importance of capitalism to these processes, and especially to the decline of medieval romance and the rise of narrative realism, the key to understanding the relationship between magical realism and romance will not only be found in the "bourgeois cultural revolution," but in colonialism and particularly in the productive collusion between realism and the negotiation – or negation – of cultural difference. To the list of processes Jameson identifies as being enacted by realism we must add that of othering, including the specific form of othering that involves defining and hierarchising what is real and what is not. Historical or imperial romance must be distinguished from their medieval antecedents on the grounds of their realism, and magical realism originates as a postcolonial response to this logic. Returning to Valdez Moses for a moment, the conflation of magical realism and Scott's historical romance elides the importance of magical realism's quality of writing back to the realist paradigm, and hence to the historical processes that informed it. Underpinning these processes are the various legacies of colonialism that informed the development of the genre.

By foregrounding texts' treatment of the supernatural, important disjunctions between medieval romance, nineteenth-century romance and magical realism become apparent. Notably, magical realism takes from medieval romance not necessarily themes of love and adventure, of devotion to one's lady or the allegories of quest, honour and passion, but something altogether more fundamental: the relationship to the real that is implied by the intermingling of the magical and the everyday, the equivalence that is presumed between real and supernatural. The task of the critic then becomes to understand why magical realism appears to reach back over the realism that was so important to Cervantes and was sustained by Scott's secular Romanticism, to the romance paradigm itself.

I would like to propose that the task of understanding magical realism's relationship with romance is best approached by considering the ways romance has conditioned the imperialist imagination, and the ways in which magical realism, at least in its postcolonial manifestations, returns romantic and exoticist tropes to their points of origin in ambivalent acts of reclamation and assertion that are almost always associated with the practice of a cultural politics of one form or another.

Spain's "conquest" of the Americas began while the chivalric romance was the pre-eminent literary genre of all Europe and while many of its values held sway over the minds of would-be adventurers and a public hungry for miracles. The writings of the early Spanish explorers and conquistadors are filled with the exotic expressed in a language of awe (Camayd-Freixas 89). Some Latin American writers and intellectuals of the mid-twentieth century, notably Alejo Carpentier, concerned with the status of Latin American nations in global cultural and political economies, saw the link between romance and Latin America as presenting an opportunity for re-evaluating the ways in which Latin America was perceived, especially by Europe, and for asserting Latin American unity and cultural autonomy. For Carpentier, the exoticism with which the conquistadors had characterised the Americas provided nothing less than corroboration of the uniqueness of Latin America, or what he called "the marvellous real":

> Here the strange is commonplace, and always was commonplace. [...] Even though the adventures of Amadís of Gaul were written in Europe, it is Bernal Díaz del Castillo, who in *The True History of the Conquest of New Spain* gives us the first authentic chivalric romance. And constantly – we must not forget this – the conquerors saw very clearly aspects of the marvellous real in America; here I want to recall Bernal Díaz's phrase as he contemplates Tenochtitlán/Mexico City for the first time [...]: "We were all amazed and we said that these lands, temples and lakes were like the enchantments spoken of by Amadís". Here we have the European man in contact with the American marvellous real. ("Baroque" 104)

Carpentier uses the romantic accounts of European explorers against the rationality of modern Europe (and against the artifice of Europe's attempts, via surrealism, to break from that rationality) in order to "identify" a Latin America that exists outside of the possibility of rational understanding, one that he elsewhere asserts can only be understood through faith. For Carpentier, the fact that early explorers could only understand the New World through the language of romance was a cause of celebration because it supports his own attempts at establishing a founding myth for Latin America. Romance thus comes to support the early Carpentier's project in terms of both its objects of fascination – the exotic, the mysterious, the strange – and in terms of its modes of perception in which the antinomies of reason and unreason that characterise rational thought are undone.

Carpentier turned away from magical realism after *The Kingdom of This World*, but the combination of stylistic innovation and cultural theory in that novel and its prologue proved productive for later purveyors of the magical realist mode. For the purposes of constructing a genealogy of magical realism as postcolonial romance it is significant indeed that, in an act of homage from one Latin American writer to another, Mario Vargas Llosa in 1971 praised *One Hundred Years of Solitude* under the moniker "Amadís in America." Vargas Llosa claims that "[b]esides writing a fine book, García Márquez has unintentionally, perhaps unwittingly, succeeded in restoring a narrative tradition interrupted centuries ago, reviving the broad, exuberant, majestic notion of literary realism held by the founders of the novelistic genre in the Middle Ages" ("Amadís" 56–57). Implicitly refuting Ian Watt's idea that the novel developed concurrently with realism in the eighteenth century, Vargas Llosa suggests an alternative history that sees romance as the true progenitor of the novel, and an expanded, marvellous realism as its natural mode of expression. Like Carpentier, Vargas Llosa holds Cervantes responsible for "deal[ing] a fatal blow to the novels of chivalry with his ridicule" (59) and thereby consigning future writers to settings and styles constrained by realism. The shift in allegiance from Cervantes to Amadís and Don Quixote can once again be seen to underpin the Latin American reclamation of the space of romance. García Márquez himself has, in his ironic way, provided substantial evidence for the presence of a connection between romance and magical realism, claiming that "[t]he first masterwork of the literature of magical realism is the Diary of Columbus" (qtd Palencia-Roth 152), and signalling a debt to Carpentier in his Nobel Prize acceptance speech.[9]

The connection between magical realism and romance holds for contexts other than those of Latin America. In *The Rhetoric of English India* Sara Suleri's attempt to locate romance as an allusive context for Indian postcolonial literature leads her to propose that both colonial and postcolonial fictions were "equally obsessed with magic realism," with the difference that the former "take on the structure of romance" (181). Here Suleri's use of the term can be faulted for the reasons noted earlier, namely that it fails to register magical realism's distinctive naturalisation of the supernatural. Kipling's *Kim* or Forster's *A Passage to India* constitute examples of the sub-genre of imperial romance, as it is perceptively analysed by John McClure, among others, but they are not examples of magical realism. Kim or the Marabar Caves, resonant though these figures may be with the suggestion of the unknowable, are not explicitly supernatural. Furthermore, the antinomy in such texts between what can and what cannot be known is deliberately left unresolved in order to generate the sense of the elusive and the mysterious on which this kind of romance depends. By contrast, magical realism appeals to a postcolonial writer like Salman Rushdie because it resolves the antinomy that underpins imperial romance, thereby destabilising the binaries – coloniser and colonised, knowledge and inscrutability, western and other – upon which the colonial fictions depend. If, therefore, as Suleri argues, the "burden of postcolonial writing" is "to invert the terms of [...] Orientalist mythmaking" (181), then the function of Kipling's putatively marvellous Kim is inverted by Rushdie's indisputably clairvoyant Saleem in *Midnight's Children*. *The Satanic Verses* goes one step further, figuring the historical/mythical nemesis of the crusaders, Saladin, as, alternatively, a mild-mannered Indian immigrant to London, and a fire-breathing horned-and-hoofed devil. This is imperial romance standing on its head, and it is enabled, mostly, by the possibilities offered by magical realism's return to the structures of medieval romance.

By way of conclusion, it should be noted that emphasising magical realism's engagement with European literary models does not automatically undermine the distinctive postcolonial possibilities of the mode. On the contrary, viewing magical realism as postcolonial romance may reinforce recent critical revisions of the history of medieval romance itself. Claiming that "the point at which a narrative shaped itself into the pattern we now recognise as medieval romance" begins with the creation of Geoffrey of Monmouth's *Historia Regum Britannie*, around 1139, Geraldine Heng foregrounds the extent to which medieval romance is part of the discursive economy of early imperialism:

> Geoffrey's exemplar materialises [...] as a form of cultural rescue in the aftermath of the First Crusade, a transnational militant pilgrimage during which Latin Christian crusaders did the unthinkable – committing acts of cannibalism on infidel Turkish cadavers in Syria, in 1098, with the attendant traumas of shock, pollution and self-denaturing that accompany the violation of

horrific taboos – and cultural fantasy was instantiated in order that the indiscussible, what is unthinkable and unsayable by other means, might surface into discussion.

Geoffrey's innovation shows how romance's preferred method is to arrange for an apparatus of the intimately familiar and pleasurable – figures of gender, sexuality, and varieties of adventure – to transact its negotiations with history. (2–3)

In addition to showing the extent to which romance drew much of its impetus from early religious/imperial encounters with otherness, Heng's emphasis on fantasy as "cultural rescue" from historical trauma flatly contradicts sentimental readings of fantasy – and by extension, of magical realism – as representing spaces of "remystification" and "re-enchantment." The magic of romance, fantasy and magical realism alike can only be understood properly within the historical and cultural contexts from which it arises, and upon which it seeks to comment. At the same time, lack of attention to the formal distinctions between and within these genres makes it impossible to be clear about the nature of the particular literary, cultural and political contributions that each strives to make. Drawing upon the insights of formalist analysis of magical realism, and then considering the reasons why writers choose to engage this mode at particular times leads the critic to some of the ongoing concerns of postcoloniality: the urge to reclaim what has been stolen or lost, to critique the assumptions and conventions of the metropolis, to recover and affirm identities and to assert autonomy in the face of hegemony. An historicising approach to magical realism helps make clear the extent to which realism is perceived by many postcolonial writers as being epistemologically allied to the kinds of reason and rationality that, by means of a productive alliance with colonialism, brought to the colonised world so much of the dark side of the Enlightenment, and so very little of its light.

3
Faith, Idealism, and Irreverence in Asturias, Borges, and Carpentier

The re-assessment of the history of magical realism undertaken in the previous chapter confirms that there are in principle no geographical constraints on where magical realism might be found, just as there are no limits to the purposes for which it might be deployed. Be this as it may, there are regions where magical realism has taken root and flourished, where writers have used it to respond to individual and cultural artistic imperatives and have learned from one another as they extend the creative and critical potential of the mode. Most obviously, Latin America is the unavoidable starting point for any serious critical engagement with magical realism. Why this should be the case is the implicit question addressed by this chapter.

Magical realism, or ideas closely associated with it, is present in the key texts of the "ABC" of modern Latin American literature: Miguel Ángel Asturias, Jorge Luis Borges, and Alejo Carpentier. Recent criticism tends not to include Borges's work directly in the category, but, as will become clear below, he is nonetheless the founding father of the irreverent strand of the mode.[1] Given the conceptual and terminological relations between Romance, idealism and magical realism outlined in the previous chapter, what is striking about these three writers is the extent to which their approaches to questions of mode and style have been influenced, in small but significant ways, by the legacy of German idealism. All three writers confronted questions about the nature of Latin America, and the role of the Latin American artist. Ambivalently positioned both inside and outside metropolitan culture, they could neither accept the terms of Western cultural hegemony nor reject them entirely. What they have in common philosophically is that they take as a target that modern paradigm of rational causality that arrogates to itself the right to determine with finality what is real and what is not. Borges uses idealist tenets for epistemological purposes. For the most part, he works from within the paradigm of causality, bringing to light the unexamined assumptions underpinning causal world-views, and manipulating these assumptions in order to show up their contradictions. The early Carpentier and Asturias, by contrast, are profoundly concerned with cultural ontology. They draw on the expanded realities of the Afro-Caribbean and the Maya to challenge the terms of what Stanley Tambiah calls causality, from the outside. These positions, as the remainder of this book aims to show, provide useful paradigms for understanding subsequent literary experiments with magical realism like those of Okri and Rushdie.

I   Borges: idealism and irreverence

Borges's admiration for idealism has been well-documented (Martín; Sturrock 20–30 and 61–76; Zamora "Swords" 35–38). In his "Autobiographical Essay" he tells us that he learned German while living with his family in Switzerland, where his father sought treatment for failing eyesight, between 1914 and 1919. The language of instruction at the College of Geneva was French, which Borges failed, and he took up the study of German on his own, reading Kant, Heine, Meyrink, and later Schopenhauer, who was to become his favourite philosopher. Schopenhauer likely appealed to Borges because facets of his philosophy corroborated already-held doubts about the laws of cause and effect and about the nature of time. As a child Borges's father used a chessboard to teach him Zeno's paradoxes. Later, "without mentioning Berkeley's name, he did his best to teach me the rudiments of idealism" (23). Back in Buenos Aires in 1921, Borges frequented a Saturday-night *tertulia* run by Macedonio Fernández, one of his father's lifelong friends. Fernández's eccentric idealism exerted an influence on the young Borges, Edwin Williamson notes, through his belief in the " 'unreality' of the material world and in the non-existence of the 'I', or individual subject" – ideas Borges would have encountered in Schopenhauer (97).

Novalis, especially attractive to Borges because he was a poet as well as a philosopher, clearly fits into this paradigm. Borges and

Novalis have many interests in common: Paracelsus and Plato, cabbalism, the role of the encyclopaedia, the relationship between art and philosophy, and the dream of uniting sign and signified, to name just a few. Borges signals the presence of a direct link between his own projects and those of Novalis in the essays "The Mirror of Enigmas", "A New Refutation of Time," and "Avatars of the Tortoise." He translated extracts from Novalis's *Fragments*, in the October 1938 edition of *Destiempo*, the literary magazine he founded with Bioy Casares. 46 years later, in his poem "Someone Shall Dream," he can still be found quoting the German thinker and providing a virtual paraphrase of some of his ideas (Williamson 225, 471). It is in "Avatars of the Tortoise," a version of which was published as early as 1929, that Borges's most explicit alignment with Novalis emerges:

> Let us admit what all idealists admit: the hallucinatory nature of the world. Let us do what no idealist has done: seek unrealities which confirm that nature ... "The greatest magician (Novalis has memorably written) would be one who would cast a spell so complete that he would take his own phantasmagorias as autonomous appearances. Would this not be our case?" I conjecture that this is so. We (the undivided divinity operating within us) have dreamt the world. We have dreamt it as firm, mysterious, visible, ubiquitous in space and durable in time; but in its architecture we have allowed tenuous and eternal crevices of unreason which tell us it is false. ("Avatars" 243)

This passage is, significantly enough, taken from Borges's analysis of Zeno, reminding us that the link between idealism and paradox had been forged long before he wrote this essay. Borges's engagement with literary or philosophical material is often caustically ironic, toying with reader expectations in order to defamiliarise established notions of order or causality. Here paradox is the key to an anti-materialist conception of reality based in the idea of the world as hallucination or dream. The language of exhortation gives the passage an almost manifesto-like quality, and indeed the search for "tenuous and eternal crevices of unreason" did constitute a large part of Borges's writerly career. Many of his short narratives can, in one way or another, be seen to participate in this logic, or anti-logic, of paradox, idealism and scepticism, and the effect is often the same: to blur the boundaries between self and non-self, object and subject, original and copy, dream and waking, reason and unreason, fantasy and reality.

Viewed in the light of Beiser's doubts about the absolutism of Novalis's idealism, discussed in the previous chapter, Borges's explicit claim to epistemological alignment with Novalis is not as straightforward as it seems, though. Borges's reading of Novalis corresponds to the subjectivist interpretation of German idealism criticised by Beiser. The epistemological thread emphasised by Borges is Berkeleyan: this is the Novalis who wrote in his study of Hemsterhuis, "we *know* only insofar as we *make*" (qtd Beiser 438). Beiser emphasises a different strand of Novalis's thinking, one which stresses antisubjectivist notions of "self-alienation" and "enlivening," and one in which subject and object are related in organic terms, "such that each becomes what it is only through the other" (432–433).[2]

For our purposes what is important is that, conceptually, Borges's inscriptions and explorations of idealism allow us better to place his writing with regard to the tradition of magical realism that was to succeed him. It will be recalled that, in terms of Novalis's original formulation, a "*magischer Realist*" was the mirror image of a "*magischer Idealist*." The latter term fits Borges better than does the former because, for all their shifting, ludic qualities, Borges's projects are antithetical to those that conventionally underpin realism and literary magical realism depends on realism even as it strives to expand or subvert it.

Borges did in fact brush closely against magical realism, as it is being defined in this book, on several occasions. Williamson notes that in 1926 he published a review of a German translation of "Turkish Tales" in which he commented on the ways in which "the marvelous and the everyday are entwined [...]. There are angels as there are trees: they are just another element in the reality of the world" (176). Williamson correctly suggests that in this review Borges "discovered the basic principle of what came to be known [...] as Latin American 'magic realism' though he would never use the term as such, and his blending of fantasy and reality would be quite different from that of 'magic realists' such as Alejo Carpentier, García Márquez or Isabel Allende" (176n). The reason for this difference is to be found in the influence of an idealism which ultimately denies the materiality of the world – and hence forecloses on the possibility of mirroring it through literary realism.

Fiction, Borges notes in his review of "Turkish Tales," "was capable of putting modern man in touch with something 'primitive' that had been lost" (Williamson 176). These ideas fed into an early essay, "Narrative Art and Magic" (1932). In this essay, Borges makes clear that, with the exception of the "ponderous psychological variety" of the novel, narrative causality is governed by "a very different order, both lucid and primitive: the primeval clarity of magic" (80). The understanding of magic here is one based on that developed by Sir James Frazer, but Borges overwrites Frazer by suggesting that "the only possible integrity" for the novel lies in the embrace of a magic "in which every lucid and determined detail is a prophecy" (82). Borges suggests that causality, the illusion of which lies behind so much naturalistic narrative, is itself a form of magic. One of the central strategies that Borges derives from Berkeley is the idea that causality can only ever be inferred, never proven. Yet, despite Berkeley, since Aristotle's *Poetics*, causality has assumed the status of a real, invisible force that orders narrative. His comments in "Narrative Art and Magic" might very well stand as a manifesto of his intentions in one of his most famous works of short fiction, "The Garden of Forking Paths" (1941) which shows the principle of order to be arbitrary, and indicates the extent to which theories of cause and effect depend for their validity on assumptions that cannot be wholly proven. Time and again in his short fictions, Borges sets out to demonstrate just how arbitrary this principle of order really is.

Though he is not concerned with the naturalisation of the supernatural that is the defining quality of magical realism, Borges is therefore still a crucial founding figure for modern magical realism. The strand of idealism he draws upon helps to clarify one important difference between what will later be identified as the faith-based approach of the early Carpentier, Asturias and Okri on the one hand, and the more discursive orientation of later magical realists like Rushdie on the other. Unlike the early Carpentier and Asturias, Borges is concerned not with bringing the magical into the domain of the real, but with calling into question the very foundations of both categories. This is a philosophical distinction, to be identified on the level of the text and the ideas being asserted by it, but it has its contextual correlative in questions about the relations between writing and identity. Where, as Erik Camayd-Freixas has shown,

Carpentier's and Asturias's magical realism was closely bound up with questions of cultural identity and the yearning for authentic modes of expression, Borges, by contrast, was sceptical of such literary expressions of cultural nationalism.

This is not to say that Borges's writerly world-view was not profoundly conditioned by his culturally marginal status as an Argentine, and hence a postcolonial subject. Beatriz Sarlo states that "there is no writer in Argentine literature more Argentine than Borges" (3). For her, Borges's dialogue with the "residual gauchesque tradition" in Argentine literature, and his "fictionalisation of the theory of the intertext" exist as poles on a continuum of literary engagement (2). It is the condition of being on the "edge," the "margins," the *"orillas"* of the metropolitan literature that gives Borges the distance to re-evaluate key questions to do with referentiality, originality, and the nature of meaning (50). Sergio Waisman, in his study of Borges and translation, telling subtitled *The Irreverence of the Periphery*, picks up these ideas, showing how the Borges's questioning of the primacy of the original text leads to a productive creative irreverence. I would like to consolidate these ideas by arguing that "irreverence" is a key signifier of the ways Borges translates cultural marginality into an idiosyncratic yet highly influential critical and creative methodology that has been of profound relevance to one strand of magical realism.

Borges himself uses the term irreverence in a lecture called "The Argentine Writer and Tradition," presented in December 1951, at the height of Peronist cultural nationalism. He begins in characteristic fashion:

> I wish to formulate and justify here some sceptical proposals concerning the problem of the Argentine writer and tradition. My scepticism does not relate to the difficulty or impossibility of solving this problem, but to its very existence. I believe we are faced with a mere rhetorical topic which lends itself to pathetic elaborations; rather than with a true mental difficulty I take it we are dealing with an appearance, a simulacrum, a pseudo problem. (211)

Borges takes issue with three existing "solutions" to the question: the first, dealt with in detail (since it constituted a key aspect of Peronist cultural policy), is the proposal that Hernández's *Martín Fierro* should be canonised and that Argentine writing "should abound in differential Argentine traits and Argentine local colour" (214). The second proposal is that Argentine writing should adhere to the tradition of Spanish literature; this suggestion is quickly rejected (217). The third is that "in Argentina we are cut off from the past, that there has been something like a dissolution of continuity between us and Europe [...]. We Argentines find ourselves in a situation like that in the first days of Creation" (217). This last position would be one that would inspire a great number of Latin American writers including Carpentier, García Márquez, Octavio Paz and others, but Borges does not go into any detail, dismissing it on the grounds that European and colonial history is still "very close to us" (218).

Borges solves the problem of the relationship between the Argentine writer and tradition by declaring that it is not a problem at all. In the face of the cultural nationalist assertion that Argentine writing should eschew all that is European, he asserts:

> I believe our tradition is all of Western culture, and I also believe we have a right to this tradition, greater than that which the inhabitants of one or another Western nation might have [...]. I believe that we Argentines, we South Americans in general, are in an analogous situation [to that of Jews and the Irish]; we can handle all European themes, handle them without superstition, with an irreverence which can have, and already does have, fortunate consequences. (218)

On one level, the Argentine writer might be said to have a greater right to "Western culture" precisely because he or she is not bound by the usual constraints of the Western world-view and its identity politics. On a deeper level, Sarlo, Waisman and others have rightly drawn the link between Borges's ludic subversions of theories of originality in texts like "Pierre Menard, Author of the Quixote" and the cosmopolitanism that emerges in "The Argentine Writer and Tradition." As Sarlo puts it: "If no originality is attached to the text, but only to the writing or reading of the text, the inferiority of the margins vanishes and the peripheral writer is entitled to the same claims as his or her European predecessors or contemporaries" (33). It is worth pointing out, though, that Borges does not in fact assert an equal right to "European themes" but a *greater* one. The hyperbolic gesture conceals a host of clues related to what Borges means by irreverence.

Infinite intertextuality, the repudiation of the referential illusion (felt to be an ethical as well as an epistemological imperative), the idea that literature can construct space and time, the decentring of the subject, the refutation and subversion of binaries of all kinds – these are all are aspects of what Sarlo calls "the freedom of a marginal working in the margins" (28). Borges's fascination with paradox, and with the idealist and sceptical philosophies of Berkeley, Hume, Novalis and Schopenhauer, exists in an unavoidable relation with his position as a postcolonial subject. Irreverence thus signifies a response to a situation of marginality, an attitude to authority, and an orientation towards the dominant systems of knowledge and representation of that authority.

Borges, through his idiosyncratic extensions of the ideas of philosophical idealists initiated an irreverent, discursive approach to writing which is very different from that of the early Carpentier or Asturias. In the irreverent magical realism developed in the wake of Borges, magic is present not as a signifier of alternative realities but as a means by which the assumptions underpinning narratives of the real can be examined in terms of their status as discourses among other discourses. Frequently, this discursive approach is associated with other forms of irreverence – religious, cultural, or political. The text I have most closely associated with this practice is Salman Rushdie's *The Satanic Verses* to be discussed in Chapter Five. As will become clear in the next chapter, it is also an approach which, in more qualified ways, enables the magical realism of Gabriel García Márquez's *One Hundred Years of Solitude*.

II   Asturias: faith and cultural ontology in *Men of Maize* (*Hombres de maíz*)

Miguel Ángel Asturias's 1949 masterpiece, *Men of Maize*, is probably the most developed example of an ontological, faith-based magical realism in existence. As the notes assembled by an international team of scholars to accompany Gerald Martin's critical edition suggest, it could also be the most anthropologically-informed novel ever written. These two features are clearly related, for it is impossible to appreciate the novel's magical realism without some knowledge of

Asturias's Mayan and Aztec sources, particularly the *Popol Vuh*, the *Book of Chilam Balam*, the "Legend of the Suns" and the *Sacred Hymns of the Nahuas*. As Martin points out in his introduction to the novel, *Men of Maize* also draws on ethnography, Guatemalan folk culture, Spanish Golden Age literature, Darwin, Marx and Freud, to say nothing of the insights and methods of surrealism (xxiv). These sources are artistically mediated through the filters of Asturias's emotional experience – childhood contact with Guatemala's *ladino*[3] and Indian population, the claustrophobia of living under the dictator, Jorge Ubico, between 1933 and 1944, the alcoholism and despair that followed the break-up of his first marriage, and the death of his mother in May 1948.[4]

In a 1959 interview, Asturias described his writing as "American magical realism [...] as in the indigenous texts." For his characters, "magic is something like a second language, like a complementary language for understanding the universe" (qtd Camayd-Freixas 170). These comments are emblematic of what I am calling the faith-based, ontological tendency in magical realist writing. This assumes for literature the task of describing a reality understood to exceed the scope of conventional narrative realism. In this novel, as in other examples from postcolonial literatures, such an approach often emerges from a pact between post-positivistic anthropology and avant-garde modernist prose. *Men of Maize* is especially successful in this regard, largely because it displays such a high degree of self-consciousness and technical skill in its assertion of the primacy of myth-based perceptions of reality over those informed by empirical rationality.

Asturias's capacity to translate the world-view of the indigenous population of Guatemala into fiction should not be overestimated. He spoke no Indian languages, and, as he said to Luis Harss and Barbara Dohmann of his knowledge of the Indian world, "I heard a lot, assumed a bit more, and invented the rest" (433). His preferred method of invention was the technique of automatic writing, and his antagonism towards rationalism was heavily influenced by the surrealist movement. As Camayd-Freixas suggests, one way of reading of *Men of Maize* is as a mixture of Lautréamont and the *Popul Vuh* (176). Nevertheless, the local frame in which this magical realism is expressed is undeniable and it will be necessary, therefore, to approach Asturias's magical realism in terms of both its surrealist and Romantic impulses, and for what it tells us about his search for a Guatemalan identity. A close focus on the roles and functions of codes of realism and of the fantastic is required. It is especially those textual spaces where the two codes meet and intertwine with one another that need to be investigated if a fuller sense of the novel's meaning is to be generated, and its place as the founding text in a strain of magical realism – largely neglected by contemporary critics – is to be fully understood.[5]

Notwithstanding the optimistic note on which the novel ends, *Men of Maize* reads like a document of loss. Whichever dimension of the novel one wishes to emphasise – whether ecological, cultural, historical, psychic or existential – nostalgia is the most pervasive of Asturias's effects and is the means by which he is able to evoke a sense of an original human wholeness, now lost. This wholeness or unity is represented as a dreamlike union with nature and also, in a Jungian sense, as the union of the male and female principles of the psyche. The novel's epigraph, "Here the woman,/ and I, asleep" alludes to this dreamtime of sacred unity, and also locates the source of this mythical wholeness in terms of Asturias's Aztec and Mayan sources.[6] Both of these imaginary states of wholeness are presented in the novel as shattered by the effects of capitalism and colonialism. It is especially deforestation and the exploitation of the land for the purposes of growing maize (a crop sacred to the Maya) for profit that is responsible for the rupture of union between human and earth. Consequent on this rupture is the impossibility of sustaining the inclusive transcendental matriarchy suggested in the constant references to the earth as mother.

Men of Maize not only attends to the ruptures wrought by conquest and capitalism; it celebrates resistance, and serves as a call-to-arms of sorts. According to Martin, Asturias's elder son, Rodrigo, was one who responded quite literally to this call-to-arms. He assumed the name of Gaspar Ilóm, the Indian protagonist of the novel, himself based on a historical figure of Indian resistance, and became a guerrilla commandant for an Indian-oriented resistance group, the "Organisation of the People in Arms" (xxvi). Martin also points out that in its conclusion the novel puts forward a socialist alternative to the distribution of natural resources in Guatemala which is demonstrably similar to that proposed in 1944 by Guatemala's first and only socialist government. On a more abstract level, *Men of Maize* harnesses indigenous myth-based modes of perception as a strategy of resistance to the dominant terms of modernity – especially those that enforce particular modes of knowledge formation at the expense of others. Having established a basis for the transcendental in ecological and psychic terms, Asturias goes so far as to gesture towards ways in which all humans can attempt to recover their connection with these lost origins. In showing how this process might take place, a number of cultural assumptions are invoked that derive directly – and explicitly – from the milieu of German idealism, as will become clear later in this chapter.

The starting point for an enquiry into the novel's ontological magical realism is its very opening lines, which dramatise the moment of rupture between what we are crudely calling "magic" and "the real." As we have seen, the epigraph evokes the double wholeness of union with earth and woman. This mythical dreamtime is also the literal sleep of the Indian leader, Gaspar Ilóm, who is lying with his wife, Piojosa Grande, on his reed mat in the forest. But both mythic and literal sleep are shattered by the recriminations of the earth:

> "Gaspar Ilóm lets them steal the sleep from the eyes of the land of Ilom."
>
> "Gaspar Ilóm lets them hack away the eyelids of the land of Ilom with axes ..."
>
> "Gaspar Ilóm lets them scorch the leafy eyelashes of the land of Ilom with fires that turn the moon to furious red ..."
>
> Gaspar Ilóm shook his head from side to side. To deny, to grind the accusation of the earth where he lay sleeping with his reed mat, his shadow, and his woman, where he lay buried with his dead ones and his umbilicus, unable to free himself from a serpent of six hundred thousand coils of mud, moon, forests, rainstorms, mountains, birds and echoes entwined around his body. (7, ellipses in original)

Immediately obvious in Gerald Martin's translation of the language of the earth's accusations are patterns of repetition which, as Martin's annotations suggest, are characteristic of litanies and spells and are frequently found on Mayan codices (315 n4). The model of language employed in the early stages of the novel is one that has affinities with oral traditions of ritual and storytelling. The structure of the novel as a whole is based on patterns of repetition and metaphoric elaboration similar to those present in the novel's incantatory opening lines. The unity of the novel cannot therefore necessarily be gauged by conventional chronology or character development but rather through a sometimes elaborate set of coded associations (Prieto 9; Christ 440). This structure, and the magical model of language that underpins it, is an important means by which the novel (and other ontological magical realism, like that of Okri) attempts to overcome the perceived linearity of the rationalist models of thought from which realism emerges.

Gaspar Ilóm, unwillingly awoken by the recriminations of the earth which has itself been disturbed from its magical sleep, reluctantly undergoes a birth of sorts. He must untie himself from the coils of the serpent – both the metaphysical dream-union with the earth, and his commitments to wife, children, rancho – to emerge individuated and separated from nature and clan. Martin notes that his waking is reminiscent of a theme frequent in Aztec poetry, that of the reluctant warrior chastised by a god for his unwillingness to go to war (316 n6). His mission will now be to take up arms against the maize growers. This task he performs with success until he is betrayed and poisoned by the *ladinised* Indian, Tomas Machojón and his wife Vaca Manuela. Seeing him poisoned, his wife flees from him, completing the violation suggested in the novel's epigraph, for now Gaspar has lost both sleep and "the woman." Gaspar defeats poison and death by "drinking down the river" (24). But when he sees his men massacred by soldiers he throws himself into the river, leaving the realm of the real to become a purely mythical symbol of resistance.

Before they die, the "firefly wizards" of Gaspar's group – men with magical powers – call curses on the traitors and soldiers for having murdered "the one who succeeded in throwing the noose of his word round the fire running wild in the mountains of Ilom" (28). This phrase – comparable with what in African orature would be called a praise-name[7] – is repeated at various points in the novel and suggests both the novel's main themes and the model of language that underpins it. In structural terms, the most obvious feature of what Seymour Chatman calls "story" concerns the ways in which the firefly wizards' curses come to be fulfilled.[8] One by one those responsible for Gaspar's murder – including, in the case of the Zacatones, their families – are punished with death or sterility. Fire is the dominant motif of the novel, and signifies as much the literal fires which threaten the forest as the cosmic forces that Gaspar is able to enlist to protect them. Ariel Dorfman has gone as far as to assert that fire is both one of the novel's protagonists, and its formal principle: "words are flames, they sputter, they refuse to be enclosed, they hop like gleaming yellow rabbits, they die down and then rise up again with an uncontainable rhythm of revenge" (393). Gaspar's praise name suggests that, like the firefly wizards whose curses are proved efficacious by their fulfilment in the novel, he has access to a magical language in which word and thing and word and deed are one. Indeed, in the "praise name" itself, the metaphorical and the literal are inseparable. The double metaphors of "word-as-noose" and of "fire-harnessed" do not displace the phrase's literal meaning – that Gaspar was able to stop the maize growers from burning the forest. Such processes, whereby literal and metaphorical, which often correspond to a distinction between fantastic and real, myth and history, are folded into one another are highly characteristic of the novel as a whole.

The earth demands that retribution on the maize growers enact a symmetry with regard to what it has itself lost. Gaspar must

> hack the eyelids of those who fell the trees, singe the eyelashes of those who burn the forest, and chill the bodies of those who dam the waters of the river that sleeps as it flows and sees nothing until trapped in pools it opens its eyes and sees all with its deep water gaze. (7)

Men of Maize's fascination with eyes and eyelids, seeing, sleep and blindness supports its project of calling into question the assumptions by which normative empirical rationality determines what is "real" and what is "magical." Throughout his novel, Asturias reverses the semiotic hierarchies between waking and sleeping, sight and blindness that prevail in modernity. Instead of merely signifying inactivity or disability, sleep and blindness are associated with orders of knowledge unavailable to the waking or seeing mind. This reversal is primarily ecologically directed, for the slash-and-burn clearing of the forests undertaken by the commercial maize growers is removing the magical mantle under which the earth – and Gaspar Ilóm – had been dreaming. The implication is that the kind of knowledge generated by a system that privileges waking and seeing – which is the same system of knowledge that privileges real over magical – leads directly to separation from nature, disenchantment and ecological disaster.

In terms of the novel's portrayal of the search for psychic wholeness, expressed as the quest for the Jungian anima, the process of semiotic reversal is even more dramatic. In Part Five we encounter Goyo Yic, the blind Indian whose wife, María Tecún, has deserted him. Desperate to find her, he consults a healer who chastises him for being ungrateful for his blindness, and warns him that sight will "stop [him] seeing the flower of the amate, the flower hidden within the fruit, the flower only blind men see" (109). Yic does not heed the warning, and, by ritual means, the healer cures him of his blindness. From this point until the end of the novel, when he is reunited with his wife, Yic is in a state of decline. He becomes a peddler and wanders the country getting women to speak by offering them trinkets, for he knows María Tecún only by ear. Eventually he realises that "in the recesses of his consciousness he searched for her no longer. He had lost her" (123). María Tecún is repeatedly associated with the flower of the amate, a tree which, paradoxically, has no flower (120, 127); she is said to be inside of Goyo Yic (126), though he can no longer find her there; but she is, above all, not a woman, but Woman, as is clear from her mythical elevation to Maria the Rain at the novel's end (305). Goyo Yic's acquisition of sight thus has consequences similar to the "waking" of the land through deforestation, or the rivers through damming. In Yic's case, loss is narrated in terms of psychic rather than ecological processes – by gaining the ability to see surface reality, he loses the ability to perceive deeper, hidden truths.

The voice of the earth will not be heard after Gaspar Ilóm awakes. The novel appears to describe a progression from the mythical dreamtime of the epigraph to the disenchanted semi-modernity of Asturias's contemporary Guatemala. Consequently, the parts of the novel that deal with *ladinos* or Europeans are characterised by a more objective narration than those dealing with Indians (though rapid shifts of focaliser and an intermingling of subjective and objective points of view are common throughout). However, Asturias installs this apparent progression with the intention of subverting it. He does this in Parts Five and Six by demonstrating the power and veracity of myth in the lives of characters who are culturally removed from the world of Gaspar and his people. These sections are set anything between twenty and fifty years after the murder of Gaspar Ilóm. Chronology is of less relevance to Asturias's intentions, though, than are the processes by which events of the past are contained in popular memory, where they acquire the status of legend. The novel dramatises the relationships between history and myth at a number of points and in several different ways, but it is always the mythic dimension which proves more important than the historical. Even when the actual, material circumstances of the myth's coming into being are well-known, Asturias insists that it is not the story itself that is important, but the patterns of truth that can be discerned underneath it.

Machojón, condemned by the curse of the firefly wizards for his parents' betrayal of Gaspar Ilóm, is carried into the heavens by a swarm of fireflies. His disappearance gives rise to rumours, which are then manipulated into the semblance of reality by the sharecroppers for their own purposes. When Señor Tomas, Machojón's father, discovers that the sharecroppers have manufactured the legend about his son, his madness leads him to take on the shape of the legend and ride through the flames himself, thus concluding a cycle that leads from myth to rumour to reality and then back to myth. Similarly, María Tecún, Goyo Yic's runaway wife, leaves her husband for purely practical reasons (if she stays she fears that she would be condemned to a perpetual state of impregnation) but within a few years has become a mythic symbol of the departed woman and her name has entered the popular vocabulary. Though the myth of the *tecuna* is named after a real person, and derives from a patently personal history, María Tecún's story does not reside in the domain of history as it is conventionally understood. Her literal departure is but an echo of the earlier departure of Gaspar Ilóm's woman, Piojosa Grande, which in turn reminds us of the rupture of the novel's epigraph and its opening lines. Whether it is sacred or popular, myth, for Asturias, provides a point of connection and interpenetration between everyday reality and the forces that flow below its surface.

The processes by which myth is valorised over history in *Men of Maize* are nowhere clearer than in the responses of the *ladino* muleteer, Hilario Sacayón, to the two most important myths in the second part of the novel, the popular myth of the *tecuna*, and the pre-Columbian belief in nahualism (metamorphosis into one's spirit animal). Hilario does not believe in either myth and has particular reason to doubt the myth of the *tecuna*. His scepticism has its roots in the fact that, once, while drunk, he invented a story about a woman called Miguelita de Acatán. The story took on a life of its own and became a legend in itself. Songs are now sung about her, masses are held to pray for her, and searches for her birth certificate in the parish registry have been undertaken. But when Hilario tries to tell the old innkeeper, Ramona Corzantes, also known as Nana Monchada, that he made Miguelita up, she refuses to believe him, claiming that she heard about Miguelita from her grandmother. In the face of his insistence on the story's fictionality, her response is revealing:

> We often think we've invented things that other people have forgotten. When you tell a story that no one else tells anymore, you say: I invented this, it's mine. But what you're really doing is remembering – you, through your drunkenness, remembered what the memory of your forefathers left in your blood, because you must realize that you're a part not only of Hilario Sacayón, but of all the Sacayones that have ever lived, and on your mother's side, of all the Arriazas, all folks from around these parts [...]. If it hadn't been you it would have been someone else; someone would have told it, so that it wouldn't be forgotten, because its existence, true or false, is part of the life, part of the nature of these places, and life cannot be lost, it's eternally at risk but it cannot be lost eternally. (204)

Asturias puts into the mouth of Nana Monchada a set of folkloric homilies that reject modern individualism and its models of creativity. Individual authorship of ideas or stories is simply not possible in this faith-based orientation to reality – and nor are categories like "true" or "false."[9]

Hilario is not convinced by the argument of the old innkeeper, however. A more personal, cathartic experience is required. Here the second major myth of this part of the novel, nahualism, finds its significance. Hilario has been sent by his German employer, Don Deferic, to ensure that the postman, Nicho Aquino, makes it safely over the so-called María Tecún ridge, where runaway wives – *tecunas* – are said to lure their husbands to their deaths. Hilario is familiar with the myth of the nahual, and knows too that Nicho's speed in delivering the mail is said to be the result of his capacity to transform into a swift-footed coyote. When Hilario glimpses a small animal near to María Tecún ridge he is immediately thrown into doubt as to whether he has seen a coyote or a person. The doubt plagues him. Later, when Nicho's disappearance is confirmed, he realises that "Señor Nicho and the coyote he ran across up on María Tecún Ridge were the same person" (221). Crucially, the way in which he comes to this knowledge is not through the senses:

> For a moment he saw himself, pistol in hand, aiming at the hide of that coyote on María Tecún Ridge, which was not a coyote, which was not a coyote at all, he knew it, with all the faculties of the soul which are not in the senses, he knew it, his consciousness had accepted as irremediably real something which previously had been a mere story as far as he was concerned. (225–226)

The repetition of "he knew," and the fact that Hilario's certainty is reached through the "faculties of the soul which are not in the senses" aligns his insight with Goyo Yic's blindness. Hilario's cathartic revelation is therefore explicitly connected to a different order of knowledge from that of observation or empirical validation, which Asturias has already linked with separation, alienation and ecological disaster. After his revelation, Hilario is an altered man. He drinks and talks less, and tells no one about his experience, because to reveal the "sacred" and "intimate" link between him and Nicho would "break the mystery" and "violate the secret nature of certain profound and remote relations." He becomes "possessor of a hidden truth" (266). The metamorphosis of Nicho Aquino from man into coyote, the most sustained magical realist event in the novel, is confirmed by the authority of detailed, if highly stylised, objective third person narration later on in the chapter. In this way, the novel endorses the lesson offered to Hilario Sacayón by Nana Monchada. Stories are not to be judged by whether they are obviously true or false, real or invented, but by the extent to which they access deeper, more hidden truths about nature and the human psyche. Within Asturias's novel, these truths can be identified by means of recourse to the sense of original transcendental unity described in the epigraph.

Supporting this process of elevating myth over the real are a series of explicit references to German idealism that make for revealing comparisons with Borges and Carpentier. The key figure here is the Bavarian trader, Don Deferic. Deferic becomes maddened by the disappearance of Nicho Aquino, fearing that the latter has fallen victim to the lure of the mythical temptations of the *tecuna*. His dialogue with his wife, Doña Elda – which is, we are told, conducted in German – is worth quoting at length to demonstrate how, through the bombastic Bavarian, Asturias harnesses Romantic ideas to his cause:

> Doña Elda, his wife, tried to calm him, urging him not to be carried away by legends, legends are just stories, they exist only in the imaginings of poets, are believed in by children, and then only by grandmothers.
>
> The German [*El bávaro*] replied that her way of thinking was completely materialist, and materialism is absurd, because matter is by nature something that passes away. What would Germany be without its legends? Where did the German language drink the better part of its spirit? Did the primary substances not spring from obscure beginnings? Has the contemplation of infinity not revealed the nullity of all that has limits? Why without the tales of Hoffmann...
>
> Doña Elda agreed that the legends of Germany were true; but not those of that poor settlement of Chuj Indians and louse-infested Ladinos with shoes on. Don Deferic pointed his finger at his wife's breast like the barrel of a pistol and accused her of having a European mentality. Europeans are fools, they think only Europe has ever existed. (197, ellipsis in original)

Deferic, a minor character, is portrayed with a great deal of sympathy in the novel. He refuses to take advantage of the distraught Nicho Aquino, offering him money instead, he helps rescue a trapped monkey, he embraces his muleteer employee, Hilario Sacayón. He is also rapturously associated with Germanic looks and with stereotypical Romantic attributes ("The German smiled. His blue eyes, the blue mountains, the blue skies"; he "plays violin on moonlit nights [and] wears a flower in his buttonhole" (162, 195)). Stephen Henighan has pointed out that in later works like *Los ojos de los enterrados*, Asturias's characters "are reduced to national stereotypes," and the Wagnerian Deferic may well anticipate this tendency. More to the point, Deferic's presence in *Men of Maize* complicates Henighan's claim that Asturias elaborates a Guatemalan national mythology "because he does not believe that Guatemalans, and, by implication, other Latin Americans, can participate on favourable terms in the kind of transnational cultural relations dramatized in Carpentier's fiction" (1021). Deferic's installation of Germany as the touchstone of culture connected with mythology, and his simultaneous rejection of Eurocentric prejudice, allows Asturias to draw on the cultural authority of Romantic idealism to reinforce the claims to legitimacy of non-rational modes of thought indigenous to Guatemala. The idealist refusal of absolute boundaries between self and not-self, between subject and object, appears at this point precisely in order to make available transnational mythopoeic relations between Germany and Guatemala, Europe and Latin America.

It is important to be cautious about too closely identifying the implied author of *Men of Maize* with Deferic, for whom "materialism is absurd" and who seems really to believe that the contemplation of infinity has "revealed the nullity of all that has limits" (154). The difference between absolute idealism and literary magical realism is not merely a question of form or genre since serious ethical issues attend Deferic's perspective. These come into view shortly after Deferic sets out his idealist agenda. Speaking of the victims of the *tecuna* myth, Deferic claims that "those people are sacrificed so the legend may live." His wife reacts strongly to this idea, calling Deferic's ignoring of the plight of the victim "detestable." Deferic retorts: "The gods have disappeared, but the legends remain and they, like the gods before them, demand sacrifices. Gone too are the obsidian knives which tore out the hearts of sacrificial victims, but the knives of absence which wound and madden, remain" (199). Probably the most famous lines of the novel, Deferic's comments clearly reinforce its central themes, which are also those of much ontological, faith-based magical realism: materialist conceptions of reality are flawed; myths and legends are not fictional, not make-believe, but rather provide a means of recovering psychic and ecological wholeness; the elemental forces flowing below the visible surface of things demand and exact sacrifice. But these comments also appear, problematically, to endorse the necessity of human sacrifice.

Asturias, who lived in Paris from 1924 to 1933, would have known that George Bataille and his circle openly celebrated the anti-bourgeois spiritual charge of human sacrifice, to the point of obtaining a volunteer victim and planning a sacrifice in Paris in the 1930s.[10] It is this spirituality, the "occult force" mentioned earlier by Doña Elda, that Asturias wishes to draw upon in his invocation of human sacrifice. In Deferic, Asturias found a way to justify the presence and reality of such qualities of spirit by recourse to a simplified version of German Romantic idealism. But Deferic's comments are troubling on an ethical level in terms of their unspoken relations to historical incidences of bloodletting motivated by mythical or cultural belief systems. Written wholly or in part by 1935 (Prieto 91) but published only in 1949, Asturias's enthusiastic portrayal of a myth-inspired Germanness seems at best insensitive to the historical realities of Europe in the previous decade. Despite his rejection of Eurocentrism, the cultural politics of Deferic's approving reference to ancient Mesoamerican human sacrifice appear, on close inspection, similar to those of a thinker like Ernst Jünger or his contemporary, Oswald Spengler, whose influence on Carpentier will be explored in the next section of this chapter. Indeed, Theodor Adorno's comments on Spengler are strikingly relevant to Deferic: "in Spengler the tendency of the German idealists to fetishize broad general concepts in their theories and then impassively sacrifice the existence of the individual human being to them – a tendency Schopenhauer, Kierkegaard, and Marx attacked in Hegel – becomes undisguised joy in actual human sacrifice" (61). Adorno, himself profoundly affected by Nazism, suggests that a crucial ethical failing of idealism is its uncompromising celebration of the idea over the individual, a position that seems to underpin Deferic's comments.

Asturias's novel, by contrast, does attend to the marginal and the marginalised, and Doña Elda's criticisms suggest a more ethical reading of her husband's claims, one grounded in the perspective of the victim of sacrifice rather than its perpetrator. Gerald Martin has noted how in *Men of Maize* "women characters are defined as devious and treacherous when it is they who are victims" (Introduction xxv).[11] The postman, Nicho Aquino, himself is, in many ways, also a victim, and the novel's later detailed exploration of his experience (including his metamorphosis into a coyote) constitutes a further demonstration of a potential distance between Asturias and the indifference of Deferic. Asturias moderates Deferic's idealism by refusing to allow individual persons and things to be subsumed by "broad general concepts." The reconciliation between ideal and real thus constitutes a meaningful sense in which *Men of Maize* can be called magical realist, one congruent with Novalis's original use of the term. In chapter six of this study I shall explore the resonances Asturias's approach has with an important later example of magical realism, Ben Okri's *The Famished Road*.

III   Carpentier: ontology into discourse in *The Kingdom of This World* (*El reino de este mundo*)

In magical realist critical lore, Alejo Carpentier is famous for having proposed in 1949 that Latin America is ontologically imbued with *lo real maravilloso americano* – the marvellous real of the Americas. Other places and other times may have been in touch with the marvellous – Marco Polo believed that certain birds flew with elephants in their claws, Luther saw a demon and threw an inkpot at his head, Victor Hugo believed in ghosts – but these are isolated, trivial examples. On the whole, by contrast with the authentic Latin American marvellous, "the tiresome pretension of creating the marvellous that has characterised certain European literatures" is nothing more than "poverty of the imagination" ("Marvellous Real" 86). The surrealists, Carpentier avers, are particularly guilty in this regard, for they have forgotten that

> the marvellous begins to be unmistakably marvellous when it arises from an unexpected alteration of reality (a miracle), from a privileged revelation of reality, an unaccustomed insight that is singularly favoured by the unexpected richness of reality, or by an amplification of the scale and categories of reality, perceived with particular intensity by virtue of an exaltation of the spirit that leads it to a kind of "extreme state". To begin with, the phenomenon of the marvellous presupposes faith. (86)

The fact that the marvellous as a concept comes from Europe, specifically from André Breton, seems to make no difference to Carpentier. Nor is he particularly concerned with elaborating the problematics and implications of his concept of faith. As

Camayd-Freixas points out, his appeal to faith signals the extent to which his conclusions, and perhaps even his thought itself, is "deliberately irrational" (100). But, as is the case with much to do with magical realism, Carpentier's unreason has a reason of its own.

We have already noted in the previous chapter the ways Carpentier used the romantic accounts of European explorers against the rationality of modern Europe (and, it should be added, against the artifice of Europe's attempts, via surrealism, to break from that rationality) in order to "identify" a Latin America that exists outside of the possibility of rational understanding. For Carpentier, the fact that early explorers could only understand the New World through the language of romance was a cause of celebration because it supports his own attempts at establishing a founding myth for Latin America. Romance thus comes to support Carpentier's project in terms of both its objects of fascination – the exotic, the mysterious, the strange – and in terms of its modes of perception in which the antinomies of reason and unreason that characterise rational thought are undone. Carpentier did not invent the cultural logic that underpins the move, however. According to Roberto González Echevarría, Carpentier's theory of *lo real maravilloso americano* depends heavily on the anti-rational cultural nationalism developed by the German thinker of the Weimar years, Oswald Spengler. Spengler was, in turn, profoundly influenced by the legacy of Romantic thought. It is thus possible to find in the relations between Spengler and Carpentier another path of influence connecting Romantic idealism to the literature of modern magical realism.

González Echevarría perhaps exaggerates the extent of Spengler's importance – Carpentier was influenced by many others, notably Pierre Mabille, Massimo Bontempelli, and Eugenio d'Ors. Primitivism, surrealism and Carpentier's own childhood encounters with Afro-Cuban ritual are also important elements to be considered (Chiampi 42; Camayd-Freixas, 34, 93–148). Spengler may well have served to confirm already-held attitudes rather than to stimulate them in the first place. Nevertheless, it is clear from Gonzalez Echevarría that Carpentier read Spengler in the translations of the *Revista de Occidente*, and when examined closely, the parallels between Spengler and the early Carpentier's cultural myth-making are telling. It is important to note, however, that for various reasons outlined by Gonzalez Echevarría, this influence pertains only to the early part of Carpentier's writing career. After *The Kingdom of This World*, Carpentier was to break with his attempts at using magical realism, as the term is defined here, to evoke the marvellous real of the Americas.

Though Spengler himself acknowledges only Goethe, Hegel, and Nietzsche, Theodor Adorno claims that his doctrine of the soul stems directly from Schelling, and it is not hard to see the influence of German idealism on his overall thinking (Adorno 69). Spengler's concern was with elaborating a set of ideas in which Prussian values provided the backbone for a nationalist socialism that would be able to stand up to Marxist and liberal forms of rationalism. As Herf puts it, Spengler, like Jünger, was governed by "the essentially Romantic intuition that external artefacts – political and cultural institutions, architectural forms, economic organisations – are the outer images of something internal and hidden: the soul or 'life'" (52). Carpentier was to adapt these ideas in the service of "a search for origins, the recovery of history and tradition, the foundation of an autonomous American consciousness" (Gonzalez Echevarría 107).

As González Echevarría shows, ironies abound in the selective ways in which Spengler's ideas were taken up by Carpentier. The pessimism Spengler expressed about the future of *Kultur* was generalised to that of Europe as a whole. Europe became only one culture among many, a culture which, moreover, was in a state of decline, unlike ascendant America. The approach to history and myth developed by Spengler in support of a narrow German cultural nationalism, when applied to the Latin American context, facilitated the kind of conflation of myth and history discernible in the prologue to *The Kingdom of This World*. In Carpentier's translation of Spengler's ideas, Latin America would have to be characterised by spontaneity, a certain fusion between landscape and consciousness, a culture felt rather than thought (González Echevarría 55–57). It was these qualities that he set out to demonstrate in the prologue to *The Kingdom of This World*. Spengler's call for myth to re-invigorate German culture thus presents the opportunity for Carpentier to boast that "America is far from using up its wealth of mythologies" ("Marvellous Real" 88). In Spengler's account myth is not separate from history – indeed, history is simply the external manifestation of hidden forces, and here too Carpentier follows in step. After all, "what is the entire history of America if not a chronicle of the marvellous real?" (88).

When the essay that introduces the concept of *lo real maravilloso americano* is read in conjunction with the novel it prefaced, it becomes clear that faith-based magical realism, with its characteristic mixing of natural and supernatural, is the mode of narration that, at this early stage of Carpentier's career, he felt best suited the exigencies of representing the marvellous Latin American world-view.

Carpentier's writing of *The Kingdom of This World* was inspired by a visit he undertook to Haiti in 1943. There he became aware of the possibility of "establishing certain synchronisms, American, recurrent, timeless, relating this to that, yesterday to today" ("Marvellous Real" 84). The most significant of these "synchronisms" – although it was not made explicit by Carpentier himself – was that which lay in the conjunction between the philosophy of history inherited from Spengler and the specific history of the Haitian revolution. If the Latin American "marvellous" was to be distinguished from that of the surrealists on ontological and telluric grounds, then these ought to be apparent in the history of the New World itself. *The Kingdom of This World* is an attempt to demonstrate that this is indeed the case and can be read as a vindication of his proposition that the history of the Americas is characterised by the real presence of the marvellous. *The Kingdom of This World* covers, in a problematically incomplete fashion, the events of the Haitian revolution, and can therefore be read as a fictional rewriting of a particular history, one which makes bold claims for the place of faith and magic in understanding the Haitian revolution.[12] Drawing closely on the remarkable history of the slave revolt, the novel manipulates this history by emphasising its repetitive qualities, cyclicality and its complicity with nature in order to demonstrate a transcendental idea of culture, and specifically of Latin America. It is significant, though, as we shall see, that Carpentier's novel directly confronts and rejects this ahistoricism in its latter half.

In the original prologue to *The Kingdom of This World*,[13] Carpentier makes specific the connection between history and the marvellous: in the text "a succession of extraordinary incidents is narrated, which occurred on the island of Saint Domingue in a definite period that does not reach the duration of a human lifetime, allowing the marvellous to flow freely from a reality strictly followed in all its details" (*El reino* xv). This assertion provides a basic summation of the most important elements of the novel and of its author's intentions in writing it. The "succession of extraordinary incidents" refers to the process by which Saint Domingue,[14] now Haiti, through a series of uprisings moved from being a colony of France to an independent republic in the late eighteenth and early nineteenth centuries.

Carpentier displays in his novel a fidelity to historical detail that is at times astounding.[15] From 1939 he had been working on a study of the history of Cuban music which was published as *La música en Cuba* in 1946. In the course of his research for this book, he uncovered and investigated a great deal of historical material, much of which he used as sources for the events, characters and ideas in *The Kingdom of This World*. The most significant of these sources were the writings of a resident of the colony, Moreau de Saint ᴵᵛᵉ́ry,[16] though Carpentier also made extensive use of diaries, correspondence and other archival sources. Carpentier's novel can thus be read in dialogue with other historiographical representations of the Haitian revolution such as C.L.R. James's classic study, *The Black Jacobins*, first published in 1938. The story told in James's groundbreaking history is that of how slaves, largely uneducated and poorly equipped, defeated their erstwhile masters along with massive armies from the three major European imperial powers in the only successful slave revolt on this scale the world has ever seen. In so doing they accomplished what all the grand revolutionary ideas of the French could not: freedom.[17] Carpentier is less interested in this story, though, than in colonial life prior to the revolution, and in dwelling on the bitter irony that, though the ideal of freedom was worth more to most slaves than their lives, no sooner had it been won from their European masters than it was betrayed by the structures of labour organisation on the island, poverty, and the oppression of new masters. When *The Kingdom of This World* is read in dialogue with James's study, the most glaring omission on the part of the former is any mention of the role of the strategist and leader of the revolution, Toussaint L'Ouverture. Carpentier's text is not historiography, and it does not distinguish fictional characters and events from those that are genuinely historical. It ignores the most important events and leaders of the revolution. Finally, and most importantly to our purposes, Carpentier insinuates aspects of the belief systems of his central character into the otherwise documentary style of the narration in a way that, initially, aligns his narrative mode with the ontological magical realism of Asturias. These early examples of magical realism are expressions of Carpentier's desire to demonstrate that quality of faith that grants access to the marvellous real.

The focaliser of those parts of the novel in which the Afro-Caribbean world-view is invoked is a slave, Ti Noël. As a boy or young man, Ti Noël witnesses colonial life and takes part in the historical poisoning campaign which took place in the 1750s, led by Macandal, portrayed as a fellow slave on Lenormand de Mézy's plantation. In Part Two of the novel Ti Noël is present at the call-to-arms led by Bouckman in 1791 and participates in the sack of the Lenormand plantation and the rape of his erstwhile mistress. He narrowly escapes execution after the insurrection is put down, and is restored to Lenormand, who escapes the troubles in Saint Domingue by fleeing, with Ti Noël, to Santiago de Cuba. Here the narrative deviates from Haitian history at the very point at which Toussaint L'Ouverture begins to turn the tide against the imperial armies, preferring to focus on the dissipate lifestyles of the refugee planters in Cuba.[18] Like those of Toussaint, the wars of independence led by Dessalines are represented only obliquely in *The Kingdom of This World*. Instead we follow the experience of Pauline Bonaparte as she journeys to the Antilles with her husband, leader of the French forces sent to reclaim the colony from the slaves. Pauline is attended by Soliman, a devoted slave, and the two dabble in Voodoo to ward off the yellow fever epidemic that kills her husband.

Ti Noël is in Cuba throughout this period, returning to Haiti only around 1816. Part Three sees his return to the devastated Lenormand plantation as an old man, but free, since slavery has been abolished forever in Haiti. However, Ti Noël is soon pressed into the construction of a palace and citadel for the tyrant, Henri Christophe, and he experiences the incredible brutality of Christophe's system of forced labour. The narrative focuses at this point on Christophe himself, describing in detail the stroke and the insurrection that leads to his suicide, and his immurement in the very stone of the citadel he was constructing. The fourth and final part of the novel describes the experiences of Soliman, who had served as valet to Christophe in Rome where Christophe's family has gone into exile. After Soliman dies of malaria, the narrative returns to Ti Noël, still living on the ruined plantation with his loot from the sack of Sans Souci. He is quite content, though senile, and enjoys a certain elevated status in the peasant community. Following the re-unification of the country and the ascendancy of Boyer, a new system of forced labour, overseen by the Mulatto aristocracy, is introduced to the area. Despairing of the cycles of recurrence that seem destined always to lead to oppression, Ti Noël decides to forsake the world of humans and, remembering the supernatural powers of Macandal, transforms himself into a succession of different animals. He is not content in animal guise, though, and, in a cathartic revelation, realises that he cannot escape his duty to the "Kingdom of This World." He declares war on his new masters but immediately disappears in a "great green wind" with which the novel ends.

The first example of magical realism occurs very early in the novel. Ti Noël, only a boy, accompanies Macandal on his search for plants that might be used as poison. They visit the house of an old woman, Maman Loi, apparently a witchdoctor, who lives alone in the mountains:

> Macandal showed Maman Loi the leaves, the plants, the fungi, the herbs he carried in his pouch. She examined them carefully, crushing and smelling some of them, throwing others away. At times the talk was of extraordinary animals that had had human offspring. And of men whom certain spells turned into animals. Women had been raped by huge felines, and at night, had substituted roars for words. Once Maman Loi fell strangely silent as she was reaching the climax of a tale. In response to some mysterious order she ran to the kitchen, sinking her arms in a pot full of boiling oil. Ti Noël observed that her face reflected an unruffled indifference, and – which was stranger – that when she took her arms from the oil they showed no sign of blister or burn, despite the horrible sputter of frying he had heard a moment before. As Macandal seemed to accept this with complete calm, Ti Noël did his best to hide his amazement. And the conversation went placidly on between the Mandingue and the witch, with long pauses while they gazed afar. (Trans. Harriet de Onís 25–26)

On first reading, this intrusion of the supernatural may seem gratuitous. Maman Loi plays no further role in the narrative and there seems no link between the bizarre action of plunging her arms into a pot of boiling oil and her knowledge of plants that might be put to use in Macandal's poisoning campaign. The passage is, however, instructive on a number of levels. It is unlikely that Maman Loi lives alone because she has been manumitted; more likely is that she is a *maroon*, a runaway, forgotten by the masters of the plantations because of her scant usefulness and monetary value. But her usefulness is of an order invisible to the whites as they are unaware – displaying an ignorance that will later kill many of them – of the kinds of knowledge (the "law" suggested by her name) that she possesses. Voodoo, the term used in the novel to identify the religious practices that unite the slaves and underpin their revolts, is a vital signifier of slave belief.[19] Crucially, it is represented by Carpentier in this novel as strongly located in a bond between nature and culture, a bond illustrated by Maman Loi. The divide between European and slave ways of perceiving reality is thematised throughout the novel, and it is the inability to appreciate and follow black religious practices that causes the downfall of the whites. Furthermore, the bubbling pot of oil can be read as evocative of the kinds of torture that slaves were subject to on the plantations, which frequently included being burned in various ways.[20] Maman Loi's immunity to harm from the oil thus figures her supernatural powers in a way that places her and Macandal outside the capabilities of white knowledge and power, and firmly within the Afro-Caribbean cosmogony. The incident also anticipates Macandal's later burning at the stake, though there are telling differences between the representations of each, as we shall shortly see.

The episode crystallises a distinction between rumour and reality. Throughout the novel, Afro-Caribbean beliefs are presented in an objective, distant and non-committal way as reported occurrence or popular legend. In the extract above, however, rumours about the supernatural are shifted onto a literal plane by the witchdoctor's actions. The reader is confronted with magic not as the belief of another, but as something actually occurring in an otherwise realistic context. The magical realist principle of equivalence is at work here, though with an important difference: Ti Noël himself finds it hard to believe what he has seen. Macandal, however, shows no amazement at the event and thus Ti Noël's coming to terms with the sudden presence of the supernatural in the midst of the natural should be read as part of the education he receives about African culture and history from Macandal. This influence is introduced in the first chapter and is central to Ti Noël's cathartic revelation in the last. More importantly, perhaps, Ti Noël's mental processing of the event can be read as an analogy of the reader's experience. The implication is that the reader, like Ti Noël, should accept the spiritual authority over these matters embodied by Maman Loi and Macandal, and hence move towards the kind of faith that empowers perception of non-rational dimensions of reality.

Ti Noël is a fictional character, whereas Macandal is drawn directly from historical source material. This difference presents a major obstacle to Carpentier, for, unlike Asturias, he is not able to reject wholly the rational basis on which history affirms the importance of the observed, the verified and the documented. By paying close attention to the interaction between codes of real and supernatural in an apparently magical real episode that lies at the heart of *The Kingdom of This World*, we can begin to outline the ways in which history begins to win its contest with myth in Carpentier's mind. Within Carpentier's oeuvre, the break with the concept of *lo real maravilloso* which Roberto González Echevarría has identified in *The Lost Steps* is anticipated in important ways in the difficulties Carpentier has with sustaining an ontological magical realism, apparent in the Maman Loi episode, that is equal to the task of portraying the Afro-Caribbean world-view. On an aesthetic level, we can re-frame the problem in terms of González Echevarría's observation of a tension that exists in Carpentier between two different views of art. The first, influenced by Spengler and the Afro-Caribbean movement points towards transcendence and an onto-theological view of art for which Carpentier's insistence on faith serves as the key marker; the other, derived largely from Ortega y Gasset's notion of "dehumanised art" is "an art devoid of transcendental pretensions – a literature that by its free play of metaphors uncovers its own game of illusion" (68). This was a tension present in surrealism itself, and is one which corresponds roughly with the distinction between ontological and discursive magical realisms I am drawing in this study. In this sense, *The Kingdom of This World* – and particularly the passage to be discussed shortly – is an appropriate bridge between the extreme onto-theology of *Men of Maize* and the eclectic, dualistic brand of magic that we will explore in *One Hundred Years of Solitude*.

After the initial success of his poisoning campaign, Macandal is betrayed and hunted by the planters and the colonial militia. He goes into hiding for more than four years, during which time the slaves "display a defiant good humour." They rejoice at the news of sightings of certain animals, for they know that, "[a]s he had the power to take the shape of hoofed animal, bird, fish or insect, Macandal continually visited the plantations of the Plaine to watch over his faithful and find out if they still had faith in his return" (41). The mention of faith is again important, suggesting the confidence the slaves have in Macandal's leadership, but also in his supernatural powers. But we must be careful to place this representation of Afro-Caribbean belief on the side of rumour rather than reality, for the narration is not committing itself to verifying these supernatural rumours as it did in the Maman Loi magical realist episode. However, when Macandal is caught and taken to be publicly executed, in a much-discussed passage, the stage is set for Carpentier to show himself in possession of the faith he has been advocating all along. He carefully outlines the difference between white and black worlds in terms of the whites' astonishment at the "indifference" of the blacks to Macandal's fate, and its counterpoint, the blacks' certainty that Macandal, who had many times before entered the world of the insects, would slip his bonds by transforming into a mosquito. Initially, it seems that Carpentier will side with the slaves and narrate the execution in the terms provided by magical realism:

> Macandal was now lashed to the post [...]. The fire began to rise toward the Mandingue, licking his legs. At that moment Macandal moved the stump of his arm, which they had been unable to tie up, in a threatening gesture which was none the less terrible for being partial, howling unknown spells and violently thrusting his torso forward. The bonds fell off and the body of the Negro rose in the air, flying overhead, until it plunged into the black waves of the sea of slaves. A single cry filled the square:
>
> "Macandal saved!" (51–52)

It is only when this description of the execution of Macandal is compared with that in Moreau de Saint-Méry that it becomes clear that there is little that is fictional about Carpentier's account.

Macandal *did* slip his bonds – temporarily – and the slaves genuinely believed that he was saved. However, in Moreau's account Macandal is nevertheless burnt to death. Carpentier's narration of the event continues by switching perspective, without break or pause, confirming the historical account rather than the slave perspective:

> Pandemonium followed. The guards fell with rifle butts on the howling blacks, who now seemed to overflow the streets, climbing towards the windows. And the noise and screaming and uproar were such that very few saw that Macandal, held by ten soldiers, had been thrust head first into the fire, and that a flame fed by his burning hair had drowned his last cry. When the slaves were restored to order, the fire was burning normally like any fire of good wood, and the breeze blowing from the sea was lifting the smoke toward the windows where more than one lady who had fainted had recovered consciousness. There was no longer anything more to see.
>
> That afternoon the slaves returned to their plantations laughing all the way. Macandal had kept his word, remaining in the Kingdom of This World. Once more the whites had been outwitted by the Mighty Powers of the Other Shore. (52)

There is far more going on than a mere juxtaposition between the perspectives of white colonist and black slave in this key passage. The first extract presents itself as a narration of the slaves' perspective, while the second is the perspective of the colonists – but also that of documented history. Carpentier here confronts a sense of the unsustainability of representing the mythical Afro-Caribbean world-view in the magical realist manner of the Maman Loi episode. The key phrase which punctuates the passage is "very few saw." As the earlier discussion of the relationship between sight and knowledge in *Men of Maize* made clear, Asturias was able to sustain and validate a mythical perspective because he rejected the very basis – empirical validation – on which historical truth is usually constructed. In Carpentier's version of the execution, the slaves' belief that Macandal escaped depends on the fact that "very few saw" – what? Did Macandal burn or did he fly away? Read closely, Carpentier's narrative confirms the presumption that truth and reality lie in the empirically-validated historical record – what was objectively seen and recorded at the execution – rather than in myth. The slaves' jollity is thus based on rumour, not reality. Macandal's mythical status is guaranteed and is felt in the slave revolts that follow, but this presence is symbolic, not real, and he makes no further appearance in the novel.

Carpentier never develops the magical realism of the Maman Loi episode. This might seem a strange claim to make, given that, at the end of the novel, Ti Noël, despairing of "this endless return of chains, this rebirth of shackles, this proliferation of suffering, which the more resigned began to accept as proof of the uselessness of all revolt" (178), decides to forego the human world and transforms himself into a succession of different animals. At this point in the narrative, Ti Noël must be close to 90 years old, a remarkable feat at a time when life expectancy was 35 (Richard Young 21). Already on his return to Haiti we are told that he "had long since acquired the art of talking with chairs, pots, a guitar, even a cow or his own shadow" (108), and he is fond of distributing baronetcies and bizarre honours to local peasants, and of issuing orders "to the winds" (172). The metamorphoses can be read as products of a diseased mind of the same order as his delusions of grandeur. The principle of equivalence between the codes of the natural and the supernatural on which magical realism depends is threatened here by the possibility of a rational, psychological explanation for the apparently magical events. But let us ignore this possibility for the moment and focus instead on the intentions behind Carpentier's representation of human-animal metamorphosis, keeping in mind that Asturias also utilised this trope in the final part of *Men of Maize*. By contrast with Asturias, Carpentier's metamorphoses are so clearly didactic in intention that we must conclude that magic – or delusion – is engaged not for the purpose of revealing a deeper layer of reality concealed from Western eyes (that is, in terms of the processes of ontological magical realism), but rather for the purpose of instruction through metaphor, otherwise known as parable.

This movement is made quite clear in Carpentier's famous assertion of a moral, replete with existential and political overtones, after the failure of Ti Noël's final attempt to integrate himself into the world of animals:

> Ti Noël vaguely understood that his rejection by the geese was a punishment for his cowardice. Macandal had disguised himself

as an animal for years to serve men, not to abjure the world of men. It was then that the old man, resuming his human form, had a supremely lucid moment. He lived, for the space of a heart-beat, the finest moments of his life; he glimpsed once more the heroes who had revealed to him the power and the fullness of his remote African forebears, making him believe in the possible ger-minations the future held. He felt countless centuries old [...]. Now he understood that a man never knows for whom he suffers and hopes. He suffers and hopes and toils for people he will never know, and who, in turn, will suffer and hope and toil for others who will not be happy either, for man always seeks a happiness far beyond that which is meted out to him. But man's greatness consists in the very fact of wanting to be better than he is. In lay-ing duties upon himself. In the Kingdom of Heaven there is no grandeur to be won, inasmuch as there all is an established hier-archy, the unknown is revealed, existence is infinite, there is no possibility of sacrifice, all is rest and joy. For this reason, bowed down by suffering and duties, beautiful in the midst of his mis-ery, capable of loving in the face of afflictions and trials, man finds his greatness, his fullest measure, only in the Kingdom of This World. (184–185)

Taken from the Book of Revelations, the title of Carpentier's novel reinforces the message of the parable as it ironises the biblical promise of the seventh angel that "The kingdom of this world has become the kingdom of our Lord and of his Christ, and he will reign for ever and ever" (11:15). In Carpentier's account, finally, there is no such closure or escape from history available to human beings. The parable rejects the transcendental and indicates a commitment to the realities of "this world," which for Carpentier, are apprehensible through history and historical discourse. In form and in content, then, the parable implies a rejection of ontological magical realism. Indeed, magical realism of any kind is distinctly absent from Carpentier's next novel, *The Lost Steps (Los pasos perdidos)*. Camayd-Freixas sees this later novel as revealing "a very different Carpentier, a Carpentier conscious of the impossibility of true communion with the Other, with the primitive" (108). For González Echevarría, the break with the marvel-lous that he perceives in the later novel is crucial to the development of Latin American literature as a whole ("Novel" 86). A magical realist reading of *The Kingdom of This World* demonstrates that this novel anticipates the move towards a discursive engagement with myth and history that González Echevarría identifies in *The Lost Steps*, and, more emphatically, in *Explosion in a Cathedral* (*El siglo de las luces*). But where Carpentier's later novels abandoned experimentation with magical realism, we shall see in the next chapter how García Márquez's *One Hundred Years of Solitude* pioneered ways of using the mode specifically to address those vital questions of history and historicity that Carpentier's rejection of the ahistoricism of ontological magical realism brought into profile.

4
Magical Realism and Defamiliarisation in Gabriel García Márquez's *One Hundred Years of Solitude*

Gabriel García Márquez's 1967 novel *One Hundred Years of Solitude* (*Cien años de soledad*) is probably the most successful magical realist text ever written. Estimated to have sold more than 30 million copies in 37 languages, the novel continues to attract a startlingly diverse range of readers from around the world.[1] It appeals to Marxist critics, to literary aristocrats and Aquarian baby-boomers, to theorists of the postcolonial condition and to the Californian "stay-at-home moms" book group selected by Oprah Winfrey in 2004, who discuss it over margaritas while their kids play in McDonalds. The many reasons for the novel's popularity can best be seen in its capacity to resolve antimonies and to integrate into apparent harmony a great number of diverse concepts and ideas: most obviously – and seductively – reality and fantasy, but also serious and humorous, myth and history, epic and quotidian, psychological and transcendental, continental, national and familial. For the ordinary reader, this effortless abandonment of established categories may come as balm for the fatigue of living in the secular, disenchanted, "bewildering empirical" modern world. For the critic it poses a series of intriguing hermeneutic puzzles to do with the relationships between writing and ideology, centre and margin, form and content, and, above all, with the cultural politics of utilising a mode of representation that appears to repudiate the key epistemological premises of the modern world view.

From a definitional point of view there is little dispute that the novel's magical realism is to be found in its technically brilliant interweaving of natural and supernatural, a style which routinely allows fantastic events to be treated as if they were perfectly normal. But, as Edwin Williamson has pointed out, "critical opinion is divided as to whether magical realism is entirely self-referring or whether it establishes a new kind of relationship between fiction and reality" ("Magical" 45). Williamson recognises that, at bottom, this question can be phrased as one of influence: do the autarchic, self-referential, ludic qualities of *One Hundred Years of Solitude* make it "analogous to the *ficciones* of Borges"? Or does the novel's magical realism, in the manner of the early Carpentier (he might have added Asturias), "expand the categories of the real so as to encompass myth, magic and other extraordinary phenomena in Nature or experience which European realism has tended to exclude" (45)? In the terms used in this study, the question becomes: where on the hermeneutical axes of faith and irreverence should *One Hundred Years of Solitude* be placed? This is a question essential to the exegesis of the novel itself, but its relevance extends well beyond this individual text for the novel is often assumed by critics to be a definitive, even normative, example of the mode of magical realism. This chapter will argue that *One Hundred Years of Solitude*, better than any other novel, demonstrates a movement between the poles of faith and irreverence, an interplay of orientations that encompasses both positions, sometimes simultaneously.

On the one hand, García Márquez himself provides substantial encouragement for reading the novel's magical realism as a style appropriate to the marvellous real of Carpentier's Latin America.[2] In the manner of faith-based magical realism, his use of the mode draws on the ways his characters view the world, though this situation is complicated by the question of whether he is sympathetic to or critical of these world views. On the other hand, many critics have witnessed the long shadow Borges extends over *One Hundred Years of Solitude*.[3] Some of have gone so far as to see Melquíades as a figure of the Argentine writer, and certainly the irreverent games the novel plays with time and infinity, its constant references to encyclopaedias, labyrinths, mirrors, arcana, and an overall structure in which reality is shown be the product of writing and reading tempt one to agree with Aníbal González when he asserts that "Borges is the most important source for García Márquez's literary ideology" (71).[4] Of course, to phrase the question as a contest of influence is reductive: both Carpentier and Borges are clearly admissible as influences, as are a great number of other writers. The question is, rather, whether the philosophical orientation of the novel's magical realism is epistemological or ontological, irreverent or faith-based. This question will, I hope to show, prove especially valuable as it relates to questions of politics and historiography.

To begin, I shall address the ways *One Hundred Years of Solitude*'s magical realism can be understood in terms of its oral/popular and ethnographic/anthropological attributes. In his conversations with Plinio Apuleyo Mendoza, García Márquez cites accounts of circus animals caught in fishermen's nets in Argentina, of a Colombian boy born with the tail of a pig, of "ordinary people" in Latin America who have read *One Hundred Years of Solitude* with "no surprise at all" because they encounter nothing in the novel that they have not encountered in their own lives (36).[5] In his 1982 Nobel Prize speech he provides an historical context for this "outsized reality," that of early traveller's tales from the region. Pigafetta's record of his journey to the Americas is, García Márquez claims in the speech, "a strictly accurate account that nonetheless resembles a venture into fantasy." Vehement in his disdain for "Walt Disney-style invention without any basis in reality," and insistent that "there's not a single line in my novels which is not based on reality" (Mendoza 31, 36), García Márquez's version of the "outsized reality" of Latin America would seem to conform to Carpentier's conviction that in Latin America "the strange is commonplace, and always was commonplace" ("Baroque" 104). More proof of Latin American territorial exceptionalism is, for García Márquez as for Carpentier, to be found in the exotic versions of the New World reported by early European explorers and conquistadors.[6] Macondo, initially, is like the America of the conquistadors, a new world which demands a new mode of representation.

More specifically, García Márquez claims that the narrative mode of *One Hundred Years of Solitude* maintains phenomenological fidelity to the cultural modalities of the Caribbean coast of Colombia. This is, in his words, a region where "the exuberant imagination of African slaves, mixed with that of the pre-Columbian natives and added to the Andalusian taste for fantasy and the Galician cult of the supernatural, had produced an ability to see reality in a certain magical way" (Mendoza 51). This ethnographic dimension leads Erik Camayd-Freixas to situate García Márquez's magical realism on a continuum that includes Asturias, Carpentier, and Juan Rulfo. The magical realism of these writers derives from an "archaic perspective" which

> can be indigenous (*Men of Maize*, *The Kingdom of this World*) or provincial (*Pedro Páramo* and *One Hundred Years of Solitude*). However, the hyperbolic tendencies of primitivism assimilate the provincial into the indigenous. There is no true distinction between the modes of these novels: the folkloric and the tribal, the provincial and the indigenous, share to the same degree this primitivist textual strategy. (70)

For Camayd-Freixas, magical realism is a mode of narration characterised by "the presence of myth, legend, and the syncretism of Indian, black and peasant from the most isolated and remote regions of the Americas" (320). By focussing on García Márquez's use of hyperbole, Camayd-Freixas is able to incorporate *One Hundred Years of Solitude* into a tradition of magical realism defined by these elements, though he also concedes that the ludic and carnivalesque quality of García Márquez's primitivism "decisively changes the tone of magical realism, opening it to humour and parody, in contrast to the seriousness of a Carpentier, an Asturias or a Rulfo" (76).

Evidence in support of Camayd-Freixas's claims can be found in the repeated references in *Living to Tell the Tale* to García Márquez's extended family as a "tribe." It has long been known that much of the material for the novel, and indeed its mode of representation, derived from his own family and personal history. Until the appearance of *Living to Tell the Tale* it was not clear just how much this was in fact the case. The bifurcated nature of magical realism is suggested in the relationships between the author and the grandparents who raised him. His grandmother, who used to narrate to him "the most atrocious things without turning a hair," is credited with providing García Márquez with the method he used in writing the novel (Mendoza 30).[7] By contrast we learn in *Living to Tell the Tale* that his grandfather was "realistic, valiant and sure" (84). Overlaps between the memoirs and

One Hundred Years of Solitude include: the grandfather, a colonel, who fought in the War of a Thousand Days, who moved to Aracataca out of remorse for having killed a man in a duel of honour, and later devoted himself to making little gold fishes; the grandmother, who made little candy animals, and died "blind, decrepit and half senile" (*Living* 86); a virgin aunt Francisca; the "rachitic and wild" Margot who arrives unbidden and who eats earth when she is not sitting in a rocking chair sucking her thumb (89); his close friends, Álvaro, Germán and Alfonso, who share the names of the characters who befriend Aureliano in the last days of Macondo; the proliferation of the names of Iguarán and Cotes; the boom brought by the fruit company (including memories of bills being burned in decadent celebration); the banana plantation called Macondo; and the massacre of the strikers whose number remains uncertain. So many and so similar are the overlaps between *One Hundred Years of Solitude* and *Living to Tell the Tale* that the reader's credulity is at times stretched.[8] The point is that many of the characters of the novel are based on real people from the author's life; moreover, these are people whose world views make space for levitating priests, sorcery and exorcism, ghosts and terrifying saints, the mysterious foreknowledge of death, premonitions of all kinds, indeed "everything that might be necessary for writing the chronicle of a supernatural realism" (*Living* 384).

If García Márquez's magical realism arises from this familial and provincial world-view, and if, as Camayd-Freixas asserts, the "provincial" is comparable with the "primitive" then *One Hundred Years of Solitude* can be said, like *Men of Maize* or *The Kingdom of this World*, to be characterised by a faith-based orientation to magical realism. But just how far can we push this comparison? We saw in the previous chapter how Carpentier's utilisation of a magical realist mode of narration in support of his representation of *lo real maravilloso* faltered because he was unable to accept the ahistorical implications of his onto-theological insistence on faith. The second half of *The Kingdom of This World* uses myth (for example, the belief in metamorphosis to animal form) not as an alternative to history or a way of escaping it, but as a means of illuminating certain patterns of historical repetition and recurrence obscured by conventional or realist historiography. I have argued that the beginning and the end of *The Kingdom of This World* suggest different attitudes to transcendence. The former, as in the Maman Loi episode, supports its possibility; the latter, as in

Ti Noël's commitment to this world, rather than any other, its rejection. Comparisons with Carpentier need to take this difference into account, and register that *One Hundred Years of Solitude* is more likely to be located on the trajectory suggested not by the first half of Carpentier's novel, but by the second.

The differences between Asturias and García Márquez can best be seen by comparing their treatment of nostalgia. *Men of Maize*, as has been noted, is pervaded by a sense of lost origins and wholeness, and with a longing to find ways of reclaiming something of what has been lost by taking seriously myth as a conduit to truth. García Márquez, too, is tempted by myths of origins. As noted above, Macondo and its inhabitants are based on his own childhood recollections, while references to the book of Genesis, to Cortes's "new world optic," and the innocence of Macondo in the early parts of the novel all suggest something of the nostalgia contained in the epigraph to Asturias's *Men of Maize*. In the previous chapter, I showed how Asturias seeks redemption of a kind by salvaging the mythical dream time of Gaspar Ilom before he is poisoned. García Márquez – especially through the utterances of Úrsula and Pilar Ternera – toys with the non-linear, circular time scales of myth and legend. But, García Márquez recognises very clearly that the problem with nostalgia is that it "wipe[s] away bad memories, and magnifie[s] the good ones" (*Living* 19). This observation, to be found near the beginning of his memoirs, is deceptively straightforward. Beneath it lies a complex set of relationships between the personal and the political that constitutes a major theme of *One Hundred Years of Solitude*, one worth examining in detail for what it tells us about the novel's attitude to time, politics, and historicity.

Nostalgia in *One Hundred Years of Solitude*, along with the solitude which it so often evokes, is part of a web of emotions which link personal responses to external events and conditions and which are experienced in similar ways by characters from different generations. But, unlike the ambivalence that attaches to the novel's treatment of solitude, nostalgia is virtually always presented in negative terms. After the wise Catalonian returns to Europe from Macondo he is increasingly caught by nostalgia for what he has left behind, just as he had suffered nostalgia for Europe in Macondo. This impossible situation, in which he is "upset by two nostalgias facing each other like two mirrors" (325), leads to cynicism and decline. Nostalgia in this sense is a trap, an illusion, and it is specifically named as such at several points in the novel. In terms of the Buendía family, the deceptive qualities of nostalgia have more serious consequences. In the novel's opening sentence – "Many years later, as he faced the firing squad, Colonel Aureliano Buendía was to remember that distant afternoon when his father took him to discover ice" (9) – nostalgia can be seen to be closely connected with the treatment of the relationship between memory, narrative time and, inevitably, death. To use Gerard Genette's terms, prolepsis yields immediately to analepsis in such a way as to undermine the expectations of linear time and to suffuse the present with the paradox of nostalgia anticipated. Though Colonel Aureliano Buendía does not die by firing squad (this fate falls to his nephew, Arcadio, whose last moments are similarly tinged by nostalgia), it is suggested that it is nostalgia itself that later succeeds in killing the Colonel where a lifetime of wars had failed. Having successfully resisted the lure of nostalgia (unlike his father) through the obsessive manufacture of little gold fishes, late in life, hearing once more the sounds of the circus, "he knowingly fell into a trap of nostalgia and relived that prodigious afternoon of the gypsies when his father took him to see ice." After the parade has passed, he sees once more "the face of his miserable solitude." He urinates on the chestnut tree, home to his father for so many years, and dies standing with his forehead against the trunk of the tree (218–219). Nostalgia here, as in numerous other examples, is linked both backward and forward in narrative time to other instances of nostalgia, but the chain does not make a circle, for it is interrupted by death.

Nostalgia is the most important cipher of what Gerald Martin identifies as a view of time that is demystified in the novel. Drawing on sociological readings of *One Hundred Years of Solitude* such as that of Agustín Cueva, Martin has famously asserted that "no misreading could be more serious for Latin American literary history than the 'mythreading' of its most famous work, *One Hundred Years of Solitude*" ("Social" 117). For him, the novel is "a socialist – though not a 'social realist' – reading of Latin American history" (103). Martin goes so far as to discern a "determinedly optimistic conception of the march of history" in the novel, a point to which I shall later return (105; *Labyrinth* 234–235). In Martin's view, critical use of the term magical realism is therefore to be excoriated because it is so often used as "an ideological stratagem to collapse many different kinds of writing, and many different political perspectives, into one single, usually escapist, concept" (107). Yet, as we might expect from the foremost critic, translator and archivist of Asturias, who has himself used the term, albeit somewhat uncomfortably, to apply to *Men of Maize* ("Introduction" xxii), Martin is conscious that magical realism is, in and of itself, not automatically guilty of an escapist conflation of difference. Thus, by way of concession, he begins to engage with the concept in terms relevant to this discussion:

> There is a world of difference between the view that tacitly assumes that reality itself is or may be fantastic, or that the imagination is autonomous (Borges, Lezama Lima, sometimes Cortázar) and a perspective which takes seriously the religious beliefs or myths, the fantasies or illusions of the fictional characters, whether by reproducing them "anthropologically" or by critically demystifying them (Asturias, Carpentier, Rulfo, Roa Bastos and – in this but not all cases – García Márquez). If the term [magical realism] must be used, it is best confined to the latter kind of writing, in which, essentially, there is a dialectic between pre-scientific and scientific visions of reality, seen most clearly in works which combine the mythological or folk beliefs of the characters with the consciousness of a twentieth-century observer. (108)

Here, once again can be seen the hermeneutic poles I am identifying as irreverence and faith. If we define magical realism formally, that is in terms of the coherent presence in a narrative text of codes of the natural and the supernatural, represented on an equal basis with one another, then it should be readily apparent that either or both of these views might provide the rationale for the presence of magical realism – the former being conditioned by a sceptical irreverence to the claims of realism, the latter by a desire to enlarge realism's purview to make space for alternative world views. Martin opts for a faith-based definition of magical realism, with the signal difference that, where a writer like Asturias reproduces myth ethnographically, García Márquez engages in a politically-motivated attempt to demystify the magical world-view of his characters, though his sympathy for these characters complicates the matter somewhat.

Martin's argument depends on a distinction being drawn between the perspectives of the characters and of the author in *One Hundred*

Years of Solitude. To understand the importance of this distinction, we need briefly to consider the impact of Colombian history and politics on the constitution of García Márquez's poetics. In Colombia, like most Latin American countries, independence from Spanish rule effectively meant the devolution of power into the hands of wealthy *criollo* landowners, who divided themselves into Liberals and Conservatives. Internecine discord between these groups has been a feature of the Colombian political landscape. In understanding the violence that has been such a defining feature of Colombia's history, the problem posed to the social sciences is, as Stephen Minta observes, "to understand the logic of a more or less continuous conflict which has drawn large numbers of Columbians of all classes into violent confrontation in the name of elite power politics with which they might have been expected to have little sense of identification" (9). Outside of the elites themselves, affiliation to Liberal or Conservative often follows lines of familial and social obligation rather than dispassionate and rational analysis of the political situation. Minta notes that in 1978 García Márquez himself was involved in promoting a left-wing candidate to contest Liberal and Conservative hegemony. The result was a disaster with the left-wing candidate garnering less that 3 percent of the total vote. Breaking the hold of traditional political affiliations, and promoting a socialist politics based on reason rather than passion, has long been a preoccupation of García Márquez, and is manifest in much of his journalism, and in the establishment of newspapers and magazines (7).

Implicit in Martin's argument is the notion that *One Hundred Years of Solitude* should show signs of this political and educational cause. Magical realism in his reading thus becomes a marker of false consciousness, of a mind-set stultified by "the general effects of colonial history upon individual relationships," incapable of breaking the hold of traditionalist affiliations and dysfunctional modes of relating to others. Key aspects of the novel – "circularity, irrationality, fatalism, isolation, superstition, fanaticism, corruption and violence" – can thus be understood as having nothing to do with any magical reality, but rather with the proletarian struggle against injustice, signified most dramatically by the massacre of the strikers, which is "the secret thread that can guide us out into the light at the end of the labyrinth" (111). Thus, when Aureliano Babilonia finally completes the process of decoding Melquíades's manuscripts, he "breaks out of false circularities, meaningless repetitions, the prehistory before the dawn of proletarian consciousness." Significantly, this ending also "turns the reader who is reading about him back out into the history outside the text." The apocalypse of the novel's final pages signifies – with a euphoria stemming from the success of the Cuban revolution on the one hand, and the Boom of the Latin American novel on the other – "the end of neocolonialism and its conscious or unconscious collaborators" (115).

Martin's materialist reading of *One Hundred Years of Solitude* is the most compelling attempt to understand the novel's magical realism in the light of the political background of its author. It fits well within the paradigm of demystificatory faith-based magical realism of the kind identified in the previous chapter at the end of *The Kingdom of This World*. Ti Noel, it will be remembered, renounces the allure of mythical metamorphosis in favour of commitment to the political here and now of this world. García Márquez's apocalypse similarly puts an end to the city of mirrors and mirages, to the fictions of alternative realities and second chances. Magical realism is used to debunk the notion of magical reality.

Persuasive though it is, a materialist reading of the novel's magical realism does not supply the final word on the matter. Having noticed that magical realism can be based either in "reality-as-fantasy" or anthropological starting points – corresponding roughly to the irreverence/faith split I am identifying – Martin concedes that García Márquez refuses to fit comfortably into the second of his categories:

> García Márquez is by no means always clear about the distinction [...]. Our difficulty is that the two levels are really separable only on the abstract plane of analysis, so seriously does the omniscient narrator take the beliefs of his characters. García Márquez uses a battery of complementary literary techniques – above all, caricature, hyperbole, bathos and condensation of every kind – to unite the two levels in each and every anecdote of his narrative. (108)

Martin recognises that the ludic, metafictional, idealistic streaks present in *One Hundred Years of Solitude*'s "caricature, hyperbole, bathos and condensation" mean that its magical realism cannot be designated as only ontological or faith-based. Magical realism is not limited to a reproduction of the world views of its characters. What, then, is the nature of this irreverent dimension, and how does it relate to the novel's anthropological projections? The answer is to be sought through a return to a concept already much discussed in García Márquez criticism: defamiliarisation.

When discussing his development as a writer, García Márquez stresses his fierce determination to learn to write well, to develop a distinctive voice. This process is linked on the one hand with a sense of political responsibility, as in his famous comment that "the writer's [...] revolutionary duty [...] is to write well" (Mendoza 59). On the other hand, his memoirs make repeatedly clear that this process will be one of discovering "a structure that was credible and fantastic at the same time but had no cracks" (*Living* 296; see also 384, 464). What does "writing well" actually mean? In his influential definition of the function of art Viktor Shklovsky claimed art exists in order that

> one may recover the sensation of life; it exists to make one feel things, to make the stone *stony*. The purpose of art is to impart the sensation of things as they are perceived and not as they are known. The technique of art is to make objects "unfamiliar," to make forms difficult, to increase the difficulty and length of perception because the process of perception is an aesthetic end in itself and must be prolonged. (12)

Shklovsky identifies the "games of nonrecognition" played by writers in order to make the familiar seem strange. Such techniques include withholding the name of the object, describing an event or object as if for the first time, or naming corresponding parts of another object instead of the object described. All of these techniques are relevant to *One Hundred Years of Solitude*. Excellent early examples are the inventions, such as ice and magnets, brought to Macondo by Melquíades's gypsies in the opening paragraph of the novel. Writing well, then, can be measured in the capacity of the writing to counter the "automatism of perception" decried by Shklovsky, the habitualisation that "devours works, clothes, furniture, one's wife, and the fear of war" (12).

Magical realism in *One Hundred Years of Solitude* is a writerly technique as much as it is the representation of a world-view. García Márquez's poetic prose clearly returns a freshness and an aesthetic appreciation to familiar, ordinary objects. What is less obvious are the ways these effects are linked to a self-conscious defamiliarisation of the relationship between reader and text. Apparently straightforward processes of object defamiliarisation are embedded in the subtle games of belief and disbelief, faith and irreverence which lie at the heart of García Márquez's ironic, hyperbolic narrative strategy. This process is apparent in the novel's opening sentence, and in a more sustained way in its first episode:

> Every year during the month of March a family of ragged gypsies would set up their tents near the village, and with a great uproar of pipes and kettledrums they would display new inventions. First they brought the magnet. A heavy gypsy with an untamed beard and sparrow hands, who introduced himself as Melquíades, put on a bold public demonstration of what he himself called the eighth wonder of the learned alchemists of Macedonia. He went from house to house dragging two metal ingots and everybody was amazed to see pots, pans, tongs and braziers tumble down from their places and beams creak from the desperation of nails and screws trying to emerge, and even objects that had been lost for a long time appeared from where they had been searched for most and went dragging along in turbulent confusion behind Melquíades' magical irons. "Things have a life of their own," the gypsy proclaimed with a harsh accent. "It's simply a matter of waking up their souls." (9)

The gypsies represent at this point the only regular contact Macondo has with the outside world. The carnivalesque spectacle presents the opportunity for García Márquez to use the innocence of Macondo, in Shklovsky's words, "to make objects 'unfamiliar,' to make forms difficult, to increase the difficulty and length of perception." In this case it is the magnets that are defamiliarised, a process extended to all objects through Melquíades's bold claim. The episode refreshes familiar understandings of magnets by reminding the reader of their unique and extraordinary capacity to combine the invisible with the visible, to exert imperceptible yet real forces of attraction.

It can safely be assumed that, unlike the Buendías at this time, most readers of a novel of this nature would be familiar with the capacity of a magnet to attract metal objects. More scientifically-minded readers would understand that magnets achieve this because electrons orbiting the nuclei of certain atoms, especially of ferromagnetic elements, produce magnetic fields. The reference to the "learned alchemists of Macedonia" sets up an awareness that we are encountering in Macondo a pre-Enlightenment conception of science, one in which the magical has not yet been detached from the real. But this is not an example of faith-based magical realism because magnets are not, to the reader, magical, though they are perceived as such by the characters. A rift is installed between implied reader and character, a rift that reflects that between the modern and pre-modern. This is why Williamson sees García Márquez as generating in the reader "a mixed reaction of sympathy and comic detachment": sympathy because he/she desires the pleasure of encountering the familiar made strange; comic detachment because García Márquez "tips the wink at his reader, as it were, creating a complicity behind the backs of the characters" (47).

Like Martin, Williamson interprets the novel's magical realism as part of a problematic Buendía world-view, in this case by asserting it to be "a symbolic equivalent of the solipsism that underlies magical realism" (47). What Williamson fails to notice is just how far García Márquez's hyperbole raises the stakes of the game.[9] *These* magnets, small enough to be dragged through the town, are so powerful as to attract kitchenware at an unlikely distance, and even, unbelievably, are able to extract nails and screws embedded in beams. The ice so admired by Jose Arcadio Buendía is, incredibly, to be found in an unrefrigerated wooden chest on an afternoon in the tropics in a town that has yet to be electrified. Such magical realist details foreclose on the suggestion of linear development and on the condescending collaboration of the reader and author identified by Williamson. García Márquez's joke turns out to be not at the expense of the characters, but at the expense of the reader who assumes a realistic (which after all implies a scientifically acceptable) correspondence between the description and what is described. This is magical realism not as a world-view, not just as object defamiliarisation, but as a technique for defamiliarising the assumptions of realism itself.

A movement between faith and irreverence can be seen more clearly in relation to the episode of the insomnia plague. In what I am calling faith-based magical realism, the story of the plague would need to derive from myth or legend, whether "indigenous" or "provincial" to use Camayd-Freixas's terms. Magical realism would be used in order to afford legitimacy to these supernatural occurrences within a realistic narrative framework. The novel provides some support for this reading since the plague does indeed follow Visitación and her brother, Guajiro Indian royalty now working for the Buendías after being forced to give up their kingdom. Dean J. Irvine asserts that the plague is "a fable from an immemorial time in Visitación's age-old indigenous culture" (67). Lorna Robinson, drawing on the work of Walter Ong, similarly suggests that, in addition to its biblical resonances, the plague serves to mark the passing from an oral to a literate culture, evoking a sense of the devastation of indigenous cultures and the loss of Indian culture generally. Later in the novel it is amnesia that allows almost all memory of the banana company massacre to be erased, and the plague thus foreshadows this important event in the narrative.

Intriguingly though, the episode can also be read as providing García Márquez with the opportunity to indulge in a game of textualisation, a Borgesian experiment designed to show up the tensions between signifier and signified and between writing and knowledge that has little, if anything, to do with the perspectives of Visitación and her brother, though it may have everything to do with the discursive mechanisms by which their history has been suppressed. As the insomnia affliction worsens, the townsfolk try to overcome it by exhausting themselves:

> They would gather together to converse endlessly, to tell over and over for hours on end the old jokes, to complicate to the limits of exasperation the story about the capon, which was an endless game in which the narrator asked if they wanted him to tell them the story about the capon, and when they answered yes, the narrator would say that he had not asked them to say yes, but whether they wanted him to tell them the story about the capon, and when they answered no, the narrator told them that he had not asked them to say no, but whether they wanted him to tell them the story about the capon, and when they remained silent the narrator told them that he had not asked them to remain silent but whether they wanted him to tell them the story about the capon, and no one could leave because the narrator would say that he had not asked them to leave but whether they wanted him

to tell them the story about the capon, and so on and on in a vicious circle that lasted entire nights. (44–45)

The target of García Márquez's defamiliarisation has now shifted away from objects and towards processes: storytelling, writing, remembering. The notion of storytelling as a game takes on a different dimension in this episode, as language begins to break down under the pressure of dysfunctional communication acts. The narrator of the story ensnares his listeners in a labyrinth from which there is no escape, because there is no answer that can satisfy his hyper-literal imperative. The labyrinth, like the hall of mirrors, is a hallowed space for García Márquez: there the real, the literal, and the rational become distorted and deviant. Such is the case with the story of the capon.

Embedded in a novel like *One Hundred Years of Solitude* the effect of the episode is metafictional and self-conscious: language is not the privileged vehicle of revealing truth or history but instead may be a trap, a snare, a deception, exhausting or pleasurable. Thus, the method devised by Colonel Aureliano Buendía to stave off amnesia, the labelling of objects with first their names, and later entire descriptions of their purposes, turns out to be useless because no one can remember what the letters mean. It is only when Melquíades returns from death, like a *deus ex machina*, that memory is restored to Macondo. The episode calls into question the integrity of the novel's narration and of its language. It shows the importance of writing as an antidote to forgetting, but simultaneously calls into question the relationship between words and things. Ultimately, what is at stake is the past itself, the value of which is central to escaping a destructive cyclicality, but which can only be accessed through the problematic mediation of memory and its apparatus, writing.

The question of how to interpret the insomnia plague episode can be related back to Melquíades's explanation for the magnets. Melquíades's claim, that "things have a life of their own" draws on a genealogy of ideas that leads us back to what Stanley Tambiah calls the paradigm of participation, as discussed in Chapter One. The belief that things have souls is shared by animism, paganism, strands of Romanticism, and, more recently, New Age spirituality.[10] But the truth is that Melquíades does not know exactly what makes the metal objects follow him in such "turbulent confusion." What he *does* know is what makes for a good story about the process. This is why, when José Arcadio Buendía tells him he wants to use the magnets to extract gold from the earth, Melquíades proves his honesty by informing him that the magnets won't work for that purpose. Like García Márquez, the gypsy has a healthy sense of the power of storytelling – "writing well" – and this process has little to do with mistaking stories for truth in the manner of Asturias's Nana Monchada, for example. In these examples, García Márquez's magical realism can be seen to have moved away from the belief in the power of literature to convey an expanded, spiritual dimension to reality.

But while García Márquez's strategic defamiliarisation of the meaning-making processes that underlie narrativisation clearly serves a metafictional function, as Roberto González Echevarría caustically observes, "it is a commonplace, almost an uncritical fetish, to say that the novel always includes the story of how it was written, that it is a self-reflexive genre. The question is why and how it so at specific moments" (94). Self-reflexivity is a feature likely to be found in both faith-based and irreverent magical realism. I would like in what remains of this chapter to consider the deconstructive implications of the irreverent dimensions of *One Hundred Years of Solitude* specifically as they pertain to historiography and historicity.

Many critics have explored in detail the ways *One Hundred Years of Solitude* registers Colombian and Latin American. Present are specific events (for example, the Treaty of Neerlandia) and characters based on historical personae (Colonel Aureliano Buendía as the Liberal commander, General Rafael Uribe Uribe). Present also is a general narrative of Latin American history, from discovery and conquest to the colonial era, the republican period, intermittent civil war, U.S. neo-colonialism and beyond. On a different level, webs of affective contiguity (solitude, nostalgia, pride, stubbornness) spun to link characters from different generations have the effect of sketching the outlines of a psycho-social history of Colombia and perhaps of Latin America itself. In this last point we are reaching the boundaries of a positivistic historiographic practice; these limits are flagrantly transgressed by the inclusion of events and occurrences that fall decidedly outside the boundaries circumscribed by historiographic representational conventions. García Márquez approaches history with an anguished awareness that positivistic and official historiography is woefully inadequate to understanding the bloody history of

Colombia. But, crucially, he does not reject rationality in the way that Asturias does in *Men of Maize*. Rather, he develops the notion suggested in the caesura between the perspective of master and slave in *The Kingdom of This World* that magical realism can exhibit a commitment to the political here and now.

The relationship between faith-based (magical realism as representation of a provincial world-view) and irreverent magical realism (magical realism as deconstruction of the processes of narrativisation) can best be seen in the light of what many critics regard as the novel's most important episode, the massacre of the banana company workers. Here what Martin somewhat pejoratively identifies as the "view that tacitly assumes that reality itself is or may be fantastic, or that the imagination is autonomous" finds its expression in an historicised exploration of the construction of reality through the rhetoric of the powerful. Jose David Saldivar, among others, has pointed to the historical basis of the episode while acknowledging that it shows how history can operate like a text, constructing discourse about the past in ideologically-motivated ways. Thus, when in the novel the "mournful" lawyers declare that the company "did not have, never had had, and never would have any workers in its service because they were all hired on a temporary and occasional basis" this point is immediately extended to signify that "the workers did not exist" (246). In the presence of such radically distorted power relations, a statement of about contracts becomes a denial of existence. Similarly, in stark contrast to José Aureliano Segundo's first-hand experience, the official version of the massacre is that

> there were no dead, the satisfied workers had gone back to their families [...]. [T]he military denied it even to the victims of the relatives who crowded the commandants' offices in search of news. "You must have been dreaming," the officers insisted. "Nothing has happened in Macondo, nothing has ever happened, and nothing ever will happen. This is a happy town." (252)

For Saldivar, this episode confirms the extent to which García Márquez is preoccupied with "showing the limits of historical discourse" by "showing how historical, governmental and news media discourses are constructed." All texts, including García Márquez's are, in this view, "written to deceive their readers" but the difference is that García Márquez is "self-conscious about his fiction" (39). This kind of scepticism about literature, about conventional understandings of the ways language functions, linked to a awareness of marginality and oppression is a key element of what I am labelling irreverence – an approach which chooses to play games with the conventions of representation in order to subvert assumed truth and establish opposition to dogma or power. García Márquez's insistence on the ways rhetoric constructs reality is a politicised and historicised version of Borgesian (anti-)logic, present most visibly in "Tlön, Uqbar, Orbis Tertius" in which story the writing of a place brings that place into being.

García Márquez has something of a love-hate relationship with Borges. As Mario Vargas Llosa points out, there are huge differences between the "supreme intelligence and absolute asexuality" of Borges and the passionate, bloody, spontaneous world of Macondo (188). Politically they are poles apart: Borges "hated Perón, he opposed the Cuban Revolution, he spoke out in favour of the abortive Bay of Pigs invasion, he supported the Argentine Conservative party, he accepted a medal of honour from Chilean dictator Pinochet within months of the bloody coup in Chile" (King xiii). Philosophically, Borges's idealism is not compatible with the materialist starting points of García Márquez's socialism. Yet Borges has been a presence in García Márquez writing life since his youthful days in Barranquilla when he and his friends "waited for the travelling salesmen from the Argentine publishers as if they were envoys from heaven" (*Living* 122).[11] Many years later, García Márquez had the following to say to Mario Vargas Llosa:

> With Borges something happens to me: Borges is one of the authors that I have read most and perhaps the one I like least. I read Borges for his extraordinary capacity for verbal artifice; he's a man who teaches one how to write [...]. I believe that Borges works with mental realities; it's pure evasion [...]. This literature does not interest me personally. I believe that all great literature must be founded on concrete reality. (Vargas Llosa 188–189)

The extraordinary levels of ambivalence displayed by García Márquez in these comments stem from a perceived tension between form and content, between admiration for Borges's artistry and disdain for the purposes to which it is put. Implicit in these comments is the suggestion that it might be possible to synthesise Borges's "verbal artifice," his evasive "mental realities" with a literature "founded on concrete reality." This is, I believe, exactly what García Márquez achieves in *One Hundred Years of Solitude*.

At the heart of García Márquez's magical realism is the notion of "radical historicity" discerned by Roberto González Echevarría via Borges. In González Echevarría's *Myth and Archive*, Melquíades's room in the Buendía house, which González Echevarría calls the "Archive," is the domain of history and is linked to similar enclosures in other Latin American novels and to the wider processes by which the Latin American narrative developed out of a dialogue with historical documents, scientific discourse and anthropology. García Márquez's success, according to González Echevarría, lies in the fact that he has managed "to punch through the anthropological mediation and substitute the anthropologist for a historian, and to turn the object of attention away from myth as an expression of so-called primitive societies to the myths of modern society: the book, writing, reading" (29).

Time in García Márquez's "Archive" initially appears, from the progressive decoding of Melquíades's manuscripts, to partake of a certain linearity, though different characters experience it differently. For the Buendías outside the room, it is circular and repetitive, as we have seen. In fact, González Echevarría sees the order of the Archive as

> not that of mere chronology, but that of writing; the rigorous process of inscribing and decoding to which Melquíades and the last Aureliano give themselves over, a linear process of cancellations and substitutions, of gaps [...]. The Archive [...] is not so much an accumulation of texts as the process whereby texts are written; a process of repeated combinations, of shufflings and reshufflings ruled by heterogeneity and difference. It is not strictly linear, as both continuity and discontinuity are held together in uneasy alliance. (*Myth* 24)

Here temporality and historicity are understood to be constructions mediated by writing, then fractured to reveal the marks of heterogeneity and difference. This view of historicity is one that might be said to be shared by Michel Foucault, who was, like García Márquez, influenced by the irreverent critical epistemologies of Borges. Famously, in the preface to *The Order of Things*, Foucault notes:

> This book first arose out of a passage in Borges, out of the laughter that shattered, as I read the passage, all the familiar landmarks of my thought – our thought, the thought that bears the stamp of our age and our geography – breaking up all the ordered surfaces and all the planes with which we are accustomed to tame the wild profusion of existing things, and continuing long afterwards to disturb and threaten with collapse our age-old distinction between the Same and the Other. (xv)[12]

In its emphasis on laughter and the overturning of binaries this passage, which, as Patricia Tobin points out, represents "the moment when rule-constrained structuralism is brought low by rule-breaking deconstruction" (65), suggests that a more detailed comparison between Foucault, Borges and García Márquez is a worthwhile critical project. The original title of Foucault's work is *Les Mots et les choses*. *One Hundred Years of Solitude*, as has been noted, is very much a novel about things: things having a life of their own, things lost and found, named and forgotten. García Márquez's poetics are invested in the defamiliarisation of things, and of the relationship between things and words as is clear in my discussion of magnets, ice and the insomnia plague. In terms of the novel's treatment of history, both García Márquez and Foucault are concerned with defamiliarising the relationship between history and writing.[13]

Where *One Hundred Years of Solitude* might be said to go beyond Foucault is in its recognition that history needs not only to be confronted with writing, but with reading. The attempts of various Buendías to decipher Melquíades's manuscripts parallel the reader's own hermeneutic journey through the novel. When, in the novel's final, epiphanic passages, Aureliano Babilonia finally succeeds in deciphering the parchments with the help of the Encyclopaedia, by means of a magical realist trick they turn out to have been telling the very story of his family that we have been reading. But here a note of caution is in order for, as González Echevarría points out (25), the parchments are not, as many readers might think, the novel itself. The epigraph has been omitted, and the passages skipped by Aureliano have either been ignored or restored. The novel's self-reflexivity is not unbounded, precisely because the place of reading must be guaranteed in the temporal model under elaboration.

The merging of embedded and implied readers that takes place at the end of the novel has been described as generating "ontological vertigo" (qtd in Irvine 62). Dean Irvine uses Brian McHale's thesis on the ontological orientation of postmodern fiction to account for this process. Irvine writes: "For Aureliano Babilonia [...] reading as a mode of interpretation gives way to a mode of being. So, too, for the implied reader of the novel, a mode of interpretation is transformed into a mode of being" (62). I do not think that it is questions of ontology that are relevant to the end of *One Hundred Years of Solitude*. Aureliano's moment of anagnorisis, far from transforming reading into being, is specifically linked with death, being's negation. Similarly, as the implied reader reaches the final few lines and then closes the book, he or she is, as González Echevarría puts it, "slain" in the role of reader (28). Indeed, the novel's emphasis on discourse takes place at the expense of ontology, because being, reading and knowing can only take place in the present: "[E]ach reading of the text is the text, that is to say [...] each of these readings corrects the others, and each is unrepeatable insofar as it is a distinct act caught in the reader's own temporality. In this sense, we, like Aureliano, read the instant we live, cognizant that it may very well be our last" (26). González Echevarría calls this a "radical historicity." "Writing well" takes on its most revolutionary aspect when, like Foucault, García Márquez defamiliarises the assumptions of official and continuous historiography. The most powerful tool available to him in prosecuting this task is magical realism, and the most direct object of critique is temporality itself.

It is a significant achievement of the novel that it manages to sustain its faith-based strand of magical realism in the teeth of its deconstructionist urges. It will be recalled that faith-based strands of magical realism require the reader to suspend his or her disbelief in order to "re-believe," that is to perceive reality in a more multi-dimensional way than is common in the modern, secular and disenchanted world. This way of seeing frequently corresponds anthropologically to the world-view of a non-Western culture, though it should be added that certain popular modes of reading the novel pay scant heed to this dimension, focussing instead on the novel's capacity to re-enchant the

Western reader.[14] *One Hundred Years of Solitude*'s faith-based magical realism resides in the ways it gives form to the world-view of his characters, which may stand in – in concentric metonymic circles of sympathy – for his own friends and family, for the inhabitants of his coastal region of the Caribbean, and from there on to Colombia and Latin America itself.[15] This magical realist world-view is evoked with considerable sympathy at times and it serves as the means for a powerful defamiliarisation of ordinary objects. But ultimately it is shown to be harmful in that it is part (and only a part) of the Buendias inability to love, their isolation, failures, solitude and still-born futures. Since the Buendias can be read metonymically, the judgement that falls upon them falls equally upon Latin America as a whole.

But there is a second dimension to faith-based magical realism which is not to be found in *One Hundred Years of Solitude*: that which depends on a set of assumptions about the capacity of literature, especially the novel, to convey accurately the phenomenological and ontological dimensions of this world-view. In this respect, *One Hundred Years of Solitude*'s magical realism differs from that of Asturias and the early Carpentier (and Okri, as we shall see), because the ludic, Borgesian, inversionary, deconstructive mental games played by García Márquez serve metafictional and deconstructive functions, allowing him to defamiliarise the processes of narrativising, storytelling and historiography with the paradoxical result that his magical realism actually comes to demystify his magical realism. Erudite and eclectic in its sources and thoroughly aware of its own artifice, *One Hundred Years of Solitude*'s magical realism finally comes to mark an engagement with discourse about reality, rather than reality itself. In this sense, the novel is the foremost representative in a tradition of utilising magical realism as a means of interrogating ideas about history, culture and identity, to say nothing of literature itself. The model of magical realism provided by *One Hundred Years of Solitude* can be productively applied to other magical realist texts, most notably those of Salman Rushdie. As García Márquez registers and exaggerates the movement from faith into discourse encountered in *The Kingdom of This World*, so Rushdie pushes the possibilities of irreverence to their extreme in *The Satanic Verses* as we shall see in the next chapter.

5
Migrancy and Metamorphosis in Salman Rushdie's *The Satanic Verses*

There is no novel more irreverent than Salman Rushdie's *The Satanic Verses* (1988). The fatwa pronouncing death on Rushdie for his alleged apostasy towards Islam, from which the Iranian government has distanced itself, but which is also periodically "renewed" by the Iranian Revolutionary Guard, confirms the incendiary, religious sense in which this novel is irreverent. But as my discussion of Jorge Luis Borges makes clear, there are other senses in which irreverence is a useful term for describing certain kinds of postcolonial writing. Borges claims in "The Argentine Writer and Tradition" that the Argentine writer has a greater claim to the ideas, traditions and texts of Europe than does the European. Eclectic, idealist, sceptical, and parodic, his writing bulldozes binaries of all kinds, inverts established hierarchies, plays games with time and infinity, seeks out those "tenuous crevices of unreason" that fissure the rational-empirical world view. Irreverence in the Borgesian sense is a ludic, critical attitude favoured by intellectuals and writers marginalised by reasons of geography, race, or culture, yet who are still able to avail themselves of the cultural resources of the centre. Rushdie is just such a writer, and his magical realism exemplifies the irreverent strand of the mode.

The Qur'an is the text that will forever be most closely associated with *The Satanic Verses*, but the novel deliberately and self-consciously assumes as intertexts a massive range of Eastern and Western cultural references that extends from Aeschylus to Isaac Asimov, the Mahābhārata to Madonna, the Rig-Veda to Bollywood films.[1] The sheer range and diversity of Rushdie's intertexts along with his disdain for distinctions such as high/low, past/present, sacred/profane or East/West are important elements of his irreverence. More profound is his deliberate extension of a sceptical philosophical stance into a fictional critique of the ways power serves its own interests by generating consensus about the nature of being and reality. This extension of the Borgesian approach to questions of politics and historicity was identified in my discussion of García Márquez's *One Hundred Years of Solitude*. Rushdie has of course read and absorbed both Borges and García Márquez, and both Latin Americans cast a shadow over *The Satanic Verses*.[2] Rushdie differs from García Márquez in at least one crucial respect, though: whereas García Márquez is still partially sympathetic to faith-based epistemologies, Rushdie is at pains to foreground them – in different forms – as problems.

Rushdie himself has displayed an ambivalent relationship with the label magical realism. In a 1983 interview with Chandrabhanu Pattanayak he comments on the similarities between his work and that of García Márquez by referring to both as magical realism. Talking to Ameena Meer in 1989, however, he distances himself from the term on the basis of its being applicable solely to "a group developed and named of [sic] South American writers in the generation around Borges and after" (Meer 111). Later in the same interview, however, he indicates a rueful acceptance of the term in respect of his own writing by stating about his future intentions (in retrospect, ironically): "no more magical realism" (122). Exactly what the term might mean to him if it is not used to designate a literary movement is uncertain, for his critical opinions offer little formal distinction between surrealism, magical realism and fantasy. And if literary critical taxonomies are complicated by Rushdie's extra-fictional statements, the case is worse as far as his fiction goes. As Shaul Bassi has pointed out, Rushdie's novels "contain events that are bizarre but plausible (babies exchanged in the cradle), and highly improbable but not impossible (a child with three mothers, a man ageing at double speed), or quite incredible (a woman with glass skin; two men surviving a fall from the sky)" all of which are often uncritically assumed to constitute his magical realism (47).

What *is* clear from his interviews, journalism and fiction is that Rushdie feels an affinity for writers "for whom the processes of naturalism have not been sufficient" (Meer 111). He grounds this preference in the conviction that realism is inadequate to the task of describing the world because there no longer exists the kind of consensus between writer and reader that might have existed in the nineteenth century (Brooks 57). The rupturing of this consensus, in British literature at least, is related to the changing demographics of Britain itself, and suggests, once again, that colonialism and its legacies constitute the unavoidable context for this discussion. Though Rushdie's fiction is resistant to categorisation, and though his anti-realism is expressed in different ways, the particular configuration of non-naturalistic prose that it resembles more frequently than any other is magical realism. Magical realism is important to Rushdie for, as will become clear, it allows him to exercise his preference for non-naturalism without foregoing the kinds of political and cultural engagement that are usually associated with social realism. And, importantly, a focus on magical realism, narrowly defined, will enable comparative analysis within and across national and linguistic boundaries.

Given the pride of place that Rushdie occupies in the postcolonial canon, the implications of the imprecision identified above extend beyond the obvious obstruction of clear-eyed perceptions of what magical realism is and does. When Homi Bhabha makes the extravagant claim that "'magical realism', after the Latin American boom, becomes the literary language of the emergent postcolonial world" (*Nation* 7), it is under the influence of the remarkable coincidence between his own intellectual labours and Rushdie's fictional projects. In the broadest terms, both Rushdie and Bhabha attempt to re-interpret modernity in the light of the historical fact of colonialism and all its multiple consequences. Magical realism is doubtless one of the ways in which Rushdie undertakes this project, but linking it inevitably to the narration of the postcolonial world does a disservice to postcolonial writing, to magical realism and to those subjects of the postcolonial world outside the intellectual circuits within which celebrities like Rushdie and Bhabha travel. As Timothy Brennan has pointed out (*Rushdie* 36–37), the primacy enjoyed by cosmopolitan novelists like Rushdie, Vargas Llosa and Allende often takes place at the expense of a recognition in the West of the drama, poetry and testimonial of the developing world, as well as of the aesthetic choices allied to what Barbara Harlow has called "resistance literature," which usually have little to do with magical realism. Furthermore, the assumption that magical realism constitutes a single "language" of narration obscures that entire category of texts that engage with modernity and its assumptions on ontological terms very different from the discursive approach of a García Márquez or a Rushdie. Pronouncements like Bhabha's are dismissed by Aijaz Ahmad as "routine features of the metropolitan theory's inflationary rhetoric" (69). For Ahmad it is the "affinities of class and location" that lead to Bhabha's "exorbitant celebration of Salman Rushdie." Ahmad's critiques of "the market-economy of theory" and of Rushdie are thus closely related, and will be revisited later in this chapter.

The definition of magical realism being utilised in this book, which views magical realism as a mode of narration that naturalises the supernatural, is very different from Bhabha's. Narrow definitions are a means of avoiding overhasty generalisations and inappropriate comparisons, insisting on the need, on a textual level, to justify the use of the term. In the case of *The Satanic Verses*, this is not difficult. The first paragraph of Rushdie's novel concludes: "Just before dawn one winter's morning, New Year's day or thereabouts, two real, full-grown, living men fell from a great height, twenty-nine thousand and two feet, towards the English Channel, without benefit of parachutes or wings, out of a clear sky" (3). A few pages of metaphysical speculations, songs and somersaults later both of these "real, full-grown, living" men are walking soggily along England's shore. No rational explanation for their survival is offered. Neither of the two was hallucinating or dreaming the experience, nor can the fantastic nature of their fall from twenty-nine thousand and two feet be explained away in terms of poetic or metaphorical license. Despite the humour of the passage, there is also nothing banal about the situation they find themselves in: their flight from India to Britain, despite hi-jack and aerial explosion, is emblematic of the journeys undertaken by millions before and since, including Rushdie himself, in search of places to study, live, work and, hopefully, to belong. They have, however, entered the country illegally, without passport or identification, and Saladin is about to feel the very literal blows of British racism. Here are coherent codes of the natural and the supernatural arranged in a state of equivalence with one another; here, in other words, is magical realism. But what does it mean?

When Farishta, cracking jokes as he tumbles towards the ground, is described as "pitting levity against gravity" Rushdie provides the key to his narrative strategy: the literal and the metaphorical are locked into one another like the embrace of Gibreel and Saladin as they fall through the clouds. The magical realism of *The Satanic Verses* operates on a similar basis to that of *Midnight's Children*, that is, primarily, though not exclusively, through an exploitation of language. Hyperbole, the splitting, fusing and blurring of the literal and the metaphorical, and an emphasis on the constitutive and performative over the merely descriptive capacities of language, are all central to Rushdie's modes of narration and strategies of representation. Much of the magic of the earlier novel, as Neil Ten Kortenaar has shown, derives from the literalisation of metaphor – Ahmed Sinai's icy testicles, the consequence of the freezing of his assets, being the most humorous case in point. On a more sustained level, the metaphor of state as person is common in historical discourse, and underlies the basis of the link between India and Saleem. Gibreel and Saladin's literal falling from the sky anticipates death – the death of old identities, old selves – while the fall towards the "bosomy earth" is itself figured as a metaphorical passage through the birth canal. It is also aligned explicitly with Satan's fall from heaven, suggesting the metaphysical questions about good and evil that will dominate the novel. Also invoked are Alice's fall down the rabbit hole, hinting at the importance of the fantastic and the bizarre; and the fall of Icarus in Ovid's *Metamorphoses*, suggesting hubris, and facilitating the intrusion of "hybrid cloud-creatures" and questions about mutation, metamorphosis, metaphor – all of which bring us back to the dominant trope of birth, and the novel's most important question: "How does newness come into the world? How is it born?" (8). The novel announces its magical realism in the same breath as its concern with immigration and the condition of migrancy in general. Put simply, Rushdie's magical realism allows him to explore more discursive terrain, more quickly and more pointedly, than would otherwise be possible. That his themes will be those of culture and identity, belief, selfhood and change, is already apparent.

There are many instances and examples of magical realism in *The Satanic Verses*, each of which can be examined in detail. The most important of these, for the purposes of this chapter, is the metamorphosis of Saladin Chamcha into a devil, and his subsequent return to human form. Because this transformation involves a devil who is modelled, in important literary (rather than theological) respects on *the* Devil, Rushdie's debts to Defoe, Blake and Bulgakov will be emphasised, and because the transformation is also from a man into beast of sorts, Rushdie's classical references to Ovid and Apuleius will be closely examined. In foregrounding these sources, I do not mean to diminish the efforts of critics like Suleri, Jussawalla, and Aravamudan to observe the extent to which Eastern aesthetic forms, especially the Urdu *ghazal* (lyrical love poetry) and Indian cinema, have influenced both the novel's narrative structure and its thematic content. However, as Brennan notes, *The Satanic Verses* is "primarily about a very secular England" (*Rushdie* 147), and there is an important link in place between Rushdie's representation of this England – especially of a London "visible but unseen" – and his reliance on the sources I intend to investigate. Saladin's metamorphosis is intimately related to the demonisation of immigrants by the police and by an institutional culture designed to protect notions of cultural purity. This metamorphosis needs to be read in the terms that irreverent, discursive magical realism, as it was identified earlier, demands: not as an escape from history, but the contrary, an engagement with reality that seeks to defamiliarise the usual terms on which discourse about history, culture and identity is founded.

If we apply a strict definition of magical realism to Rushdie's novel what we find is that the parts of the text most offensive to Muslims are not themselves magical realist. Rushdie himself has attempted to defend his novel by pointing out the multiple distancing techniques he has utilised to avoid the Jahilia sections being read as real (MacCabe 65). The most important of these defences is the fact that such sections are presented as the dreams of a man suffering from severe schizophrenia and therefore are doubly unreliable. To be sure, these are no ordinary dreams, recalling as they do the Tao Te Ching, Lewis Carroll, and Borges. Borges's most obvious use of dreams to achieve his unreality effects is in "The Circular Ruins." The story, which cites Carroll in its epigraph, tells of one who achieves his life's work of dreaming another man into reality at the point at which he realises that he himself is no more than the product of someone else's dreaming. Rushdie borrows this idea to cast a reproductive metaphor linking Gibreel and Mahound: "I emerge, Gibreel Farishta, while my other self, Mahound, lies *listening*, entranced, I am bound to him, navel to navel by a shining cord of light, not possible to say which of us is dreaming the other" (110). This image draws together ideas about birth, dreaming and being, inspiration, anxieties about selfhood and ontological instability. Though Rushdie is, in Borgesian fashion, blurring the binary between self and other, the novel does not manage to sustain this exchange and for the most part Gibreel is the dreamer, Mahound the dreamed. Their dream/ hallucination qualities, and the fact that the Jahilia sections are subordinate to and framed by the London sections, mean that their status must be charted on different sets of co-ordinates from those utilised by magical realism. Such nuances may not, in the end, matter much to an offended Muslim, but literary criticism ignores details like these at the peril of its own credibility.

Gibreel also dreams the Ayesha narrative into being and so, within the novel as a whole, the status of this narrative cannot be quite the same as that of the framing narratives of Saladin and Gibreel. From a magical realist perspective, the Ayesha sections are more interesting than the Jahilia sections because of the deliberate and self-conscious way they evoke what Rushdie has called García Márquez's "village world-view" ("García Márquez" 301). Rushdie, who sees himself as an urban writer, has publicly expressed his pleasure at having written a passage about rural India (Meer 112). The elements of fantasy centre on the magical butterflies that attend Ayesha, which recall the cloud of butterflies that hover around Mauricio Bablionia in *One Hundred Years of Solitude*.[3] But there is more going on here than mere tribute. Rushdie's butterflies can be read as an objective correlative of the states of faith induced in and by Ayesha, suggesting perhaps that it is the "provincial," faith-based strands of García Márquez's magical realism that impress Rushdie more than his irreverent ones.[4] If we ignore the fact that Gibreel dreams the whole sequence into being, it is in fact possible to read this "lepidopteral blessing" (477) as an example of faith-based magical realism.

The Ayesha sections develop in interesting ways one of the key themes of the novel: a contest between faith and doubt. The satanic verses of the novel's title are not only the passages of the Qur'an allegedly admitting the possibility of worship of gods other than Allah (114). They are also the verses of Robert Browning's *The Pied Piper of Hamelin* recited by Mirza Saeed to the pilgrims in an attempt to dissuade them from following Ayesha (484), and they are Saladin's insinuating rhymes recited over the telephone to a jealous and paranoid Gibreel (445). What links the three instances is an association of the verses with doubt, explicitly asserted to be the opposite of faith (92). It is manifoldly clear that Rushdie's preference throughout is for doubt over faith. Yet, although Mirza Saeed is a powerful voice against the unreasoning adherence of the pilgrims to Ayesha's authority, the presence of the butterflies and the ending of the section, which leaves the reader uncertain about whether a miracle has actually happened, complicate interpretations of the novel which see it as straightforwardly denigrating faith.

Evidence in favour of the miracle includes the testimonies of the Sarpanch, Sri Srinivas, Osman and Mrs Qureishi, the doubters who followed the crowd of pilgrims into the water and later, independently, allege to the police that they saw the sea divide. Mirza Saeed is an exception: he too followed the crowd into the water but did not see the parting of the waves. However, some time later, as he is dying, the butterflies and Ayesha return to him in a vision of himself splitting open, joining with others, and walking to Mecca across the seabed. This kind of spiritual anagnorisis is distinctive of Stanley Tambiah's "participation," a "sense of encompassing cosmic oneness" (109) far removed from Rushdie's usual sceptical irreverence. These examples suggest that attitudes of faith and irreverence in *The Satanic Verses*, as in *One Hundred Years of Solitude*, rather than being at odds with one another, are intertwined. The point should not be stretched, however, because the two hundred "gawpers" on the beach witness neither the butterflies nor the parting of the sea. The CID detective investigating the case claims that "drowned bodies are floating to shore, swollen like balloons and stinking like hell" (505). Saeed's witnessing of the miracle can be read as a classic "death bed vision" which anticipates that of Changez in the next chapter, a phenomenon too limited to the realm of the individual psyche to be magical realist. Rushdie is only toying with faith-based magical realism; his real interests lie elsewhere.

The parts of *The Satanic Verses* that are most clearly magical realist – and hence that will be the concern of this chapter – are those located in the city of London in the 1980s. Rushdie's narrative concerns begin to emerge in his epigraph, which cites Defoe's *The History of the Devil*, first published in 1726. The epigraph is fitting for a number of reasons: its presence is a tribute to the writer widely considered the first novelist in English; it, along with the novel's title, suggests that "Devil" – in a multitude of shifting significations – will constitute one of the most important symbols and themes of the novel; it anticipates themes of migration and exile; and, more subtly, it recalls the attitudes about cultural identity held by Defoe himself. Additionally, the narrator (along with many of the characters in the novel) is linked with the Devil from the outset (10, 93), and thus the whole novel itself constitutes a kind of satanic prose. As Martine Dutheil has pointed out, in his epigraph Rushdie selectively truncates the original passage from Defoe, which reads (elided parts italicised):

> Satan, being thus confined to a vagabond, wandering, unsettled condition, is without any certain abode; for though he has, in consequence of his angelic nature, a kind of empire in the liquid waste or air, yet, this is certainly part of his punishment, that he is *continually hovering over this inhabited globe of earth; swelling with the rage of envy, at the felicity of his rival, man; and studying all the means possible to injure and ruin him; but extremely limited in power, to his unspeakable mortification. This is his present state,* without any fixed abode, place or space, allowed him to rest the sole of his foot upon. (94–95)

The elision signals the beginning of Rushdie's reclamation of the Devil from polarising discourse which sees him only as evil. Closer scrutiny of Defoe's text reveals that this is a project which Defoe himself anticipates. Writing out of the same religious tradition as Bunyan and Milton (whose representation of Satan in *Paradise Lost* provided Defoe, as it would Blake, with a great deal of creative antagonism), Defoe's Puritanism implied a belief in the capacity of both God and the Devil to influence directly the affairs of humans. Yet, as Richard Landon points out, Defoe was also much influenced by the rationalism of Locke, Grotius and Hobbes. *The History of the Devil*, one of Defoe's more popular works of non-fiction, is thus, according to Landon, an attempt "to treat a supernatural phenomenon as if it was real and thus capable of being subjected to an historical and logical enquiry" (x). In this, the early part of the eighteenth century, clear-cut distinctions between magic, religion and science were unavailable to Defoe. He is quite able to castigate women and children for conjuring images "frightful [...] horrible [...] and monstrous [...] enough to fright the Devil himself to meet himself in the dark"

(Defoe *History* 9), while at the same time asserting that the Devil assumes female form to enter the world, where he sets about instilling lust, greed and corruption in humans. In other examples, however, Defoe shows clearly the incipient spirit of the age, pouring scorn on supposedly learned men who seek explanations in the agency of the Devil. The broad links with Rushdie's concerns in *The Satanic Verses* take the form of an historical preoccupation with the supernatural aspects of established theology, an ironic interest in the shapes and forms taken by the Devil in his earthly manifestations, and a scepticism (incipient in Defoe, pronounced in Rushdie) about the possibility of divine or diabolical agency.[5]

Rushdie's truncated epigraph highlights the migrant, exilic condition of Defoe's Satan, a key theme in *The Satanic Verses*. Defoe knew all too well the feeling of being a wanderer and of being unsettled, having been bankrupt several times, a fugitive, imprisoned, and later employed as a secret agent travelling around the country. He was, too, the great-grandson of exiles from Europe, a protector of refugees and a defender of cultural hybridity. Written in response to opposition to the enthronement of the "foreign" William III, Defoe's *The True-Born Englishman* anticipates the repudiation of cultural purity that is a key feature of Rushdie's novel, to say nothing of its satire:

> Thus from a mixture of all kinds began,
> That het'rogeneous thing, an Englishman:
> In eager rapes, and furious lust begot,
> Betwixt a painted Briton and a Scot.
> Whose gend'ring off-spring quickly learn'd to bow,
> And yoke their heifers to the Roman plough:
> From whence a mongrel half-bred race there came,
> With neither name, nor nation, speech nor fame.
> In whose hot veins new mixtures quickly ran,
> Infus'd betwixt a Saxon and a Dane.
> While their rank daughters, to their parents just,
> Receiv'd all nations with promiscuous lust.
> This nauseous brood directly did contain
> The well-extracted blood of Englishmen.

Defoe's version of Englishness as mixed, hybrid, heterogeneous, and gloriously contaminated is one which Rushdie shares. Defoe did not merely disrupt exclusivist notions of Englishness, he actively set out to create space for migrants in Britain. When in the summer of 1709 some 10 000 refugees arrived in England from Germany, fleeing famine, war with France and religious persecution, they found in Defoe their most eloquent defender. In an anticipation of the kind of rhetoric that characterises certain responses to asylum seekers in Britain today, the "poor Palatines," as they were called, were demonised by many for their perceived criminality, for taking the jobs of Englishmen, for pretending religious persecution when their motives were economic, and for the threat of numbers they presented. And in an anticipation of one of the ways in which the British government is dealing with the perceived problem today, the refugees were housed in massive camps, while it was decided what to do with them. Published in August of 1709 Defoe's *A Brief History of the Poor Palatine Refugees* is an intervention into the debate in which he aims to provide, among other things: "A full Answer to all Objections made against receiving them; and plain and convincing Proofs, that the Accession of Foreigners is a manifest Advantage to *Great Britain*, and no detriment to any of her Majesty's native Subjects" (title page). Though Defoe's Protestantism may have been a prime motive in his embrace of the Palatines, and his enthusiastic support of the economic benefits of colonialism serves as a warning that the point should not be stretched, Rushdie doubtless approves of the cultural politics that emerge in texts such as these.

The elision in Rushdie's epigraph de-emphasises the maliciousness of Defoe's Satan in order to initiate the process of generating sympathy for the Devil. My choice of wording here is deliberate and takes us down another strand of literary references that will lead directly to Rushdie's magical realist precursors. At a crucial moment in Saladin's metamorphosis from man to devil his transformation becomes public knowledge and he becomes a hero. As Mishal Sufyan recognises, the image of the Devil is one "white society has rejected for so long that we can really take it, you know, occupy it, inhabit it, reclaim it, make it our own" (287). The visible, commercialised ways in which this process begins are through the wearing of rubber devil-horns and tee-shirts, badges, posters and banners carrying the image of the "Goatman," fist raised in defiance. The song to accompany all this is, of course, the Rolling Stones' "Sympathy for the Devil," famously inspired by Mikhail Bulgakov's novel *The Master and*

Margarita. Bulgakov's novel is never referred to directly in *The Satanic Verses*. But, adding more threads to the web, Saladin, after his return to human form, sees outside the art cinema in Brickhall a poster for the 1981 Hungarian film, *Mephisto*, adorned with the lines from Goethe's *Faust*:

> – *Who art thou, then?*
> – *Part of that Power, not understood,*
> *Which always wills the Bad, and always works the Good.* (417)

Though *Faust* is a prime example of a literary engagement with the Devil, Rushdie's citation of the extract has less to do with Goethe than with Bulgakov, who used these lines as an epigraph to *The Master and Margarita*. Rushdie has claimed that the two books most influential on *The Satanic Verses* were Blake's *The Marriage of Heaven and Hell* and Bulgakov's novel (MacCabe 51). There are a great number of thematic similarities between *The Satanic Verses* and *The Master and Margarita*: the appearance of the Devil in the city and the attendant havoc his presence wreaks there; the ironic role he plays in providing moral instruction of a sort to the inhabitants; the questioning of established versions of theological truth (Biblical and Qur'anic) through an emphasis on the unreliability of the scribe; a re-writing of key moments in the history of Christianity and Islam; the interplay between dreams, reality, psychosis and the supernatural; an emphasis on performative arts, theatre in Bulgakov's case, film and television in Rushdie's; and the importance of forgiveness and compassion in human relationships. Most importantly, from Bulgakov, as from Blake, Rushdie learned the advantages of cultivating literary sympathy for the Devil. Bulgakov's Devil, Woland, is a complex and intriguing character whose diabolical interventions into Russian society take place at the expense of the hypocritical and self-serving Muscovites. Woland is linked with the writer-figure in the novel, the unnamed Master, and actually narrates the first chapter of the Master's novel, the story of Christ's crucifixion from the point of view of Pontius Pilate. This kind of literal identification of and with the Devil provides an important precedent for Rushdie.[6]

An especially interesting feature of *The Master and Margarita*, given the definition of magical realism being used here, is that Bulgakov, through the agency of Woland and his cronies, actively and relentlessly punishes those of his characters who claim not to believe in the supernatural. Rational attempts to understand Woland's powers as conjuring tricks or as hypnosis fail miserably. Decapitation, dispossession, magical deportation, public humiliation and incarceration in mental hospitals are just some of the consequences of disbelief in Woland's supernatural abilities. By contrast, Margarita's willingness to believe in Woland unlocks his compassion, allowing her to be permanently reconciled with the Master in a supernatural afterlife. The foreclosure of rational explanations for the presence of the supernatural in the heart of the real is the most important defining feature of magical realism. In its blending of grim realism with outrageous flights of fancy, the magical realism of the Moscow sections of *The Master and Margarita* clearly appeals to Rushdie's anti-naturalistic sentiments. Yet, within the magical realist frame narrative lies the Master's novel, an intricately detailed, resolutely historical and painstakingly realistic rewriting of Christ's crucifixion. Rushdie has tried to emulate this inversion whereby historical realism is the mode engaged to narrate a founding moment in religion, and the fantastic is everywhere in the representation of a modern city. But at this point the differences between the novels begin to assert themselves. By rendering fantastic his depiction of Moscow and realistic his portrayal of a moment of religious mythology, Bulgakov, writing in the darkest days of Stalinist oppression, effectively pillories the twin Soviet doctrines of socialist realism and atheism. Rushdie's treatment of fantasy, religion and history works in the opposite direction, towards a satire on that variety of faith that implies submission to the holy text, and also on other kinds of faith, as we shall see. For the purposes of this chapter, a yet more important difference is that within the frame narratives, Bulgakov's Woland has an *a priori* existence with respect to the other characters, whereas Rushdie's devil metamorphoses out of a man as the consequence of the actions and attitudes of those around him, and later shifts back into human form involuntarily.

These metamorphoses, and the ways they are indexed to a trio of authors of classical antiquity, need to be examined more closely before we can consider their import for an understanding of the politics of selfhood and belonging that underlie Rushdie's concerns with racism and with migrancy. In harnessing Ovid, Lucretius and Apuleius to his narrative purposes, Rushdie sets up a series of parallels that his novel is only able to hint at. It is as if, having shown the relevance of the *Ramayana* and the *Mahābhārata* to his anti-naturalistic methods in *Midnight's Children*, he sets out to do the same for the Western classical tradition in *The Satanic Verses*. Holed up in south London, transforming steadily into a cloven-footed devil, Saladin Chamcha receives a lesson in classical literature from Muhammed Sufyan, retired schoolteacher and proprietor of the Shandaar Café. The discussion is, as one would expect, about metamorphosis. Sufyan's immediate reaction to Chamcha's startling appearance is to quote jestingly from Apuleius's *The Golden Ass* – if Apuleius's protagonist, Lucius, was able to transform from a man into an ass and back again, there is hope yet for Chamcha. This flippant citation conceals a complex set of interrelations with Apuleius's text that will be examined shortly. Some time later, embarrassed by the satanic fury induced by his suggestion that "possession of his body could be terminated by the intercession of a mullah," Sufyan tries to console Saladin with classical precedent:

> "Question of mutability of the essence of the self," he began, awk-wardly, "has long been subject of profound debate. For example, great Lucretius tells us, in *De Rerum Natura*, this following thing: *quodcumque suis mutatum finibus exit, continuo hoc mors est illius quod fuit ante.* Which being translated, forgive my clumsiness, is 'Whatever by its changing goes out of its frontiers,' – that is, bursts its banks, – or, maybe, breaks out of its limitations, – so to speak, disregards its old rules, but that is too free, I am thinking... 'that thing', at any rate, Lucretius holds, 'by doing so brings immediate death to its old self'. However," up went the ex-schoolmaster's finger, "poet Ovid, in the *Metamorphoses*, takes diametrically opposed view. He avers thus: 'As yielding wax' – heated, you see, possibly for the sealing of documents or such, – 'is stamped with new designs And changes shape and seems not still the same, Yet is indeed the same, even so our souls,' – you hear, good sir? Our spirits! Our immortal essences! – 'Are still the same forever, but adopt in their migrations ever-varying forms.'" (276–277)

In his hesitation and self-interruption, his elision of articles and his archaisms, Sufyan brushes against the boundaries of caricature. But Rushdie's obvious sympathy for his character reconciles the dramatic comedy of the vignette with the symbolic importance of the opposition Sufyan sets up between Lucretius and Ovid. Sufyan is a Muslim, a haji, and Rushdie's choice of reference points is apposite to questions of being and religion. Lucretius's *De Rerum Natura*, drawing from the atomic theory of Epicurus, is a poem designed to illustrate the non-intervention of the gods in earthly matters. For Lucretius, humans are material entities; any belief that we might survive the destruction of our physical selves is regarded with extreme suspicion. Ovid, on the other hand, was influenced in the final book of *Metamorphoses* by Pythagoras, whose belief in metempsychosis, or the reincarnation of souls, is well-attested. Apuleius himself claimed that Pythagoras learned his spiritual beliefs from the Brahmins of India (*Apologia* 16), and this assumption is now common, though historical evidence is scarce. Sufyan's obvious preference for Ovid – he hops from foot to foot as he declares, "For me it is always Ovid over Lucretius" – suggests a sneaky parody on Rushdie's part, for it is potentially scandalous to try to reconcile Ovid's apparent support for theories of reincarnation with Sufyan's Muslim beliefs. Saladin Chamcha, however, finds little of comfort in either position: for him acceptance of Lucretius implies "that some demonic and irreversible mutation is taking place in my inmost depths" while the Ovidian position suggests that "everything now emerging is no more than a manifestation of what was already there." Saladin suggests a third option, derived, most likely, from Shakespeare's *Othello* (yet another important intertext for *The Satanic Verses*): his horns, he suggests, fittingly for one whose "old friend and rescuer is also the nightly lover of his wife," are those of a cuckold (277).

Suggested in the very scripting of Sufyan's speech is Rushdie's preference for the Lucretian model. He cites the original Latin, and allows Sufyan to struggle through possible translations, thus providing a subliminal commentary on the way in which words, sentences and meanings are carried across and altered from language to language, culture to culture, even across millennia. At this point in the narrative, Saladin's interpretation of the Lucretian position as describing his condition as "demonic and irreversible" is not strictly tenable. By removing the gods from the equation, Lucretius proposed a model of identity that emphasises flux and alteration. Nothing is irreversible, nothing is absolute and, most importantly for Saladin, the "demonic" nature of his metamorphosis must be read in its human rather than its transcendental dimensions. This human dimension is most obvious in the extent to which Saladin's devil-form is dependent on the behaviour and attitudes of those around him. As tensions rise in Brickhall, with murder on the streets, detention and interrogation, wild rumours of occultism, "everyone, black brown white, had started thinking of the dream figure as *real*... Saladin Chamcha was getting to be true" (288). This process of validation contributes, along with his desire for vengeance against Gibreel Farishta, to Saladin's alarming growth as a devil. Confronted by the extremity of his situation,

> he chose Lucretius over Ovid. The inconstant soul, the mutability of everything, *das Ich*, every last speck. A being going through life can become so other to himself as to *be another*, discrete, severed from history. He thought, at times, of Zeeny Vakil on that other planet, Bombay, at the far rim of the galaxy: Zeeny, eclecticism, hybridity. The optimism of those ideas! The certainty on which they rested: of will, of choice! But, Zeeny mine, life just happens to you, like an accident. No: it happens to you as a result of your condition. Not choice, but – at best – process, and, at worst, shocking, total change. Newness: he had sought a different kind, but this is what he got. (288)

By confronting the Lucretian position with a fatalism founded in despair, Saladin pushes it to an extreme that denies the possibility of any stable sense of purpose, meaning and identity.[7] Saladin's position is contradictory, though: if he is "severed from history" what is the "condition" or "process" that causes life to happen to him? He is, instead, for the first time in his life, deeply aware of how enmeshed in history he is, both the history of colonialism, and that of contemporary London. His metamorphosis, it must be emphasised, is not one that happened to him "like an accident." It is, among other things, a punishment for the false, essentialist view of identity that characterised his life prior to his fateful visit to India.[8] Zeeny's interruption into his thoughts serves to remind us that, long before he turned into a devil, she had confronted him with the consequences of his repudiation of India. Her alternative to Saladin's Anglophilia is not an essential Indianness (one we might extrapolate from Sufyan's version of Ovid) nor is it a nihilistic disavowal of the possibility of any stable identity (the extreme version of Lucretius). It is, rather, similar to that espoused by Rushdie's friend and interlocutor, the postcolonial theorist, Homi K. Bhabha.

Bhabha's and Zeeny Vakil's hybridities are not entirely the same: Bhabha's is a "restless, uneasy, interstitial hybridity: a radical hetero-geneity, discontinuity, the permanent revolution of forms" (Young *Hybridity* 25) that may be closer to the position Saladin finds himself in as he chooses Lucretius over Ovid than to the more optimistic ver-sion of hybridity embraced by Zeeny. That Saladin moves closer to Zeeny's position is clear, however. Having returned to human form, he receives a televisual gift, a demonstration on "Gardener's World" of the "chimeran graft" – not this time a hybrid mythological mon-ster, but two trees, bred into one. Remembering the tree his father had planted for him at birth, and subsequently chopped down in his Bombay garden, and faced with the image of the hybrid "firmly planted in and growing vigorously out of a piece of English earth," Saladin reasons: "If such a tree were possible, then so was he; he, too, could cohere, send down roots, survive" (406). Realisations such as these are linked with Saladin's "cure": not only is he not subjected to involuntary metamorphosis again, but the novel itself moves towards a conclusion that is the most naturalistic passage Rushdie has writ-ten. Not surprisingly, Zeeny is the one to whom Saladin turns, liter-ally and metaphorically, for "another chance" at the novel's conclusion – a final, ringing endorsement of her insistence on the need for a valorised hybridity.[9]

The Ovid-Lucretius dialectic suggests Rushdie's concern with the impact of migration on the individual psyche, but his narrative project in *The Satanic Verses* extends to the communal experiences of minority cultures living in the West, or more specifically in London in the 1980s. In the part of the city that is "visible but unseen" – that part inhabited by diasporic communities, embattled immigrants, asylum seekers – the nature of the real, the believable, the normal cannot be taken for granted lest it prove to be yet another instrument of oppression. Rushdie's point that realism is inadequate to describe a world in which consensus may not exist between reader and writer is clearly being played out here. After the migrations into Britain that have taken place since the 1950s, competing cultural views of the world and of reality regularly confront one another in cities like London. Yet this contest is usually unequal. Certain ways

of seeing (and of not seeing) attendant on specific cultural configurations dominate others. To the extent that it is intended as a literary intervention, Rushdie's novel attempts to reverse the usual view
of the city in English literature. As he put it, the London of *The
Satanic Verses*

> is not an invisible city in the sense that Calvino's cities were invis-
> ible cities, fantasy cities; [it] is a real city whose streets I know; you
> know, it would be possible to guide anybody down those streets
> and to show them the locations out of which, and the kind of life
> experience out of which, the experiences in the book come. But
> that city is certainly in English literature, and even in English
> society, ignored, not looked at – in fact, unseen. So there you have
> the experience of a lot of people, millions of people now in Britain,
> invisible to the rest, and I wanted to try and make it visible. (Ball
> interview 105)

Rushdie is not correct to say that this part of the city has been
ignored by English literature – as Brennan points out (*Rushdie* 149),
G.V. Desani's *All about H. Hatterr* was published as early as 1948, and
other diasporic narratives with which *The Satanic Verses* can be set
in dialogue include Samuel Selvon's *The Lonely Londoners* and George
Lamming's *The Emigrants*. Rushdie is, in effect, guilty of participat-
ing in a discourse that renders this literature "unseen." His almost
absolute espousal of non-realist forms of narration is made at the
expense, at least in this case, of an appreciation of the political possibilities of alternative aesthetic choices. Nevertheless, there is no
doubt that his commitment to anti-naturalism is intimately connected with his political sensibilities. The London sections of *The
Satanic Verses* are set in 1983, about the time Rushdie started writing
the novel. Just two years previously, Britain had experienced the
worst race-related violence in its history, to the extent that 1981
became known as "Year of the Riots." In January, 15 000 people –
the largest black demonstration ever – had taken to the streets in
London to voice grievances over press indifference to black deaths.
In April the Metropolitan Police had launched "Operation Swamp
81" to tackle burglary and robbery, provoking severe violence in
Brixton. In six days, officers stopped 943 people and arrested 118.
Violent disturbances followed in Liverpool over four nights in July

leading police to use CS gas for the first time in Britain. In response, some 1000 people gathered outside a police station in Manchester, new riots erupted in Brixton and further disturbances took place all over Britain (Manoraj et al. 8) Rushdie's sister, Sameen, was one of the victims of the charged mood of the times, harassed and assaulted by racists on the London Underground (Haffenden 52). Read within this context, the London of *The Satanic Verses* is as real and histori-cal as Rushdie asserts. At times, though, the surface of Rushdie's city is distorted into surreal and fantastic forms, such as when the weather in London is tropicalised. But Rushdie is able to avoid hav-ing to choose between the poles of realism and fantasy by utilising a magical realism that allows the supernatural to exist within the framework of the real city. The most visible, dramatic and signifi-cant demonstration of this technique is Saladin's reversible transfor-mation into a devil.

This metamorphosis, the most important aspect of the novel's engagement with magical realism, is best understood through a reading of the influence of the final member of his trio of classical sources, Apuleius. Where lines from Ovid and Lucretius were selec-tively introduced to conceptualise themes of selfhood and change, the influence of Apuleius lies in the fact that *The Golden Ass* is a magical realist proto-novel that explores the relationships between superstition and everyday life in the Roman Empire in the second-century A.D. Very little of *The Golden Ass*'s content makes it into *The Satanic Verses*. Aside from a hubristic desire to partake in a tradition of plundering or alluding to Apuleius that includes Boccaccio, Cervantes, Shakespeare and Le Sage, Rushdie's intention in citing *The Golden Ass* is to flag the treatment of the supernatural in the clas-sical text. Nevertheless, a detailed comparison between the texts proves extremely productive. Along with Ovid's *Metamorphoses*, by which it was clearly influenced, and from which it takes a second title, *The Golden Ass* serves as an important point of reference for Rushdie because it works towards legitimising the presence of both metamorphosis and witchcraft in *The Satanic Verses*. Accompanying Sufyan's offer of "Apuleian sympathy" to Saladin, a passage of free indirect narration informs us that Apuleius was a "priest" who "denied the accusation of having bewitched a rich widow yet confessed, somewhat perversely, that at an earlier stage in his career he had been transformed, by witchcraft, into (not an owl, but) an ass" (243). This biographical sketch curiously misrepresents Apuleius and underestimates his novel. Apuleius was a noted orator and a Platonic philosopher; his priesthood in the imperial cult constituted a political rather than a religious appointment and is not necessarily related to his explorations of religion and magic (*Florida* 16). Rushdie seems to imply that *The Golden Ass* should be read as an account of Apuleius's own experience, but the prologue of the novel clearly announces, in metafictional style, its status as a "Milesian discourse," a "series of different stories" and as "amusing gossip" (7). It is not Apuleius who was transformed into an ass, but his narrator, Lucius, and there are good reasons for reading *The Golden Ass* as a satire on credulity, rather than, as Rushdie seems to imply, as testimony to the power of belief.[10]

There are other motives, overt and covert, at play behind Rushdie's inclusion of Apuleius. He was "a colonial of an earlier empire" (243) and he is drafted into service in support of a genealogical linkage between migrancy and writing. This linkage is demonstrated through the double mapping of metamorphosis onto language, outwards towards translation, and inwards towards metaphor. This process is supported by the degree of self-consciousness displayed by Apuleius in the prologue to his novel, where his narrator points out the value of translating from his native Greek into Latin, claiming that "this linguistic metamorphosis suits the style of writing I have tackled here" (7). In pointing towards the linguistic as well as the literal qualities of metamorphosis, Apuleius is extremely close to Rushdie's preoccupation with the links between translation and cultural identity in migration. The starting point for *The Satanic Verses* could be Rushdie's narrator-surrogate's assertions in *Shame* that "I, too, am a translated man. I have been *borne across*. It is generally believed that something is always lost in translation; I cling to the notion [...] that something can also be gained" (29). In both Rushdie and Apuleius, the narrative position is ambivalently located both inside and outside the dominant culture to which such statements are addressed. And in both cases, the writer is materially comfortable enough to turn such an ambivalent location to his advantage, to investigate and celebrate the "newness" that hybridity engenders.

Instead of the owl, symbol of wisdom, whose shape he desires to adopt, Apuleius's Lucius is transformed into an ass. That this transformation is punishment of some kind is clear, and signals further links between the texts, for we have already noted that Saladin's metamorphosis served punishment on him too. Lucius's life prior to metamorphosis had been far from pure in the Platonic sense that would have been familiar to Apuleius. E.J. Kenney thus suggests that *The Golden Ass* can be interpreted in the light of Socrates' suggestion that "it is likely [...] that those who have practised gluttony and violence and drunkenness and have not taken heed to their ways enter the bodies of asses and suchlike beasts" ("Phaedo" 81e; Kenney xxvi). Read in this way, the central metamorphosis of *The Golden Ass* is a literalisation of Socrates' image. At the very least, Lucius's transformation renders material the metaphorical connection between the animal that gave Latin words like *asinus* (ass or fool) or *mulinus* (mulish) and the kinds of human behaviour such words describe.

It has already been pointed out that the device of literalising metaphors is common, if not central in Rushdie's *Midnight's Children*, and it underlies the meaning of Saladin-as-goatman/devil in *The Satanic Verses*. Protesting to the policemen who arrest him that he is a British citizen, the reply comes: "Who are you trying to kid? [...] Look at yourself. You're a fucking Packy billy. Sally-who? What kind of a name is that for an Englishman?" (163). When they concoct the story of how they discovered Saladin on the Sussex beach, the police note that there will be little objection to their story, since Saladin "looks like the very devil" (164). Later, lying in a guarded hospital, sprouting horns, hair and a tail, Saladin is confronted by a number of other metamorphosing humans: a manticore, a woman "who is now mostly water-buffalo," "businessmen from Nigeria who have grown sturdy tails." When he asks, "how do they do it?" he receives the revealing reply: "They describe us [...]. That's all. They have the power of description, and we succumb to the pictures they construct" (168). In referring to blacks and Asians as animals or devils, "they" – the police and associated institutions – metaphorically withhold humanity from them, and this metaphorical process is literalised, through magical realism, in Rushdie's text.[11]

There is an alternative to this linguistically determinate explanation for Saladin's metamorphosis, one which, like the Ayesha sections, troubles the interpretation of *The Satanic Verses*'s magical realism as wholly irreverent. Pamela Lovelace, Saladin's wife, is a distant relative of Matthew Hopkins, seventeenth-century Witchfinder-General, responsible for the deaths of about 230 "witches," and finally hanged as a witch himself in 1647 (Brians note to p. 182). The relationship becomes significant when Pamela herself becomes involved in investigating allegations of witchcraft within the police force as part of her work for the Brickhall community relations council. It is initially suggested that such witchcraft is simulated as a means of terrorising the black population of London. However, through the research of Antoinette Roberts, mother of Dr Uhuru Simba, the activist murdered in detention, it seems that there is "extensive evidence of the existence of witches' covens throughout the Metropolitan Police" (452).

The witchcraft plot is anticipated in the many ways in which magic, obeah, superstition and voodoo are present in the novel. Both Saladin and his father, Changez, ritually cross their fingers and rotate their thumbs for luck while taking off in aeroplanes (33, 41); Gibreel Farishta's mentor Mhatre was an "amateur psychic" who communicated with spirits (21); Orphia Phillips is accused of using obeah to win back her lover, but is told that "it don't signify" in the London Underground (331); and television reports are received of mermen in Guyana and lycanthropy in the Scottish Highlands (405). There is an element of ritual about the dancing and rapping at Club Hot Wax, and the wax effigies of historical figures, resonant all at once with Ovid's metaphor for the soul in migration, Guy Fawkes, Madame Tussauds and voodoo dolls, have, as the conservative lenses of the television cameras suggest, something more than a little "witchy" about them (455). In all of these cases the supernatural and magic are presented as potentially real presences or as efficacious means of action. They serve as precedents for a reading of Saladin's metamorphosis as caused by the witchcraft of the Metropolitan Police. We might therefore put forward the hypothesis that, since belief in some form of equivalence between supernatural and the natural remains a feature of some Afro-Caribbean communities of the kind to which Antoinette Roberts belongs, Rushdie is making an attempt at reclaiming this aspect of their world view from the empirical and rationalist grasp of the dominant culture. In this respect, his magical realism could be interpreted as similar to that of the early fiction of Alejo Carpentier, Asturias or Okri.

As is the case in the Ayesha sections of the novel, Rushdie is again only toying with faith-based magical realism. When Antoinette Roberts dies, assassinated, we are led to believe, by the police in order to prevent the information about their occultist practises coming to light, the dossier of evidence disappears and the witchcraft plot is, therefore, never satisfactorily resolved. Witchcraft in *The Satanic Verses* exists partly to displace the exclusive association of superstition with the Afro-Caribbean by reminding us of English history and of the superstitious social practices that continue to characterise its everyday life.[12] But, more importantly, as Pamela points out to an incredulous Jumpy Joshi, it contests all and any versions of "normality as being normal" (280). As a cause for the metamorphoses of Saladin and others it is left at the level of suggestion only. Given the broader context of the novel it is unlikely that Rushdie's goal is to legitimise the functionings of superstition. *The Satanic Verses* explicitly asserts the ethical primacy of doubt over faith, the human over the transcendental. As has been stressed previously, Alejo Carpentier's faith implied not only a confidence in the veracity of the non-rational of Latin America, but also a faith in the capacity of language to represent such putative realities. Rushdie's magical realism is based in a rejection of both of these aspects of faith; for him, culture does not have an ontological reality prior to its inscription in language, nor is language the vehicle by which culture can unproblematically be carried. His anti-naturalism, including but not limited to his magical realism, is the basis for an attack on both of these assumptions. The goal is not the inscription of new ontological realities, but the destabilisation of those already present in order to posit a different basis for the assertion of new cultural identities.

The diminution of the importance of the witchcraft plot brings "demonising discourse" into stark relief as lying behind Saladin's transformation. "How do they do it?" asks horned and hoofed Chamcha. "They describe us... That's all" comes the reply. The language of racism seems itself to be a form of witchcraft because it is so capable of inflicting violence remotely. If Rushdie's anti-naturalism is founded in the idea that language does not merely represent the world but actively constitutes it in important ways, then his magical realism serves as his most frequent demonstration of this point. In this case the performative aspects of language are harnessed to the dehumanising racism of the police and immigration controls. But, precisely because language *is* so powerful, through the process of his politicisation the image of Saladin-as-devil can be reclaimed by those at whom such demonising discourse is targeted. As Rushdie writes in

In Good Faith, "The very title, *The Satanic Verses* is an aspect of this attempt at reclamation. You call us devils? it seems to ask. Very well, then, here is the devil's version of the world, of 'your' world, the version written from the experience of those who have been demonised by virtue of their otherness" (12).

The novel's preoccupation with the status of the idea, with newness and with birth suggests that the logical extension of this reclamation is the assertion of new cultural identities. As was clear from Saladin's turning to Zeeny at the novel's end, hybridity will be the key to the coming into being of this newness, predicated in this case on the hybrid model of language. In Bhabha's post-structuralist-inflected model of culture, it is always the "'inter' – the cutting edge of translation and negotiation, the *in between* space – that carries the burden of the meaning of culture" ("Commitment" 38). Saladin's transformation served punishment on him for not accepting that there is no essential cultural location in which to ground individual identity; he is punished for looking for newness in the wrong places. Neither fully Indian, nor fully English, he is buffeted between the poles of change and fixity and, like Rushdie himself, will find that he belongs only in a hyphenated category: Anglo-Indian, Indo-Anglian, and more in the hyphen than in the substantive.[13] Homi Bhabha is clear on this point when he explains how migration opens up new identities which can be expressed in new ways:

> Renamings of the subjects of cultural difference do not derive their discursive authority from anterior causes – be it human nature or historical necessity – which, in a secondary move, articulate essential and *expressive* identities between cultural differences in the contemporary world. The problem is not of an ontological cast, where differences are effects of some more totalising, transcendent identity to be found in the past or the future. Hybrid hyphenations emphasize the incommensurable elements – the stubborn chunks – as the basis of cultural identifications. What is at stake is the performative nature of differential identities: the regulation and negotiation of those spaces that are continually, *contingently*, "opening out," remaking the boundaries, exposing the limits of any claim to a singular or autonomous sign of difference. ("Newness" 219)

This understanding of the way in which cultural identity is constituted in and through discourse is drawn as much from Bhabha's reading of Rushdie as it is from the Mexican-American performance artist, Gómez-Peña or from his consideration of the challenges facing the *gastarbeiter* in Germany. The Bhabha/Rushdie theory of culture speaks to minorities living in the West on two important levels. First, by insisting on the performative at the expense of the essential or expressive qualities of culture, those struggling with questions of value, identity and belonging are potentially able to determine themselves the ways in which "newness enters the world." Rushdie makes clear in his ironically-titled defence of the novel, *In Good Faith*, that his over-arching goal in *The Satanic Verses* is the reclamation of the ability to re-imagine and re-figure cultural locations by valorising their hybrid natures. In an often-cited passage that gave Bhabha the title for the essay cited above, Rushdie echoes Defoe's celebration of his "mongrel half-bred race":

> *The Satanic Verses* celebrates hybridity, impurity, intermingling, the transformation that comes of new and unexpected combinations of human beings, cultures, ideas, politics, movies, songs. It rejoices in mongrelization and fears the absolutism of the Pure. Mélange, hotch-potch, a bit of this and a bit of that is *how newness enters the world*. It is the great possibility that mass migration gives the world, and I have tried to embrace it. *The Satanic Verses* is for change-by-fusion, change-by-conjoining. It is a love song to our mongrel selves. (4)

Hybrid cultural formations, in this model, make possible new ways of ways of seeing the world, of engaging with it, describing it, and changing it. Second, though Bhabha's "exposing the limits of any claim to a singular or autonomous sign of difference" may not suit those who advocate a politics of contestation, it provides an important means of repudiating the kinds of claims to homogeneity on which racist and exclusionary discourse about identity is invariably founded. Again, this project lies at the heart of Rushdie's intentions. In Rosa Diamond's vision of the "unfinished business" that keeps the ghost of William the Conqueror returning to the shoreline, or in the parody of Hal Valance's greedy Thatcherism, or the whisky-soaked speculations of S.S. Sisodia, "Englishness" of a pure or essential kind is thrown open to doubt throughout the novel. Jumpy Joshi's attempted reclamation of Enoch Powell's "rivers of blood" image provides an example of a point where these two projects overlap most visibly.[14] A more recent reminder of the need for this kind of project became obvious in the 2001 election race, when Conservative Party MP, John Townend, who clearly had not read Defoe's defence of the heterogeneity of the English, nor Bhabha's postulations about the meanings of hyphens, claimed that "[o]ur homogenous Anglo-Saxon society has been seriously undermined by the massive immigration – particularly Commonwealth immigration – that has taken place since the war." According *The Guardian*, Townend had the word "coloured" in place of "Commonwealth" in the first draft of his speech (Watt and Wainright 10). Townend went on to claim that Enoch Powell would have become prime minister if voters had realised the accuracy of predictions he made in his "rivers of blood" speech in 1968.

The simple question, "what is the source of the supernatural in this novel?," yields some voluminous answers in Rushdie's case. I have emphasised here those literary referents concerned with the sympathetic representation of the Devil (Defoe and Bulgakov), those that provide a precedent for the trope of metamorphosis (Lucretius, Ovid, Apuleius) and those that have helped Rushdie in developing the potential of a mode of narration that naturalises the supernatural (Borges and García Márquez). This literary dimension is complemented by Rushdie's experiences of the 1980s Britain in which he was living as he wrote the novel, which provided him with the bulk of his subject matter in *The Satanic Verses*. What holds all of these elements together is Rushdie's heightened awareness of language, and a constant foregrounding of the ways meanings are produced by it. Magical realism's appeal to Rushdie's project in *The Satanic Verses* lies in the extent to which it is capable of reclaiming the hidden potentials of language and of definition. Where the fantastic has been thought of as an escape from history, Rushdie reclaims it by showing how it is already present in the language of history in *Midnight's Children*, and of identity discourse more generally in *The Satanic Verses*. His is a metaphorical magical realism in both the etymological and the linguistic senses of the word "metaphor." In bringing to the surface meanings obscured by our usual sense of metaphor as figurative or not real, Rushdie emphasises the extent to which all meanings are in a perpetual state of being *carried across*. Within this continually opening space of flux and contingency, he would have us recognise, lies our capacity to imagine and invent identities and futures.

6

The African World View in Ben Okri's *The Famished Road*

One of the most pressing concerns facing the critic commenting on *The Famished Road* (1991) has been the question of where to locate the work in terms of existing narrative traditions. As Derek Wright puts it: what are the appropriate "exegetic latitudes" by which to navigate through a reading of this difficult novel ("Interpreting" 18)? On a survey of the criticism that has appeared on Okri, three options have presented themselves: *The Famished Road* has been read as heir to a tradition of Nigerian writing of which Fagunwa, Tutuola and Soyinka are the most significant exemplars; as part of a configuration of recent west African novels, including works by Laing, Cheney-Coker, Sony Labou Tansi, Bandele-Thomas and others, which represents the advent of a postcolonial postmodernism in African writing; and as sharing commonalities with the projects of a global set of writers who engage non-realist narrative strategies, especially magical realism, in their writings. The first two of these options are mutually reinforcing and point in a general way towards African culture, mythologies and literature as the most appropriate markers by which to chart one's responses to the novel. The third option emphasises those places where Okri's narrative opens out onto global and generic literary, cultural, ecological and geopolitical discourses. These two currents of Okri criticism – one pointing inwards towards Africa, one outwards to the wider world – are by no means dichotomous. From the biblical refrain, "In the beginning" that opens the novel it is clear that Afrocentric approaches will have to account for Okri's eclectic, hybrid aesthetics; on the other hand, generic approaches that do not acknowledge the literary and cultural legacy of Nigeria in Okri's narrative will impoverish themselves by this silence, and, more importantly, will run the risk of reinforcing dubious Eurocentric critical practices.

In what might be read as a tacit acknowledgement of the difficulties of applying a generic category like magical realism to Okri's work, one finds in early Afrocentric commentary on *The Famished Road* a studious avoidance of the term. Taking Ato Quayson's 1997 study, *Strategic Transformations in Nigerian Literature*, as paradigmatic of this tendency, we should first note the benefits that accrue to literary-historical grounding in the analysis of Okri's work, before examining the ways in which this approach struggles to accommodate those aspects of Okri's project that are not ultimately reducible to analysis in terms of the Nigerian literary tradition as Quayson defines it. Quayson takes Yoruba oral culture as a set of "indigenous conceptual resources" (9), and his task is to identify a tradition of writing informed by "varying interdiscursive relationships" with that resource-base. This tradition is constituted out of a literature that "exercis[es] the option of mythopoesis and ritual instead of realism," expressing a "will-to-identity" identifiable through a historicised literary criticism attentive to the implications of the mythopoeic (158–159).

Quayson thus reads Ben Okri's work as being filially related to that of Tutuola and Soyinka, but moving beyond the positions of both of these writers. Contradictory aspects of the narrative strategy are explained in terms of "the novel's evocation of an orality paradigm within the space of a literary one" (129). An awareness of this duality helps us to understand the novel's apparent atemporality, the difficulties that derive from locating the narration in Azaro's consciousness while still invoking a communal world-view, and the place of tropes and symbols like the road, the abiku, and the spirit world in general. Azaro's experiences, whether they take place in the world of the living, of the spirits or in an indeterminate zone between the two is fluid and uninterrupted, with only a few exceptions, by the need to explain, to make connections with prior experiences or to provide the kinds of chronological markers that help the reader to orientate him or herself within the narrative. As Quayson points out, the technique that allows Okri to achieve these effects is an almost exclusive utilisation of the preterite tense. At the same time, the narration dodges the question of where the narrating "I" is located, thus creating the effect of events flowing through Azaro's experience without responding to the imperative, common in realism, to rationalise them in any way (*Strategic* 125). Limiting the narratorial ambit in such a way facilitates the novel's indeterminacy – a key goal of Okri's – but this indeterminacy can become monotonous and more than one critic has commented on the fatigue that is a feature of reading the novel.

Quayson's comparisons between Tutuola's work and *The Famished Road* are particularly fruitful in terms of understanding the ways in which Okri has appropriated and transformed the specific interweavings of real and spirit worlds found in Tutuola's folkloric worlds, and, more distantly, in Yoruba orature. Nonetheless, Tutuola has still not been given his due. There is certainly a difference between Tutuola's heroes and Okri's refusal of the heroic potential of the folktale in his construction of the character of Azaro, but certain textual similarities have passed unnoticed. Like Azaro, the narrator of *My Life in the Bush of Ghosts*, begins the novel as a seven-year-old boy whose mother is a market trader, and in that novel the narrator-hero encounters a certain kind of spirit known as "burglar ghosts." When the narrator asks one such ghost whether he is an "earthly person," the ghost answers, "I am and I am not" (53): he turns out to be one of the "born and die babies" – in other words, an abiku. The trope of the abiku reappears in Tutuola's *The Witch Herbalist of the Remote Town*. Moving beyond the coincidence of tropes, it might be asserted that, though the boundaries between real and spirit worlds in Tutuola are certainly more clearly demarcated than they are in Okri's novel, nevertheless the extent of interpenetration between these two domains in Tutuola's work is underemphasized by Quayson and others.[1] A useful example of this interpenetration is the "10th Town of Ghosts" in *My Life in the Bush of Ghosts*, where the narrator-hero learns that his dead cousin has brought Christianity – along with schools, hospitals and many houses "built in the modern style" – to the ghostly inhabitants of the town (149). Though this town is safely located within the mythopoeic realm, the bush in this example cannot be viewed only as an anxiety-generating space liminal to the real world: it is a hybrid space where natural and supernatural exist in a matter-of-fact state of equivalence. Putting intentionality aside, the ironic, subversive potentialities that reside in Tutuola's image of congregations of ghosts attending regular services at a Methodist

Church are undeniable. Contrary to the perspective that holds Tutuola to be only a writer of folkloric morality tales, this reading thus suggests that Okri may have learned even more from his writing that is usually recognised.

The relevance of Soyinka to Okri's writing leads us back to the key question of exegetic emphasis identified earlier. In Quayson's analysis, Soyinka's influence is examined in terms of the meanings of the road, the abiku myth and the embodying of Ogun and Sango essences in the form of Azaro's Dad.[2] Through the inscription of both of these deities, Okri is said to accomplish a "strategic elaboration" of Soyinka's persistent invocation of Ogun – one that demonstrates a link between Okri's hybrid upbringing and the "hybrid and eclectic potential" of the indigenous resource-base itself (141). This suggestive comparison is not developed, however, despite the fact that earlier in his book Quayson noted Soyinka "drawing on indigenous resources for affirming Yoruba, Nigerian and even African verities at a world level" (76). Quayson thus leaves Soyinka's influence on Okri at the level of the textual dynamics of *The Famished Road*, not examining the extent to which Okri's project, which emerges more fully in his interviews, is informed by a desire to extend and transform Soyinka's attempt in *Myth, Literature and the African World* to "forge a metaphysical African community" (77). This project will be examined in detail later in this chapter.

Throughout his analysis, Quayson uses a language very similar to that used to describe magical realism. His study of *The Famished Road* is enabled throughout by his utilisation of a "reality-esoteric axis" (134); the "real world and that of the spirits are rendered problematically equivalent in [Azaro's] experience" (124); "the spirit world remains a vital life operating between the arena of real events" (133); "equivalence is hinted at in the calibration of events between the two worlds" (136).[3] But when it comes to explicitly identifying this narrative practice, the absence of the term magical realism signals a demurral.[4] Instead, Quayson drafts in Harry Garuba's term, "animist realism," to account for Okri's narrative mode (148). While this term may describe quite well certain of the tenets on which Okri's narrative is constructed, the concern is that, as a neologism, it is as yet inadequate to the task of locating *The Famished Road* in a category of literary discourse that would enable comparison with texts from other literary traditions.

Garuba has recently returned to animism in order to address these concerns and to rethink conceptions of African modernity. For Garuba, drawing on Soyinka's assertions about the elasticity of African epistemologies, animism serves as means whereby the "modernising of tradition" and the "traditionalising of the modern" can be understood. Included in Garuba's account is a detailed assessment of the relationships between magical realism and animism, in which animism is seen as a "deep structure" generating various *paroles*, among which is magical realism. Garuba thus describes how "many of the literary techniques of the artists who have been labelled magical realist writers derive their warrant from traditional animist cultures" (275). Though Garuba does not discuss *The Famished Road* explicitly, his account corroborates the reading of novel I will undertake in this chapter, as will be seen. The problem though, as Garuba recognises, is that magical realism's "urban cosmopolitan aspect" and an "ironizing attitude" fit less well into the animist trajectory he is sketching. Garuba's answer is to see magical realism as a subgenre of animist realism "with its own connecting characteristics and its own formal difference" (275). This is only a partial solution, for Garuba does not acknowledge the possibility that magical realism might have other, alternative intellectual genealogies that do not include animism. Animism provides a possible base for what I am calling faith-based strands of magical realism. But it does not explain irreverent magical realism, as I am defining it, which has a different genealogy that includes rationalism, scepticism, idealism and postmodernism. It is the argument of these pages that magical realist critical discourse needs to develop a suitable vocabulary for dealing with such distinctions.

By contrast with Garuba, some commentators who locate *The Famished Road* in terms specific to African writing and culture explicitly dismiss the relevance of the term magical realism to the novel. In most cases, the term is rejected because the specific form and mode of Okri's narration is not seen to resemble those engaged by other magical realists. This position was initiated in an early review of the novel by Kwame Anthony Appiah, where he states: "My own sense is that there is a difference between the ways in which Latin American writers draw on the supernatural and the way that Okri does: for Okri, in a curious way, the world of the spirits is not metaphorical or imaginary; rather it is more real than that of the everyday" (Appiah

"Spiritual" 147). This same point is made in more detail by Derek Wright in an article entitled "Postmodernism as Realism: Magic History in Recent West African Fiction":

> Okri does not envisage his world as an imaginary mythic, metaphorical or parabolic construct, after the fashion of the magic realists, or as a surrealist fantasy, as in the folkloric dream-narratives of Amos Tutuola, where the fantastic events occur only in a hallucinated esoteric realm sharply differentiated from the real world. The novel's spirit realm is not an approximation to reality but a reality in its own right [...] Their [Okri's and Laing's] narratives are not intended as mythopoeic projections of other or imagined worlds but palpable representations of one that exists, ...nd to relocate their spiritual, psychic naturalism in the order of mythopoeics or to displace it into allegorical or symbolic discourse, is to unhitch them from their quasi-realistic moorings and to dilute the strength of its informing indigenous world view. ("Postmodernism" 182–183)

The very title of Wright's article gestures playfully towards magical realism. But, similarly to Appiah, Wright believes that Okri's novel lacks the specific kind of metaphoricity that he sees as characteristic of magical realism. This position echoes Okri's own claims to be utilising a multi-dimensional realism in *The Famished Road*. It is my argument in this chapter that it is exactly this feature of the narrative project behind *The Famished Road* that qualifies the novel as a magical realist text, and that thereby connects Okri with a number of writers specifically affiliated to magical realist modes of narration. The caveat to this observation is that we need to be clear that Okri's is a faith-based, ontological magical realism quite different from the irreverent, discourse-oriented magical realism of a writer like Salman Rushdie.

Wright's warning about the dangers of "unhitching" Okri's narrative from its roots serves as a timely caution against a kind of interpretation that has emerged recently. Renato Oliva has provided a reading of *The Famished Road* and *Songs of Enchantment* solely as performances of Yeatsian and Jungian ideas, erasing entirely all traces of Yoruba orature, Tutuola and Soyinka. These novels' emphasis on dreams, ritual, myth and magic suggests that such a reading might be fruitful. But the terms on which such a reading is undertaken need to be carefully spelled out if the critic is to avoid replicating a discredited essentialist universalism. From the outset, Oliva's position presents difficulties in terms of where he is speaking from, and whom he is addressing:

> While magical realism affords Caliban the opportunity to "write back" and reject some of the cultural paradigms of his colonial heritage, it is no less true that Caliban is our Shadow, and that magical realism is founded in our unconscious. Archaic man, with his primitive mentality and tendency to magical thinking survives in each of us. (172)

Who is being constructed as "Caliban" and who are the "we" in this assertion? It seems that an unqualified Eurocentrism lurks behind the innocent phrase "no less true." Oliva's is a magical realism that has been sundered from its historical and cultural roots in order that it can be utilised in the excavation of the collective unconscious:

> We all dream, and in our dreams we speak the language of magical realism [...] A dream never expresses itself in a logical or abstract way, but, rather, in figurative language that is a survival of an archaic mode of thought. This imaginal form of communication is primary and comparable to that of the child, of primitive cultures, and of the poet. (172, 174)

This assertion is extraordinary in its reproduction of the language of Victorian anthropology. In E.B. Tylor's 1871 *Primitive Culture* "survivals" are "fragments of a dead lower culture embedded in a living higher one" (vol. I, 72). Tylor's thought was irretrievably conditioned by an evolutionary scheme whereby "primitive" customs were interpreted as comparable to those of Western antiquity, and the behaviour of European children was used to illuminate that of the "savage" adult. Tylor's intellectual heir, Sir James Frazer, was credited by his contemporaries for extending Tylor's ideas into an exploration of the "unitary experience of the human race" (Tambiah *Magic* 44, 51). This "unitary experience" is now widely interpreted among anthropologists as little more than a self-aggrandising projection of the values of Frazer's own times. Though

Oliva is influenced by the ideas of analytical psychology rather than social evolutionism, when he reads Okri's magical realism as comparable to the language of "the child, of primitive cultures and of the poet," he does so in order to extract from it truths about the human condition that have become obscured to Westerners. In Oliva's hands, Okri's text becomes a vehicle for journeying into the unconscious, the pre-logical, the archaic. Like the armchair anthropologist who found everywhere he looked the evidence for his particular informing assumptions, Oliva extracts from Okri those parts of the narrative that concur with particular configurations of thought he wants to emphasise and then, like Jung or Yeats, asserts these to be universally valid observations about history or the human psyche.

Whether or not analytical psychology or Yeatsian mysticism are applicable to *The Famished Road*, these are surely not the terms on which such an approach must be founded. Oliva dilutes the indigenous world-view that informs *The Famished Road* into unrecognisability. He fails to note that Okri's harnessing of the potential of the folkloric concurs with disillusionment with political processes as they have unfolded in post-independence Nigeria, and that this process is noticeable in other African fiction (Quayson *Strategic* 148). He replicates a spurious methodology of reading texts entirely out of their contexts in order to identify universal, timeless truths. And he allows his voice to echo Okri's esoteric political philosophy in a way that is extremely problematic: in a work of academic literary criticism, what are we to make of the unqualified assertion that: "the road to redemption for the African peoples, and the restoration of all oppressed peoples, must be sought in dreams and visions," for example (188)? Financial restitution for the crimes of slavery and colonialism might be a better place to start. And yet, despite these shortcomings, one has a sense in which Oliva is responding to an impulse in Okri's work itself. Okri seems to want his reader to move beyond a reading of his novels only in terms of received ideas of Africa, wants to gesture, in other words, towards the essential and the universal.

This impulse towards universality has been explained by Douglas McCabe in terms of the novel's inclusion of a New Age perspective. McCabe shows how Okri's abiku heaven has no analogues in Nigerian oral or literary traditions. The "sociocosmic millenarianism, co-creative idealism, loving monism, self-actualisation, and detraditionalising perennialism" he finds in Okri's non-fiction is shown also to exist in the novel; indeed so much so that *The Famished Road* can be read as "an Aquarian allegory, reflecting and transmitting central tenets of the human potential movement" (10, 16). Though he is at pains to emphasise that "New Age spiritual discourse is neither the only, nor the only significant, historical shaper of Okri's text," the conclusion he reaches is that "New Age spirituality [...] is the most important cultural vector shaping Okri's novel" (2). McCabe's analysis makes clear that New Ageism is undeniably present in *The Famished Road*. But exactly to what extent, and by what routes it has travelled to be there, and in what kinds of balance it exists with other discourses, are questions that remain to be answered. A seldom-adopted path to answering such questions would be to consider the writings that precede and follow *The Famished Road*. I propose that a trajectory could be traced from realism (*Flowers and Shadows*) to modernism (*The Landscapes Within*) and then into the experiments with ritual and magic one finds in the title story of *Incidents at the Shrine*. Significantly, the short stories are written in London, and the experimental qualities that emerge in them can be linked to anxieties about loss of roots.[5] The trajectory then leads into the magical realism of *The Famished Road*, and from there into the utopian and allegorical later works. At a certain point in this trajectory "African" (a category that only emerges as important, ironically, the longer he lives in London) begins to yield to "New Age." In *The Famished Road*, this yielding is underway, but not, I believe, complete.

Having assessed the trends in Okri criticism that are, in different ways, squeamish about considering *The Famished Road* as an example of magical realism, and having also noted some of the dangers of unhitching Okri from his contexts, we must now turn to those critics who have identified it as magical realism, while respecting the historicity of Okri's writing and its indebtedness to the tradition from which it emerges. This kind of criticism was initiated by Henry Louis Gates, Jr in an early review of *The Famished Road*:

> It is the redoubtable achievement of this book [...] to have forged a narrative that is both engagingly lyrical and intriguingly post-modern. And Mr. Okri has done so not merely, as we might expect,

by adapting techniques of the magic realism associated with the great Latin American novelists (especially Gabriel García Márquez) but by returning to the themes and structures of traditional Yoruba mythology and the little-known achievements of the Yoruba novel. ("Between" 3)

The "as we might expect" is alluring here, as is the potential comparison with García Márquez. But, unsurprisingly – given that they appeared in a review – such ideas are left at the level of suggestion only. More detailed analysis is to be found in an article by Edna Aizenberg, and a book-length study by Brenda Cooper. Aizenberg's is a tentative account of the unfolding of magical realism through four successive phases: Franz Roh's post-Expressionist art; Carpentier and Asturias's "ontological brand of magical realism"; the literary "Boom" of the sixties exemplified by García Márquez's *One Hundred Years of Solitude*; and a fourth phase, "magical realism's international or postcolonial moment" which is where she places *The Famished Road* (26–28). The account isolates several different strands, themes and approaches from the various phases of magical realism and the attempt to apply these to Okri's novel is a worthy one. However, her project is hampered by a linearity that posits Okri at the end of a developmental sequence. Thus, despite her recognition on the place of Carpentier and Asturias in the sequence, it is predominantly Borges and García Márquez that serve as points of reference for her exegesis. Later in this chapter I will argue that it is Carpentier and Asturias – and especially the latter – who provide the most apposite points of reference for understanding Okri's magical realism.

Brenda Cooper's account lacks the historical perspective on the development of the concept of magical realism emphasised by Aizenberg, but her study is attentive to the African contexts from which Okri's fiction emerges, displaying a tacit awareness of the local and the generic axes with which Okri criticism has struggled. Cooper's analysis operates implicitly within the "international or postcolonial moment" identified by Aizenberg and she grounds her use of magical realism in some of the most important theoretical debates in postcolonial studies. For her, hybridity is "at the heart of the politics and techniques of magical realism" (20). This is the hybridity of Rushdie or Homi Bhabha, a celebration of intermingling, transformation, impurity. In the magical realist novel, according to Cooper, irony is the primary means by which hybridity operates. Irony serves to distance cosmopolitans from a narrow nationalism. It is also the means by which writers of magical realism come to appropriate and transform the resources that will supply the "magic" of their novels: "magical realism is born precisely out of that perilous and frail embrace between the superstitious beliefs and the ironic distance." It is, potentially, "a merging between irony and faith" (34).

Having associated hybridity and magical realism, Cooper is careful to note the challenges that have been directed at the celebration of hybridity in general and to the exotic peddling of stereotypes that some critics see in magical realism. The three African writers she discusses (Okri, Kojo Laing and Syl Cheney-Coker) are distinguishable from "the postcolonial, intellectual, global travellers who are cultural hybrids, speak with forked tongues, have ambiguous emotions about their national homelands and some of whom write magical realist novels" (51). On the other hand, the politics of the African writers needs to be understood against two tendencies in African literature: the folkloric literary experiments of Fagunwa and Tutuola, and the cultural nationalism that she identifies in the works of Ngugi, Soyinka and Achebe, for example. In a lucid way, therefore, Cooper's trio of African magical realists is represented as buttressed between cosmopolitanism, the folkloric and cultural nationalism. Despite the critical position she adopts towards all these poles, there is, however, a consistent bias that emerges towards a specific kind of magical realism, that of a García Márquez or a Rushdie, which we identified earlier as discursive in orientation:

> Magical realism at its best opposes fundamentalism and purity; it is at odds with racism, ethnicity and the quest for tap roots; it is fiercely secular and revels in the body, the joker, laughter, liminality and the profane. I say it can do these things when at its best, to emphasize that it does not, by definition, do them. In reality the novels themselves are heir to many traditions, pressures and conflicting strategies. (22)

Why "at its best"? The potential benefits of a subtle and nuanced identification of different types of magical realism are undermined here by the overt construction of a norm. Cooper's understandings of magical realism are, despite the possibilities that emerge from her detailed readings of the contexts from which magical realism arises, ultimately imposed onto the novels from the outside. This is what Olatubosun Ogunsanwo objects to in a review of Cooper's study in which he claims she has not recognised the "intrinsic and distinguishing features of [Okri's, Laing's and Cheney-Coker's] fictional art that can clearly establish their own unique form of magical realism" ("Review" 226). It is not surprising that Cooper prefers Cheney-Coker's *The Last Harmattan of Alusine Dunbar* to Okri's or Laing's novels since it much more closely resembles the norm of discursive magical realism she is working from. It is thus on the basis of a lack of suitable "ironic distance" that Cooper makes her final evaluation of her three African writers: "The fervour of cultural nationalism ultimately mutes the irony of Laing, Cheney-Coker and Okri" (222). This conclusion leads Ogunsanwo to wonder whether "magical realism is not a serious misnomer" (228). I do not believe it is. Okri's position will become clearer in two ways: by allowing a definition of his peculiar brand of magical realism to emerge from within the novel itself, and by avoiding distorting comparisons with the strands of magical realism which favour metaphor and irreverence over myth and faith.[6]

Magical realism was defined earlier as a mode of narration in which the non- or extra-rational – often associated with myth or fantasy – is represented on scrupulously equal terms with the empirical, objective or phenomenal world familiar to realism. From the opening paragraphs of Okri's novel, the duality of its narrator's point-of-view appears amenable to analysis in terms of its encoding of the magical and the real. As an abiku who chooses to live rather than to die, Azaro is uniquely positioned in both the spirit world and the world of the living. Although the novel is in important respects a sustained exercise in blurring the boundaries between these two domains, it is still possible – indeed, I am arguing that it is essential – to identify differences between the two realms. The spirit world is, as Quayson observes, at least initially derived from Yoruba belief and Nigerian literature, but the aesthetic within which it is represented is cosmopolitan and transformative in nature. One of the more important transformations of this nature concerns Okri's rewriting of the abiku myth through emphasising its similarities with myths of reincarnation, thereby factoring a fatalistic, quasi-moral, perhaps New Age, dimension into the abiku experience.[7] It is useful to describe this aesthetic as being informed by a code of the fantastic that is not answerable to the laws of physical or empirical reality. The key trope governing this code is metamorphosis, understood not as unilinear transformation, but rather as a constant, unstable shifting of form and identity that depends on processes of return and recurrence that are never resolved in the novel.

The domain of the living is governed by what Amaryll Chanady would call a code of the natural derived from the conventions of social realism. The realistic dimensions of Okri's characters can quite clearly be sketched: Azaro is a boy of around seven years of age who lives with his parents, attends a school that is never described, plays with other children and has a tendency to wander off on his own. His father, physically powerful and outspoken, earns a tenuous living as a carrier of loads, and occasionally as a nightsoil man. Azaro's mother is a trader of wares. The three share a strong bond of love, although outbreaks of domestic violence are not uncommon. Outside Azaro's family, Madame Koto is the novel's most significant character. She establishes a bar, selling first palm-wine then beer and peppersoup, and the increase in her wealth and status coincides with her courting of powerful politicians. The geography of the realistic dimension of the novel can also be readily mapped: key spaces are the room in which Azaro and his parents live, the compound, the road outside the compound, the bar, the paths and roads that lead into the forest as well as the forest itself, and the marketplace. Chronologically, a number of references locate the narrative in the run-up to this African country's post-independence elections, although there is no explicit comment on the processes of decolonisation that are immanent at the time the novel is set. The code of the natural thus seeks to document the life of the poor in the ghetto of this African city – their struggles against their neighbours, landlords, employers and politicians, and the multi-faceted encroachments of modernity on their lives.

To a greater or lesser degree, every one of the realistic components isolated above carries within it a supernatural charge. Azaro's wanderings, filtered through the bifurcating lens of his problematic ontological status, construct an alternative characterology. Through the adoption of a viewpoint which refuses the privileges and obligations of the traditional realist narrator in favour of an expanded spiritual or hallucinatory mode of narration, the code of the fantastic is effectively afforded the same semiotic status as that of the real. Thus Azaro himself is simultaneously a young child of the ghetto and a spirit child. Dad is a worker, a family man, a resident of the compound and is simultaneously "Black Tyger" a fighting hero of mythical status who defeats ghosts and can make lightning flash from his fist (301). He becomes a spokesman against spiritual as well as material poverty. Mum, significantly, is the character in the novel who least obviously carries within her a supernatural aspect. In fact, Mum's sorties into the supernatural, whether they take the form of journeys, prayers or cautionary folktales, are always intended to rescue Azaro or Dad from dreams or spiritual entrapment: to bring them back to the domain of the living. Madame Koto, like Dad, is also the bearer of a double load of signification. On the one hand, her successful entrepreneurship suggests in microcosm the roles played by capital in the modernising postcolonial state. On the other hand, she is constantly identified with witchcraft, either through her actions or by the attitudes she evokes in others.

In each of these cases, the character's actions, speech and presence can be interpreted on Quayson's "reality-esoteric axis." The same can be said for the geography and chronology of the novel. There is an abundance of examples of spaces like the road, the bar, the forest and the marketplace being represented in a natural fashion within the code of the real and then "supernaturalised" by that of the fantastic. Although this strategy is not as clear with regard to the representation of the passing of time in the novel, it is still possible to isolate the poles on the reality-esoteric axis on which this representation takes place. For example, when Azaro, in a rare moment of standing back from his experience in order to analyse it, notices how the landscape around him is changing, he formulates the change in terms of conventional units of time: "Steadily, over days and months, the paths had been widening" (104). At the other end of the reality-esoteric axis we encounter the fracturing of this conception of time: "as I kept watch I perceived, in the crack of a moment, the recurrence of things unresolved – histories, dreams, a vanished world of great old spirits, wild jungles, tigers with eyes of diamonds roaming the dense foliage" (176). As the moment "cracks," it reveals a deeper level of temporal meaning which had been concealed by the apparent unity of the concepts of "days" or "months." It appears that Okri is gesturing towards the possibility that behind the objective facade of linear conventional time lies a mythical time of return, recurrence, cyclicality.[8] Unlike in García Márquez, we should note, such notions are not installed in *The Famished Road* in order to be demystified.

There is very little in Okri's novel that cannot be demonstrated to participate in the implicit construction of a reality-esoteric axis. As he falls asleep one evening, Azaro hears "the air whispering, the walls talking, the chair complaining, the floor pacing, the insects gossiping" (21). Characteristically, any of the following signifiers might denote either its literal referent or one infused with super-natural agency: trees, the forest, stones, lizards, dragonflies, dogs, sunlight, rain, a motor-car, politics, fires, sneezing, illness, rats, chickens and so on. To the extent that things in this novel appear to have lives of their own (to paraphrase Melquíades in the opening page of *One Hundred Years of Solitude*), Garuba's notion of "animist realism" would appear to be appropriate. As Garuba has argued, the magical realism can be seen to derive from an "animist uncon-scious," strongly suggesting that Okri's novel ought to be located squarely on the hermeneutic axis I am labelling "faith." Magical realism is never as clear cut as this, however. As is the case in all of the novels discussed in this book, faith and irreverence are never far from one another. In *The Famished Road* an irreverent dimension is most noticeably present in the games the novel plays with the very "reality-esoteric" axes utilised by Quayson to make sense of the novel. For, just as the novel relies on such an axis, so it simultane-ously seeks to problematise it in order to disrupt readerly expecta-tion and to violate conventions of representation, even the provisional ones established within its pages.

The reader can never be entirely certain of the place of an object, character, space or moment on the reality-esoteric axis at any given point in the narrative. We are warned very early on that "one world contains glimpses of others" (10). Within the code of the natural, then, are a variety of narrative positions that destabilise its unity and resist attempts to define it narrowly. The same can be said for the code of the fantastic which constructs an unstable, disturbing realm where hallucination, dream and spiritual reality are often impossible to separate from one another and where bewildering shifts of percep-tion can take place in the space of a single sentence. The following description of Azaro's first visit to the marketplace illustrates the ways in which Okri is able to shift his representations along the reality-esoteric axis, and will also lead to a discussion of the role that perception plays in the novel:

> I watched crowds of people pour into the marketplace. I watched the chaotic movements and the wild exchanges and the load-carriers staggering under sacks. It seemed as if the whole world was there. I saw people of all shapes and sizes, mountainous women with faces of iroko, midgets with faces of stone, reedy women with twins strapped to their backs, thick-set men with bulging shoulder muscles. After a while I felt a sort of vertigo just looking at anything that moved. Stray dogs, chickens flapping in cages, goats with listless eyes, hurt me to look at them. I shut my eyes and when I opened them again I saw people who walked backwards, a dwarf who got about on two fingers, men upside-down with baskets of fish on their feet, women who had breasts on their backs, babies strapped to their chests, and beautiful children with three arms. I saw a girl amongst them who had eyes at the side of her face, bangles of blue copper round her neck, and who was more lovely than forest flowers. (15)

Two codes can be seen in operation here, separated by the phrase, "I shut my eyes." But what I am labelling the code of the real is suffused with carnivalesque grotesquerie that anticipates the strange mutations of the spirit visitors to the marketplace. The sudden juxtaposition of "mountainous" women and midgets, for example, renders the representation surreal, jolting it along the reality-esoteric axis away from the naturalistic. The destabilisation of the code of the real is reinforced by Azaro's sense of vertigo – a vertigo that the text itself is trying to induce in the reader. This vertigo signals that a change in perception is about to take place, and the shift is neatly punctuated by Azaro closing his eyes. The representation that follows is clearly governed by a code of the fantastic, but the grotesquerie is not dissimilar to that which was present prior to Azaro's shift in perception. This similarity alerts us to the fact that the representation of the marketplace is wholly achieved through the limited perspective of a child-narrator suffering from hunger, lack of sleep and vertigo. It is, in this sense, unreliable; however in irreverent fashion, this unreliability is a key part of the overall narrative strategy, which is to render uncertain the reality-esoteric axis that a reader may try to implement to make sense of his or her reading.

The reader cannot be sure, at this point of the narrative, if Azaro is merely hallucinating or if the spirits really are there.[9] But the passage immediately continues with the spirits themselves questioning whether Azaro can see them, ironically turning on its head the dilemma of the reader:

> I was so afraid that I got down from the barrel and started to move away when the girl pointed and cried:
> "That boy can see us!"
> They turned in my direction. I looked away immediately and hurried away from the swelling marketplace, towards the street. They followed me. One of the men had red wings on his feet and a girl had fish-gills round her neck. I could hear their nasal whisperings. They stayed close to me to find out if I really could see them. And when I refused to see them, when I concentrated on the piles of red peppers wrinkled by the sun, they crowded me and blocked my way. I went right through them as if they weren't there. I stared hard at the crabs clawing the edges of flower-patterned basins. After a while they left me alone. That was the first time I realised it wasn't just humans who came to the market-places of the world. Spirits and other beings come there too. They buy, sell, browse and investigate. They wander amongst the fruits of the earth and sea. (15–16)

In traditional Yoruba culture, the marketplace is a space where spirit and real worlds meet. Okri's spirits have much of the Tutuolan grotesque about them. But Okri deviates from a folkloric representation of this liminal space in his deliberate foregrounding of the instability of the boundary between natural and supernatural, real and magical. He examines the connection between the operation of the senses and the construction of a sense of reality – the connection between seeing and believing – by dramatising acts of perception throughout his novel. To escape the inquisitions of the spirits, Azaro must pretend not to see them, and eventually he walks right through them *as if they weren't there*. The point of this knowing, ironic short-circuiting of the reader's potential doubt is to demonstrate that the spirits *are* there.

In Okri, as in Borges, García Márquez, Rushdie and many others, irony is used to demonstrate the impossibility of knowing what is "really real." But Okri's irony, unlike that of writers who favour the irreverent strand of magical realism, is directed at the unbelieving reader, and is harnessed to a faith in the unseen possibilities of the world, and in literature to represent them. Irony of this kind is ludic, but its intent is seriously and deliberately to target the perceived distance between rational and supernatural. A focus on the strands of faith and irreverence in Okri's work reveals the opposite tendency from that in Carpentier, García Márquez and Rushdie: where these writers exhibited primarily a movement from faith towards irreverence, Okri uses irreverent writerly techniques to insist on mythical, spiritual dimensions of reality. These dimensions initially resemble the expanded reality of a putative Yoruba cosmology, but the ability to perceive multiple dimensions is immediately generalised into an African way of seeing, and from there becomes a universal resource available to all, as McCabe's New Age reading makes clear.

Symbols supporting the novel's exploration of modes of perception are photographs, masks, mirrors, windows, and glasses. These symbols are developed in a variety of ways and to different levels of complexity, but all effectively work as frames for Okri's central narrative intention, which is to relativise acts of perception in order to make space for non-Western and alternative sets of cultural modalities. The first signs of Okri's obsession with eyes and seeing are to be found in the title story of the collection, *Stars of the New Curfew*, and recur throughout his later works. In *The Famished Road* the activities and presence of the ocular organs are noticeable in the emphasis on Azaro's blinking, and through palpable, tactile images, such as when "thick green substances passed over my eyes" (313), or when a splinter penetrates Madame Koto's driver's eye and "[g]reen pus and all the fluids of sight and blood poured down the sides of his face like a burst egg" (422). Illness, hunger, vertigo, and the effects of the sun are all capable of inducing altered states of perception, impacting on Azaro's ability to perceive both natural and supernatural worlds. Blindness is figured in both literal and metaphorical terms throughout the novel, with the Old Man representing – in a problematic link between physical and moral disability – one whose lack of sight is a spiritual failing. The only points of view other than Azaro's allowed to the reader can be found when Azaro sees through other eyes: the ghost-child of the policeman, the Old Man himself, the duiker.

When *The Famished Road*'s insistence on tropes and modes of perception are aligned with Okri's critical statements about his writing, certain patterns become evident that will allow us to begin the task of assessing his place in a tradition of magical realism. Asked by Jean W. Ross about the possible relationship between his work and magical realism, Okri produced the following revealing response:

> The difference is this: the Latin American writers – let's be quite honest – are largely European Latin American writers. Their writing has, as it were, come through the journey of symbolism, surrealism, and then come right around to the reality of that particular place. That's very different from what I am saying. Whereas in Gabriel García Márquez's *One Hundred Years of Solitude* there's a scene in which the woman flies, in my book you have an effect where the kid sees spirits. If you accept the basic premise that this kid is an abiku, a spirit child, it's not unnatural that he would see spirits. If all the characters were to see spirits, that would be pushing it a bit, as far as Western thinking is concerned. I'm looking at the world in *The Famished Road* from the inside of the African world view, but without it being codified as such. This is just the way the world is seen: the dead are not really dead, the ancestors are still part of the living community and there are innumerable gradations of reality, and so on. It's quite simple and straightforward. I'm treating it naturally. It's a kind of realism, but a realism with many more dimensions. (337–338)

Okri's claims to be describing an authentic African world-view in *The Famished Road* are founded on the premises that the modes of perception available to Azaro are representative of those available to Africans, and that literature is capable of representing such cultural modalities. *The Famished Road* is, if we take Okri's comments seriously, a sustained literalisation of the very idea of a world view, a fictional performance of certain key qualities – cohering around expanded modes of perception – of a state of being known as "African." In this intention, as was suggested earlier, Okri is able to draw from a tradition of defining Africanness that finds its most thorough elaboration in Soyinka's *Myth, Literature and the African World*. Soyinka's study is conditioned throughout by an assumption that African and European culture display "essential differences" (38). African culture evidences a "cohesive understanding of irreducible truths" that has been jettisoned by Europe. It is informed by an awareness of the "elastic nature of knowledge as its one reality" (53). In this world view, as Soyinka's comments on Camara Laye's *The Dark Child* make clear, "the harmonisation of human functions, external phenomena and supernatural suppositions within individual consciousness merges as a normal self-adjusting process in the African temper of mind" (122). As far as the role played by "supernatural suppositions" is concerned, Soyinka is fulsome in his praise of the "unusual lyrical possession by the integral reality of the African world" demonstrated in Birago Diop's poem, "Breath":

> Listen more to things
> Than to words that are said.
> The water's voice sings
> And the flame cries
> And the wind that brings
> The woods to sighs
> Is the breathing of the dead. (qtd in Soyinka *Myth* 131)

Diop's poem, in its portrayal of a natural world animated by the spiritual energy of the ancestors, and in its incantatory insistence on the presence of the dead among the living ("Those who are dead have never gone away," "The dead are not under the ground," "The dead are never dead") is celebrated by Soyinka as conveying "an important, even fundamental, aspect of the world-view of traditional Africa" (133).[10] Based on his comments in the interview cited above, it is clear that this is the metaphysic that Okri would like us to derive from his novel. He objects to the label magical realism since it would appear to displace exegesis of the esoteric into the realm of the purely literary, and thence into the "European." His standpoint, as we have seen, is implicitly or explicitly supported by several critics. There is a lot more to be said about the implications of this position, however.

First, Okri's claims to the effect that, "I'm not trying in the slightest to produce any strange effects," and "this is just the way the world is seen" (337–338), uncannily echo those made by the very Latin American magical realists from whom he is trying to distance himself. For Carpentier, at least initially, faith was the key to the ability to perceive *lo real maravilloso*, and magical realism served as a means by which such ontological realities could be revealed. Faith in the presence of the marvellous was required, but also in the capacity of literature to reveal it. Okri's statements to the effect that his is a kind of realism capable of accurately representing the multiple gradations of reality in the African world are not substantially different from Carpentier's claims to be simply representing a landscape, history and culture that was already marvellous. To the extent that the tropes of the supernatural in *The Famished Road* derive either from a Yoruba cosmology that is by now extensively archived in literary and anthropological domains, or from sources that can in no sense be considered authentically African, Okri cannot defend his magical realism by claiming to share the superstitious world-view of his characters any more than Carpentier could. His faith, in this sense, like that of Carpentier, turns out to be oriented more towards literature than the supernatural itself. And faith of this kind is necessary because it is through literature that cultural identity – Latin American or African – can be asserted in both its mythic and historical dimensions.[11]

When Okri tries to distance his writing from that of the Latin American magical realists on the basis that they are "European Latin American writers" he is, in effect, underscoring even further his similarities with their project. Alejo Carpentier's marvellous real is exclusively and definitively Latin American, and what is Latin American is defined by its difference from Europe. Carpentier's marvellous –appropriated from Breton in a process described by Amaryll Chanady as the "territorialisation of the imaginary" – is constituted out of a repudiation of the "tiresome pretension of creating the marvellous that has characterized certain European literatures" ("Marvellous" 84). Surrealists are "bureaucrats" who do not look for the marvellous in reality, but will it into being by means of clichés and formulas. Carpentier consistently backs his claims that "the marvelous real that I defend and that is our own marvelous real is encountered in its raw state, latent and omnipresent, in all that is Latin America" ("Baroque" 104). That the representation of this faith, a position, as I have argued, that Carpentier was unable to sustain, took place by means of a narrative mode in which equivalence between real and supernatural was presumed, implies that coincidences with Okri's project should not be overlooked. To consolidate the point that Okri's "territorialisation of the imaginary" (the phrase Chanady applies to Carpentier) concurs in spirit with that of Latin American magical realism, García Márquez's well-known elaboration of Carpentier's position should be compared with Okri's response to Ross cited above:

> Everyday life in Latin America proves that reality is full of the most extraordinary things [...]. I know very ordinary people who've read *One Hundred Years of Solitude* carefully and with a lot of pleasure, but with no surprise at all because, when all is said and done, I'm telling them nothing that hasn't happened in their own lives. [...] There's not a single line in my novels which is not based on reality. (Mendoza 35–36)

While Okri's claims lack the baroque hyperbole of Carpentier or the subversive irony of García Márquez, his assertions to the effect that his writing simply reflects the gradations of African reality is not substantially different from their comments about the extent to which their magical realism expresses a Latin American reality "out of all proportion." Though, as we have seen, García Márquez's position is in some ways very different from that of the early Carpentier – and also of Okri – the magical realist presentation of the exotic, the marvellous and the magical as a perfectly normal aspect of everyday existence is assigned the task of exhibiting difference from Europe, where such things are considered fantastic.[12]

Magical realism of this kind begins from a desire to present the narrated cultural self as other. The perspective being outlined here concurs roughly with that of Fredric Jameson, echoed in Brenda Cooper's repeated assertion that "magical realism arises out of particular societies – postcolonial, unevenly developed places where old and new, modern and ancient, the scientific and the magical views of the world co-exist" (216). However, this position can lead to a rather naïve correlation of magic with what we might bluntly call "tradition," and realism with "modernity." Magical realism is a deliberate and intricate mode of narration and the processes by which codes of the real and of the fantastic are derived from various resource bases always require substantial amounts of authorial manipulation. Furthermore, as has been noted in this study, pre-scientific and scientific perspectives are bound up with one another in magical realism, and their complicity serves to undermine the security of Enlightenment assumptions about the nature of the real.

Once the terms on which our identification of magical realism in a given narrative are made clear – in other words, once we are able to establish whether ontological or discursive impulses are dominant – then a comparative focus on historically-located authorial projects becomes necessary. To the extent that Okri's magical realism intends to destabilise the boundary between natural and supernatural in order to effect an appreciation of a putatively African world-view in which such a boundary is held to have little value, it follows that points of connection between *The Famished Road* and other magical realist writings should respect this integral intention. In preference to the Borges/García Márquez/Rushdie paradigm, I therefore suggest that appropriate comparisons might be made between *The Famished Road* and, for example, the ontologically oriented magical realism of the early Carpentier or Miguel Ángel Asturias. Such comparison will assist in developing the notion of faith-based magical realism being presented in this book.

The Kingdom of This World is set in the Antilles in a period when the slave trade was at its zenith. While its protagonist, Ti Noël, is probably Caribbean-born, others, like Macandal and Bouckman, from whom he learns, maintain strong connections with Africa and specifically with Yoruba and Dahomean culture.[13] Carpentier and Okri are thus both concerned with imagining and representing African modes of perception and attitudes towards reality through the vehicle of Yoruba cosmology. The motivation behind this desire is to give voice to specific identities: in *The Kingdom of This World* and Carpentier's early stories, Afro-Caribbean belief systems constitute an important component of the difference between Latin America and Europe; in Okri's novel, the nature of African consciousness must be distinguished from that of the narrowly rational Western world view in order to present reality "from the inside of the African world view" – though as noted, "African" progressively tilts into a millenarian universalism towards the end of the novel and in later works.

It is not surprising therefore that the novels share a number of tropes and themes: metamorphosis (usually of humans into animals and vice versa, but including a capacity for inanimate objects to be animated or transformed); the presence of nature as signifier of orders of knowledge threatened by slavery, colonialism and modernity; the representation of national history which, when mediated by the hand of the author, reveals the presence of a mythical template for understanding history. Informed by a powerful sense of how postcolonial histories are characterised by the recurrence of oppression and exploitation, both novels utilise repetition and cyclicality as structuring principles. However, Carpentier's novel is short, erudite and focussed on the minutiae of Caribbean history; Okri's is lengthy, impressionistic and studiously avoids all chronological markers. More importantly, as has been noted, *The Kingdom of This World* backs away from the implications of its magical realism, whereas *The Famished Road* is saturated with the supernatural. For a more fitting comparison we need to consider the similarities between *The Famished Road* and Asturias's *Men of Maize*.

Gerald Martin's claim about Asturias, that "no other writer has imposed 'difference' and 'otherness' so comprehensively from the native American side" ("Introduction" xx), might, if we substitute "African" for "native American," apply to Okri's *The Famished Road* – at least up to a point. From a certain critical point of view, this claim is problematic, for "otherness" can only be perceived as "other" from a position of "same," and there can be little doubt that the success of both novels derives at least partly from the allure of the exotic for the Western reader. But such objections are better made in the light of a full appreciation of the textual dynamics of this kind of novel, which have yet to be fully understood in a comparative context.

In both cases, these novelists are responding to a tradition of writing about indigenous peoples that is anthropological and conditioned largely by the conventions of narrative realism. Both writers begin from an awareness that narrative realism is inadequate to their purposes, for it is perceived as distancing writers and readers from much that is important in the cultures they are trying to describe. When Okri asserts in an interview with Jane Wilkinson that, although he recognises the extent to which colonialism was an invasion of Africa's social structure, he does not believe that it really touched the "spiritual and aesthetic and mythic internal structures" of the continent and its people (86), he is implicitly suggesting the need to go beyond the narrative model utilised by a writer like Chinua Achebe. Similarly, Asturias rejects the realism of the *indigenista* novel not only because of his exposure to modernism and to surrealist dogma, but because it could not contain crucial aspects of the ancient Mayan and Aztec mythologies, traces of which he had perceived in the world views of Guatemalan *ladinos* and Indians of his youth, and in the texts that he had encountered through his anthropological studies at the Sorbonne.

On a wider level, the rejection of realism is also founded in an awareness – more pronounced in the case of the surrealist-influenced Asturias, but clearly present in Okri – that Western-style realism is epistemologically allied to the kinds of reason and rationality that entered into a productive alliance with colonialism – with ruinous consequences for the indigenous people of Africa and the Americas. Specifically, we might point to the obsession with eyes, blindness and seeing to be found in both *Men of Maize* and *The Famished Road*, and consider the ways in which these novels foreground and challenge the established relationship between what can be perceived and what is considered to be real. Both novels relativise acts of perception in order to problematise the empiricism that so often underlies the claims to truth of the Western world-view, the intention of both writers being to clear space for an assertion of cultural alterity. *Men of Maize* goes a step further by actively valorising blindness over sight, and by expertly locating this inversion in environmental terms: deforestation has "hacked away" the eyelids of the land, shattering its sacred dreamtime. *The Famished Road* "cycle" (and especially *Infinite Riches*) shares this ecological perspective and shares also the need to confront the capitalist logic that underlies the building of roads and the clearing of trees with a myth-based sense of the sacredness of certain aspects of nature. The imposition of difference from the native American or African sides, facilitated by ontological magical realism, can serve as an assertion of autochthony as an act of resistance to ongoing acts of colonialism.

Other correspondences between *Men of Maize* and *The Famished Road* include an emphasis on dreams and dreaming, an impressionistic and highly poetic use of language, and the representation of ritual, curse, natural medicine, animism, ancestors and metamorphosis. The presence of these shared tropes and themes is significant enough in its own right, but it is the ways in which their representation is accompanied by a deliberate blurring of the line between natural and supernatural that is the dominant similarity between the two novels. The faith-based, ontological magical realism we are dealing with here is, to re-iterate the point, not simply the product of juxtaposing "pre-scientific" and "scientific" world-views. It constitutes nothing less than a critique of Enlightenment-derived notions of reality from a myth-based point of view.

7
Conclusion

Jacques Derrida points out that the first noun in *The Communist Manifesto* is "specter." From Marx's times to our own, forces of reaction have wanted to exorcise the specter of Communism, but Derrida makes clear that Marx himself also wants the ghost, the spirit of communism, to disappear, to be replaced with the living reality of the revolution. In characteristic fashion, Derrida opposes Marx's ontology, materialist in nature, and dependent on a metaphysic of presence, with a "hauntology" of his own, a kind of ghost-driven ethics:

> If he loves justice at least, the "scholar" of the future, the "intellectual" of tomorrow should learn it from the ghost [...]. Even if it is in oneself, in the other, in the other in oneself: they are always *there*, specters, even if they do not exist, even if they are no longer, even if they are not yet. (*Specters* 176)

For Derrida, hauntology always haunts ontology (the terms sound the same in French). Awareness of absence, silence, the ghost is also awareness of the "other," and of the otherness of the other, which, as in Levinas, becomes the basis for a substitution of ethics for ontology, of respect for knowledge. Like a good magical realist, Derrida therefore counsels hospitality towards the ghost: we should "learn to live by learning [...] how to talk with him, with her, how to let them speak or how to give them back speech" (176).

Robert Young has shown how the development of French post-structuralism was implicated in the experience of a colonial politics of domination and resistance. Sartre, Althusser, Derrida,

Lyotard, Cixous and others were all either born in Algeria, or involved in the Algerian War of Independence (1), and French philosophy's return to the question of the Enlightenment, Young claims, had a great deal to do with what Foucault calls "the movement which, at the close of the colonial era, led it to be asked of the West what entitles its culture, its science, its social organisation, and finally its rationality itself, to be able to claim universal validity" (qtd. Young 9). For those violated in one way or another by colonialism, or for those concerned with trying to address this violation, Levinas's claim that "from its infancy philosophy has been struck with a horror of the other that remains other" has a special kind of resonance. For Levinas, violence is the inevitable result of knowledge's necessary assimilation of the other, because "the idea of truth as a grasp on things must necessarily have a non-metaphorical sense somewhere" (qtd. Young 12).

Magical realism in its postcolonial forms is a response to this violence. Its most characteristic feature is that it naturalises the supernatural, integrating fantastic or mythical features smoothly into the otherwise realistic momentum of the narrative. It does this in order either to expand existing categories of the real (processes often associated with faith in the possibilities of the unseen and of the novel to convey them) or in order to rupture them altogether (processes usually associated with varieties of epistemological irreverence). More specific reasons behind magical realism's hostility towards reason and realism have been explored in this book. For Asturias and the early Carpentier, personal experience of the cultural worlds of the descendents of the Maya and Afro-Cubans respectively, combined with exposure to surrealism resulted in an urgent awareness of the literary possibilities of asserting difference from Europe and all it stood for. García Márquez feels a similar urge to capture the superstitious provincial world-view of his native Caribbean coast, and this intertwines with a politically-motivated irreverence towards the conventions of realist narrative and historiography. Rushdie develops this irreverence into a full-blown critique of faith as it manifests in Islam, but also of constructions of race and identity in 1980s Britain. Finally, Ben Okri attempts to develop a magical realism capable of representing the "African world view" as it was defined by Soyinka. In all of these different incarnations, the basic formal properties of magical realism can be seen to be in place: at key moments in each novel the supernatural is naturalised and integrated into the novel's realism without being explained away. But the purposes to which each novel puts this technique are clearly different, and can only be understood in the light of the cultural, historical and political contexts with which it is in dialogue.

Magical realism in its postcolonial forms can thus be seen as a response to the "othering" that accompanies Western colonialism, supported as it is in the modern period by the universalist claims of reason. It is an attempt to escape from the violence, epistemic or actual, of rational truth's "grasp on things" by calling into question post-Enlightenment certainties about what is real and what is not. To the extent that its narrative processes constitute a challenge to those systems of thought and knowledge that fall under the label of "rationality," and to the extent to which this challenge derives an ethical charge from the fact that it emerges from the cultural margins of the "West," magical realism has much in common with post-structuralism, as Derrida's supplementing of ontology with "hauntology" suggests.

Claims like these necessarily take the form of generalisations, however, and generalisations about magical realism have been responsible for a great deal of confusion as far as literary critical discourse about magical realism is concerned. There are, as my discussions of García Márquez and Salman Rushdie make clear, important correlations to be drawn between irreverent magical realism and postmodern modes of thought. In Chapter Two, I suggested that the work of Novalis provides an historical precedent for aligning magical realism with anti-foundational thinking. My discussion of Borges in Chapter Three provides some of the necessary philosophical and literary context for this alignment. But the over-hasty alignment of magical realism with post-structuralist thinking obstructs the recognition of that strand in magical realist writing which does not seek as much to deconstruct as to explore and affirm. In Asturias, Okri, and to a lesser degree Carpentier, the novel is the vehicle for transmitting cultural codes and an expanded world-view different from that which prevails in the secular West. To return to Stanley Tambiah's terms, introduced in Chapter One, faith-based magical realism uses the causal legitimacy of novelistic realism to authorise the claims of the participatory realities of Guatemala,

Africa, and Afro-Cuba. This kind of magical realism confounds Derrida by turning "hauntology" back into ontology.

The major task of this study has been to extend the critical vocabulary for discussing magical realism in such a way that the frequent occlusion of faith-based magical realism from literary criticism can be redressed. Three general lines of enquiry have been followed. In the first chapter I examined aspects of the ways magical realism has been used in recent literary criticism, and, attempted, in so doing, to move beyond the customary deflationary quotation marks ("magical realism" or "so-called magical realism" or even "so-called 'magical realism'") which silently testify to the multitude of unresolved difficulties that attach to the term. In the second chapter, I asked questions about the origins of magical realism, looking at why and by whom this particular term was used, and what older modes and genres magical realism reacts to or resembles. The notion of magical realism as postcolonial romance was developed through exploring the conceptual genealogies of magical realism as both a term and as mode of narration. In the chapters that follow I looked specifically at the fictional strategies that fall under the label of magical realism and asked questions like: what is the source of the supernatural in this text? What kind of dialogue does it enter into with the text's more realistic elements? What literary, cultural, and historical factors lead to the appearance of this narrative strategy in this particular work of literature?

These questions have yielded some complex answers, answers which open out onto areas of enquiry which I have not been able to deal with in this book. It remains to be seen how the faith/irreverence split might help us to interpret any of the hundreds of magical realism novels beyond the very circumscribed number discussed here. It may be possible to extend the analysis beyond the domain of literary criticism, back into anthropology (from whence the impetus for the distinction came), or to make sense of historical events or other artistic phenomena. Finally, there is a sense in which the philosophical dimensions of the distinction between faith and irreverence need to be worked out more fully. The geographical, linguistic, historical and cultural diversity represented in the range of texts discussed in this book is a testimony to the ability of the magical realist mode to express not so much a new globalised aesthetic, nor a will-to-power on the part of a privileged set of migrant intellectuals, but rather an historical conjunction of literary and cultural tendencies that speaks powerfully to our need for literature to explore the limits of definition, and to provide models of identity that confirm or contest notions about the nature of modernity and the place of the postcolonial subject in it.

Notes

1 Introduction: Re-thinking Magical Realism

1. In May 2002, a banner headline in *Newsweek International* offered the world the question, "Is Magical Realism Dead?" (Margolis 52). The story was taken up in Britain less than a week later by Robert McCrum in *The Observer* under the headline, "Has Magic Realism Run Its Course?" By contrast with these last rites, a company called Mag-Well recently advertised a new kind of fluid conditioning technology with the label 'magic realism' (see Mag-Well).
2. I am glossing over critical debates about the differences between magic realism and magic*al* realism because, unlike, Maggie Ann Bowers in her book, *Magic(al) Realism*, I don't think much is at stake in this regard. I prefer the latter term because I emphasise the fact that magical realism is a kind of modified, expanded or subverted realism. For an alternative position see Hegerfeldt (1).
3. This phrase is derived from Irlemar Chiampi, who in 1980 described processes involving the "denaturalisation of the real" and a "naturalisation of the marvellous" (see 27–32). In her 1985 book, Amaryll Chanady, drawing on Chiampi, claims magical realism "naturalizes the supernatural" (151). This chapter argues that this formulation encapsulates the key feature of magical realist narrative.
4. For more detail see my essay "The Hermeneutics of Vagueness: Magical Realism in Current Literary Discourse."
5. See Radcliffe-Brown's distinctions between the "expressive" and the "technical" (143); Evans-Pritchard's between "patterns of thought that attribute to phenomena supra-sensible qualities" and those that depend on empirical patterns of thought (12); Lévy-Bruhl's between "mystical mentality" and the "conceptual" and "intellectual" (38, 382); Douglas's between differentiated and undifferentiated "fields of symbolic action" (85); and Geertz's "common-sense" and religious "orientations to reality" (122). Durkheim and Eliade are also relevant here. These thinkers have, of course, all influenced and revised each other's positions.
6. Inquiries into the natures of magic and religion reveal them to be conceptually inseparable on a number of levels. See for example Mircea Eliade who subsumes both under the label of the sacred (14), or Mary Douglas who saw Frazer's and Tylor's distinctions as nothing more than "sectarian quarrel about the value of formal ritual" (30). Tambiah elsewhere argues for magic to be interpreted as a form of rhetoric comparable with the performative utterances of linguistic philosophy ("Form and Meaning of Magical Acts" 60–72).

7. See for example Hebrews 11:1 and 2 Corinthians 5:7.
8. The term "faith-based" has taken on a number of political connotations given its centrality to George W. Bush administration policy where it is used to refer to social programmes run by religious institutions in the US. Faith in these contexts means *religious* faith, whereas I am at pains to take a broader definition of faith to mean the suspension of rational, sceptical or scientific frames of reference, and the often accompanying confidence in the claims to truth of non-empirical, extra-rational orderings of reality. In my discussion, faith is very often linked to claims about non-Western cultural modes of thought and belief. A second element to my definition of faith is specifically literary: faith in the power of the novel to be able to convey "faithfully" a record of such cultural otherness is often an intrinsic element in certain strands of magical realism. Neither of these two core aspects of my argument have anything to do with White House Policy, despite the co-incidence of terminology.

2   Magical Realism as Postcolonial Romance

1. See Guenther 34, n15; Zamora "Swords" 28–29.
2. The original passage reads:

   Pathologische Philosophie. Ein absoluter Trieb nach Vollendung und Vollständigkeit ist Krankheit, sobald er sich zerstörend, und abgeneigt gegen das *Unvollendete*, Unvollständige zeigt. Wenn man etwas Bestimmtes tun und erreichen will, so muß man sich auch provisorische bestimmte Grenzen setzen. Wer aber dies nicht will, der ist vollkommen, wie der, der nicht eher schwimmen will, bis ers kann – Er ist ein magischer Idealist, wie es magische Realisten gibt. Jener sucht eine Wunderbewegung – ein Wundersubjekt – dieser ein Wunderobjekt – eine Wundergestalt. Beides sind *logische Krankheiten* – Wahnarten – in denen sich allerdings das Ideal auf eine doppelte Weise offenbart, oder speigelt – heilige – isolierte Wesen – die das höhere Licht wunderbar brechen – wahrhafte Propheten. So ist auch der Traum prophetisch – Karikatur einer wunderbaren Zukunft.

3. I sympathise with Hegerfeldt's dissatisfaction with critical attempts to interpret literary magical realism via art-historical uses of the term (12–15). As this chapter should make clear, however, I believe that there is scope for a broad, philosophical consideration of the extent to which discursive resemblances can be traced between magical realism's philosophical, art-historical and literary manifestations.
4. For a tendentious argument that postmodernist anti-rationalism represents a comparable set of dangers, see Richard Wolin.
5. The best recent example of magical realist narrative techniques being used in the service of reactionary politics can be found in the title story of a collection of short stories by the Afrikaans writer, J.C. Steyn, *Op pad na die grens*. The cause in question here is the ideology of apartheid then dominant in 1970s South Africa.

6. See Amaryll Chanady's essay "The Territorialization of the Imaginary in Latin America" and, in a different context, Anne Hegerfeldt's defence of her identification of a number of British writers as magical realists (2–6).

7. Jameson's own discussion of magical realism relates more to cinema than to literature. Unfortunately, he never makes clear exactly what he understands the term to mean, and his description of magical realism as based on "a kind of narrative raw material derived essentially from peasant society" ("Film" 302) seems to be inadequate for similar reasons to those identified by Aijaz Ahmad in his critique of Jameson's examination of 'Third World' literature. Ahmad concedes that Jameson's plea for syllabus reform is noteworthy, and his readings of Lu Xun and Ousmane are "marvellously erudite"; it is the "suppression of the multiplicity of significant difference among and within both the advanced capitalist countries on the one hand and the imperialized formations on the other" that are troubling. (95).

8. Jameson specifically links a valorisation of romance ("the place of narrative heterogeneity and of freedom from that reality principle to which a now oppressive realistic representation is the hostage") with a defence of Marxism: "The association of Marxism and romance does not discredit the former so much as it explains the persistence and vitality of the latter". See *The Political Unconscious*, p. 91.

9. For an article that explores medieval elements in García Márquez as a form of allegory, see Christopher Little.

3   Faith, Idealism, and Irreverence in Asturias, Borges, and Carpentier

1. See, for example Camayd-Freixas 60; Loiz Parkinson Zamora "Swords" 44; Hegerfeldt 37. Seymour Menton's analysis in *Historia verdadera del realismo mágico* is an exception to this rule, but Menton's classification of Borges as a magical realist and García Márquez as a fantasist is controversial and unlikely to garner much support.

2. It may be the case that Borges, like Novalis, did in fact desire to break out of the circle of subjectivism, since solipsism was for him so closely associated with psychological traumas related to his relationships with duty, parents, tradition, sex, and his own writing. Edwin Williamson suggests that there is a cruel irony in the fact that the acclaim Borges received for *Ficciones* and *The Aleph* derived largely from their exposition of "the nothingness of personality," a notion that secretly filled him with "horror and revulsion" (444). Signs of ambivalence can be found in the nightmarish qualities of some of his inverted worlds, or in the ways he parodies idealism as well as realism.

3. The glossary to the Pittsburgh Edition of *Men of Maize* defines *ladino*: "In Spanish America generally, a mestizo or half-breed who speaks Spanish; in Guatemala, however, the term denotes any person whose speech and way

of life are Spanish, that is, 'European', even if ethnically he or she is mainly or entirely 'Indian'" (310).

4. Rene Prieto points to a link that may have existed in Asturias's mind between his mother, who was mestizo, and Indian culture (116–123). Certainly, shifts in Asturias's personal life, along with his encounters with Mayan and Aztec texts at the Sorbonne, lie at the heart of the empathy he shows for the Indians in *Men of Maize*, and which was notably lacking in his dissertation on "the Indian problem," completed in 1923.

5. Asturias became, in 1967, the first Latin American novelist to be awarded the Nobel Prize. Martin notes that he has never been as widely read in the Anglo-Saxon world as in Eastern Europe and France, though, and his achievements have been partially eclipsed by the so-called boom of Latin American literature which he, among others, made possible (xiv).

6. Asturias is quoting from Garibay's *Poesía indígena* (1940). Garibay drew the extract from "Canto de Atamalcualoyan" collected by Sahagún in Teapepulco in the sixteenth century (Martin 315).

7. See, for example, Karin Barber's discussion of the genre of Yoruba oral poetry known as *oriki*, which are "attributions or appellations: collections of epithets, pithy or elaborated, which are addressed to a subject" (1).

8. For Chatman, drawing from French structuralism, "story" is "content or chain of events (actions, happenings) plus what might be called the existents (characters, items of setting)," and is to be contrasted with "discourse" or "the expression, the means by which the content is communicated" (107).

9. Camayd-Freixas suggests, passingly, a Borgesian quality to this passage, along the lines of "Pierre Menard, Author of the Quixote" (*Realismo mágico* 192). There is an overlap with respect to the resistance towards individual models of creativity, but the differences are more telling: "Pierre Menard" is a cerebral, intellectual exploration of authorship that has little to do with the kinds of oral/spiritual communality being evoked here by Asturias.

10. For a discussion see Esther Pasztory.

11. Asturias's representation of gender issues in *Men of Maize* is sophisticated by contrast with other Latin American writers. However, as Rene Prieto makes clear, Asturias's portrayal of women also includes "feminine cruelty, mutilation and castration anxiety" (115).

12. For a reconsideration of *The Kingdom of This World*'s representation of the Haitian revolution in the light of recent historical and anthropological scholarship see Lizabeth Paravisini-Gebert.

13. Most English-speaking readers now encounter the prologue in its translated form as "On the Marvellous Real in America" in the Zamora and Faris anthology. This essay is a translation of "De lo real maravilloso americano" originally published in *Tientos y diferencias* in 1964, which is itself a rewritten and expanded version of the original prologue, which in turn had its origins in an article written for the Caracas newspaper, *El Nacional* in 1948 (Camayd-Freixas 93). Carpentier's own footnote to

the extended essay suggests that the latter part of the essay reverts to the original prologue. This suggestion is misleading as parts of the original are left out of the extended essay. References to the original prologue are taken from the 1964 Bolsilibros edition published in Havana, which reprints the original prologue along with an interesting preface in which Carpentier explicitly links the Haitian and Cuban Revolutions.

14. I refer to the French colony as Saint Domingue and the Spanish part of the island (largely untouched by the revolution) as Santo Domingo (now the Dominican Republic). In 1804, following the declaration of independence of Jean-Jacques Dessalines, Saint Domingue became Haiti, an Amerindian name meaning "mountainous." Its flag was created by ripping out the white from the French tricolour. The nation has retained its name, its flag, and its independence (apart from a period of U.S. occupation) until today.

15. See Richard Young 23–34 and González Echevarría, *Pilgrim* 131–154 for demonstrations of Carpentier's fidelity to historical detail.

16. Moreau de Saint-Méry is remembered by M. Lenormand de Mézy in the novel as "that ruddy, pleasure loving lawyer of the Cap" (78) who collected information about Voodoo practices. His *Description topographique, physique, civile, politique et historique de la partie française de l'Isle de Saint-Domingue* was originally published in 1797.

17. On an economic level, Saint Domingue's importance cannot be overstated: in 1789 it was the most valuable colony in the world, producing close to half of all the sugar and coffee consumed in the world, as well as cotton and indigo. It was the largest market for the European slave trade and accounted for between two fifths and two thirds of all of France's foreign trade (Geggus 22; James ix). In addition, it was of vital strategic and military importance to France's interests in the region. Although slave uprisings had occurred regularly in Saint Domingue in the eighteenth century, as they had elsewhere in the Caribbean, the particular significance of what took place there lies in its relationship with the French revolution, particularly with the fraught and convoluted attempts to translate the ideal of universal freedom into the reality of the abolition of slavery. The role of the Haitian revolution in world history and its relationship with the development of Western thought in the eighteenth century are relatively unexplored areas by contrast with the American and French revolutions. The reasons behind this occlusion are significant, as C.L.R. James points out (see 381–382). Susan Buck-Morss picks up on the implications of "scholarly blindness that silences the past" (834n), where Haiti, read as primary locus for slave-led quests for freedom, is concerned. Unfortunately, Buck-Morss makes little use of Carpentier, who undertakes his own detailed and sophisticated exploration of the relationship between enlightenment and slavery in his later novel *Explosion in a Cathedral* (*El siglo de las luces*). Louis Sala-Molins' work on slavery and the French Enlightenment, recently translated into English by John Conteh-Morgan, will prove informative in this regard.

18. Carpentier's deviation at this point is a clue to the fact that his real interest lies with Cuba rather than Haiti. As González Echevarría points out, Carpentier learned from Guerra's *Sugar and Society in the Caribbean* (1927) that the sugar boom in Cuba, precipitated by the fall in production consequent on the Haitian revolution, was largely responsible for the nature of Cuban economy and society in the early twentieth century (44). Doubtless, given his heritage, Carpentier also appreciated that the revolution in Haiti was responsible for the arrival of large numbers of French colonists in Cuba.

19. Voodoo or Vodou now signifies a set of religious practices common to the Caribbean in which Roman Catholicism is syncretised with elements of African religion. This development is anticipated in the scenes in *The Kingdom of This World* in which Ti Noël finds a "Voodoo warmth" in the Spanish churches of Santiago de Cuba. In the mid-eighteenth century, slaves like Bouckman and Macandal would have been born in Africa, and their ritual invocation of Ogun, transcribed by the Abbé de la Haye (67–68), refers to what is probably the first written mention of the West African deity. See Barnes (5) and McCarthy Brown (65–89) for discussions of Ogun in Haiti. The link provided by the presence of Ogun in Carpentier's Caribbean and Okri's Nigeria will be commented on in Chapter 6 of this study.

20. James documents some of these tortures: "Whipping was interrupted in order to pass a piece of hot wood on the buttocks of the victim; salt, pepper, citron, cinders, aloes, and hot ashes were poured onto bleeding wounds [...]. Their masters poured on burning wax on their arms and hands and shoulders, emptied the boiling cane sugar over their heads, burned them alive, roasted them on slow fires, filled them with gunpowder and blew them up with a match" (12–13).

4 Magical Realism and Defamiliarisation in Gabriel García Márquez's *One Hundred Years of Solitude*

1. I have taken these sales figures from Bob Minzesheimer, "*Solitude* Gets Boost from Oprah Selection." *USA Today*. 28 January 2004. <http://www. usatoday.com/life/books/news/2004–01–28-solitude-oprah_x.htm>

2. Some of García Márquez's allusions to Carpentier are obvious: *One Hundred Years of Solitude* and *The Kingdom of This World* both end in an apocalyptic wind; José Arcadio sees the ghost ship of Victor Hugues (81); others are less so: the river in which Melquíades dies is according to González Echevarría, the Orinoco of *The Lost Steps* (*Myth* 16). García Márquez's Nobel Prize acceptance speech contains further evidence of influence as will be discussed below.

3. See for example: González, Rincón, Zamora "Swords," Gyurko, Saldivar and González Echevarría. The last two will be discussed below.

4. See González Echevarría who claims that the presence of the "English Encyclopaedia" and *The Thousand and One Nights* are allusions to the Argentine writer. He singles out "Tlön, Uqbar, Orbis Tertius," "The Secret Miracle," "The Aleph" and, especially, "Death and the Compass" as being important particularly to the ending of *One Hundred Years of Solitude* (*Myth* 23).

5. Of course we ought to be suspicious of the truth value of García Márquez's comments in interviews. As he states in his memoirs, *Living to Tell the Tale*: an "immense majority of [the interviews] I have not been able to avoid on any subject ought to be considered as an important part of my works of fiction" (489).

6. Drawing on a study by Amaryll Chanady, Dean J. Irvine has noticed that the Macondo of the opening page of *One Hundred Years of Solitude* – located in a time when "the world was so recent that many things lacked names and in order to indicate them it was necessary to point" – corresponds closely to Hernán Cortés's *relacíon* to Emperor Charles V. "There are so many [things in the New Continent] and of so many kinds that because of the great number of them and because I do not remember them all, and also because I do not know what to call them, I cannot relate them," Cortes wrote in 1520 (59–60).

7. In *Living to Tell the Tale*, García Márquez calls his grandmother, "the most credulous and impressionable woman I have ever known" (83).

8. García Márquez's purported memory of the return of the many illegitimate sons of the colonel, who arrive with ash crosses on the forehead and throw a huge party (73), is so close to the description of a similar event in *One Hundred Years of Solitude* as to raise doubts about the interpolation of memory and fiction. This is of course, an appropriate state of affairs given García Márquez's predilection for blurring boundaries of all kinds.

9. Erik Camayd-Freixas provides a detailed and contextualised account of García Márquez's hyperbole that makes clear the extent to which exaggeration constitutes a core ingredient of *One Hundred Years of Solitude*'s magical realism. Camayd-Freixas recuperates this hyperbole into a ludic and sophisticated primitivism.

10. See Harry Garuba, for whom Melquíades's comment "sum[s] up the basic creed of animist belief" (272). The comment does seem to invoke animist modes of thought; however, I argue here that such claims are destabilised by García Márquez's hyperbole and irony.

11. When Editorial Losada of Buenos Aires rejected his first novel, *Leaf Storm* on the advice of Guillermo de Torre, García Márquez's friend, Alfonso Fuenmayor suggested that it might have met a different fate had it been read by Borges except that "the devastation would have been worse if he had rejected it too" (*Telling* 450).

12. Foucault is referring to the description of the "Chinese Encyclopaedia" from "John Wilkins' Analytical Language."

13. For a useful discussion of this distinction from a postcolonial point of view, see Robert Young's *White Mythologies* 78. In his discussion of how Foucault "relocates writing in relation to the history to which it had

until then been opposed," a relocation apparent in the shift between *Madness and Civilisation* and *The Order of Things*, Young stresses Derrida's intervention but makes no mention of the role played by Borges, despite the evidence of the opening lines of the preface. Similarly, though both Borges and Foucault loom large in González Echevarría's study, he does not connect them directly at any point.

14. See for example, W.L. Webb's claim that the novel "continues to inspire in readers throughout the world a devotion-like conversion to some benign new religion," taken from a review in the *Guardian*, and emblazoned on the dustcover of the Picador edition of the novel. Oprah Winfrey similarly claims on the Book Club section of her website that "through this fantastic town and its fantastic people, you will come to appreciate the magic of your own life."

15. The idea of "successive concentric circles" is drawn from an anonymous early review of *One Hundred Years of Solitude*, cited in Fiddian 12.

5   Migrancy and Metamorphosis in Salman Rushdie's *The Satanic Verses*

1. In his acknowledgements to the novel, Rushdie notes the following literary sources: The Qur'an, Faiz Ahmed Faiz, Jorge Luis Borges, W.H. Hudson, Arun Kolatkar, Lionel Bart and Kenneth Tynan. He concludes: "The identities of many of the authors from whom I've learned will, I hope, be clear from the text; others must remain anonymous, but I thank them, too." Some of these authors, film-makers and stars, poets and singers and cultural resources of a general nature include: Brecht and Weill, Godard, Raj Kapoor, Lewis Carroll, Joyce, Ovid, Lucretius, Ian Fleming, Laurence Sterne, Marcel Carné, Isaac Asimov, Shakespeare, Kenneth Graham, James Barrie, Frank L. Baum, The Arabian Nights, George Bernard Shaw, Keats, Ridley Scott, Akira Kurosawa, the Dastan-e-Amir-Hamza, cockney rhyming slang, Darwin, Lamarck, Gramsci, Elvis Presley, Charlton Heston, Bergman, Byron, Little Red Riding Hood, Tennyson, Kipling, Thackeray, Tagore, Bruce Lee, Madonna, Julius Caesar, Virgil, 1970s and 1980s horror films, Hermann Hesse, William Ernest Henley, Constantine Costa Gavras, Yeats, the Mahābhārata, the Rolling Stones, advertising slogans, Ukawsaw Graniosaw, Harriet Beecher Stowe, Thomas Hughes, James Hilton, Alfred Jarry, Herbert, Milosz, Baranczak, Gurdjieff, Isaac Bashevis Singer, Francois Truffaut, William Blake, Nabokov, Ginsberg, Yoji Kuri, Milton, Voltaire, Robert Louis Stevenson, Fanon, Rider Haggard, Omar Khayam and Edward Fitzgerald, Henry (Snr and Jnr) and William James, B.F. Skinner, Bizet, Nirad Chaudhuri, Sir James Frazer, Buster Keaton, Machiavelli, Jim Henson, Ridley Scott, Walt Whitman, Catullus, Dickens, Bentham, Marx, Aeschylus, Cervantes, Heraclitus, Herman Melville, Samuel Foote, Daniel Defoe, Eisenstein, Welles, Fellini, Buñuel, Mehboob Khan, Strindberg, Cliff Richard, Orwell, Pepys, Wordsworth, Dryden, Virgil, Edward Bond, Arthur C. Clarke. This list, which makes

no claim to be exhaustive, has, with a few additions of my own, been culled from Paul Brians' admirable *Notes on Salman Rushdie's The Satanic Verses* <http://www.wsu.edu/~brians/anglophone/satanic_verses/contents. html>. Another useful online resource is Joel Kuortti's index to the novel: <http://www.uta.fi/~f1joku/svindex2.htm>.

2. Rushdie discusses both writers in several interviews (see below). He credits Borges in the acknowledgements to *The Satanic Verses* and adduces him as an influence in an essay in *Step Across this Line* (151). In *Imaginary Homelands* he dedicates an essay to García Márquez which focusses on his magical realism. The influence of Borges and García Márquez on Rushdie will be fleshed out in more detail in this chapter.

3. Feroza Jussawalla provides an interesting alternative to the idea that the butterflies are derived from García Márquez, arguing they exemplify the kinds of fairies or winged creatures common to the Indo-Islamic tradition of the *dastan* (Smale 60). Alternatively, Paul Brians observes that Ray Guerra's film version of García Márquez's short story "Innocent Eréndria and her Heartless Grandmother" contains a magical butterfly, and was advertised with a poster featuring a young woman with a butterfly covering her mouth. Brians notes further that the heroine of the short story undertakes a lengthy foot-pilgrimage to the sea (note to p. 217). These interpretations are not necessarily mutually exclusive.

4. Of course, the Ayesha sequences are based on a actual historical episode, the so-called Hawkes Bay case. See Suleri 202.

5. Rushdie has stated that he is "very keen on the eighteenth century in general, not just in literature" and that he thinks that "the eighteenth century was the great century" (Chaudhuri interview). Whether and to what extent this interest, and his attempts to ground the transcendental in the realm of the human in *The Satanic Verses*, mean that he was attempting to become a "Muslim Voltaire," as Paul Brians suggests, is an interesting proposition that has yet to be examined in detail.

6. For discussions of the similarities between *The Satanic Verses* and *The Master and Margarita* see Balasubramanian and Gimpelevich, who observe the influence of Aleksei Skaldin on Bulgakov. Adam Weiner's *By Authors Possessed* is an excellent study of relationship between demonic themes and authorial personae in Russian prose, and provides the context for understanding Bulgakov's literalisation of the diabolical in Russian literature. Bulgakov's novel, written in the 1930s, is undoubtedly to be considered an example of magical realism according to the definition used here. It is thus an interesting example of how magical realism can arise from themes and tendencies within a national literature (one which, moreover, has no relationship whatsoever with Latin America).

7. Through this fatalism, Saladin begins to accept his physical condition, which in fact reverses within a short time. Rushdie's description of Saladin's acceptance of his demonic form in the biblical terms reserved for God – "*I am*, he accepted, *that I am*" – and his naming of this process as

"Submission" (the translation of "Islam"), is yet another of the minor parodic set-pieces that characterise the novel.

8. For the significations of "chamcha" ("spoon") in terms of relations of complicity between colonial authority and subject that is furthered in the postcolonial period by neo-colonial elites, see Brennan (*Rushdie* 85–90).

9. Rushdie is not finished with Zeeny Vakil. She re-appears in his next novel, *The Moor's Last Sigh* in order playfully to parody Bhabha's work (he had written an essay partly on *The Satanic Verses* entitled "DissemiNation") by authoring a critical work entitled "Imperso-Nation and Dis/Semi/Nation: Dialogics of Eclecticism and Interrogations of Authenticity in A.Z." (329). David Smale's suggestion that the word-game is a playful warning against the kind of convoluted use of theory in academic circles (115) is probably correct, but the allusion should also be read as confirming the contract between the writer and the critic over the importance of hybridity as a way of describing cultures in migration.

10. There is much in *The Golden Ass* that is highly critical of superstition and religious belief, especially Apuleius's treatment of various cults of belief. However, its ending continues to puzzle critics by its apparent advocacy of the Isis cult. See, however, Kenney xxix, for arguments against reading the ending of the novel as proselytism.

11. In 1999, investigating the racist slaying of Stephen Lawrence six years earlier, the Macpherson inquiry stated that the police force in Britain is infected with institutional racism.

12. For an intriguing study of witchcraft in the 1980s amongst middle-class professionals (including academics) in Cambridge and London see Tanya Luhrmann.

13. Though Rushdie has jokingly noted, with reference to the title of his collection of short stories, *East, West*: "I live in the comma...I don't feel like a slash. I feel more like a comma" ("Homeless" 162).

14. Despite these noble intentions, we should note along with Timothy Brennan (*Rushdie* 164–166), that there is an out-of-touch element to Rushdie's representation of black British protest, one that borders on condescension at times. An ambivalence attaches to Jumpy Joshi's character, as it does to several politically-involved characters, most notably the community activist Dr Uhuru Simba, whose re-naming of himself (in Swahili, "uhuru" means freedom; simba means "lion") is scorned by Mishal Sufyan. And, of course, for different reasons, the novel was burned and banned by those that Rushdie felt himself to be writing for.

6   The African World View in Ben Okri's *The Famished Road*

1. Brenda Cooper also reduces the influence of Tutuola on Okri. Tutuola is seen as partaking in an "oral tradition of morality tales, desperate to conserve the fabric of ancient societies" (86); the "language of Tutuola, [is] of myth and conservation, of pure and inviolate African ways of seeing the

world; it is diametrically opposed to the hybrid, to change" (90). It is difficult to agree with such a perspective in the light of the example from *My Life in the Bush of Ghosts* discussed above.

2. Soyinka's poem, "Death in the Dawn," and his plays *The Road* and *A Dance of The Forests* are all relevant to this discussion.

3. Robert Fraser takes issue with Ato Quayson's reading of Okri's work on exactly the grounds that it utilises a "reality-esoteric" axis (134) to understand the narrative mode engaged by the fiction. For Fraser, "there is no single delineation between what Quayson calls reality and what he persists in calling the 'esoteric realm'." Fraser is correct in assuming that this is the effect Okri is trying to generate, but, as I have argued elsewhere, it is not useful for the critic to follow him in this. The distance between text and critic required for such a reading can only detract from criticism's capacity to evaluate, elucidate, explain, and compare. See my essay "The Hermeneutics of Vagueness" for more detail.

4. See, however, Quayson's more recent work "Fecundities" where he returns to questions of magical realism. A similar tendency can be found in an article on *The Famished Road* by Olatubosun Ogunsanwo. Ogunsanwo makes glancing reference to García Márquez and Kundera, and even, provocatively, to Okri's "marvelous African reality" (43, 47), but magical realism is nowhere mentioned. In a review of Brenda Cooper's book that will be discussed later, Ogunsanwo explicitly expresses doubts about the applicability of the term magical realism to African fiction, preferring Garuba and Quayson's "animist realism."

5. For a more detailed version of this argument, which situates Okri's later work in terms of his earlier novels and short stories, see my essay on Okri in *World Writers in English*.

6. A recent study of African writing by Gerald Gaylard concurs with mine by reading Okri as magical realist and linking his aesthetics to questions of faith (291–294). But for Gaylard "faith" points towards the mysteries of the other, conceived in a Levinasian frame. Following Carpentier, I am keen to situate faith more specifically in relation to questions of cultural identity and literary strategy. With regards to Okri, this means examining closely his claims about "the African world-view," which as McCabe has shown, open out onto a New Age discourse.

7. Azaro's name, derived from Lazarus, suggests the importance that death and rebirth have in the novel. Dad symbolically dies and is reborn three times, and is also associated with Lazarus (484), and Mum's morality tale tells of the white man, re-born as a Yoruba businessman (483). *Abiku* myths and myths of reincarnation all work to support the novel's inscription of cyclicality (see note 8).

8. On the important question of whether the novel is implying that these cycles of time can be transcended, Derek Wright's response to Margaret Cezair-Thomson is instructive ("Recent", 1997). Wright argues against Cezair-Thomson's interpretation of *The Famished Road* as a "resolute, indefatigable quest for an inviolable form" (40) on the grounds that, though acts of volition are present at crucial moments, the fact that Azaro cannot ultimately will himself out of cycles of return and recurrence infuses his

character with a "riddling, aporetic quality" (10): "Insofar as this essential nature is generally inactive, he is chiefly an awareness and a mode of perception in the narrative, simply being rather than doing, a presence rather than an agent" (12). Secondly, Wright points out that Okri's invocation of cyclicality cannot be read only as a positive alternative to a Western linearity – it concurs in important respects with a fatalism that can be found in other examples of African literature. My argument coincides with Wright's position on both these counts, and hence will not examine the controversial "allegorical passages" comparing the nation-state to the *abiku*. Instead, the focus here will be on *The Famished Road* as performing Okri's hybridised ideas about modes of perception and awareness in order to establish the ontological grounds for an assertion of cultural difference.

9. Relevant here is Todorov's narrow definition of the fantastic as "that hesitation experienced by a person who knows only the laws of nature, confronting an apparently supernatural event" (25). In *The Famished Road* such moments of hesitation are deliberately provoked in the implied reader, and are inevitably followed by encouragement to accept the supernatural. In Todorov's terms, the narrative therefore moves swiftly from the fantastic into the "marvellous."

10. Soyinka's myth of an African world is criticised by Appiah in terms relevant to the comparative position argued for in this chapter. Referring to both the "nativist" school of criticism exemplified by Chinweizu et al., which he dislikes, and to Soyinka, whom he admires, Appiah argues that "the attempt to construct an African literature rooted in African traditions has led both to an understating of the diversity of African cultures, and to an attempt to censor the profound entanglement of African intellectuals with the intellectual life of Europe and the Americas" (*In My Father's House* xiii, see also 116–134). Garuba sees things differently, finding in Soyinka's notion of African epistemology a powerful means of re-assessing the nature of African modernity.

11. Okri's borrowings from the Bible are one of his more obvious attempts to harness an already existing religious/spiritual paradigm to his own mythopoeia which, though inflected with Yoruba ideas, is nevertheless cosmopolitan and eclectic in nature.

12. Okri's 1999 poem, *Mental Fight*, attempts in its conclusion to echo the inverted liturgy of Part V of *The Wasteland* (Eliot) by reciting the names of a number of literary works including *The Kingdom of This World* and *One Hundred Years of Solitude.*

13. As noted in a previous chapter, the West African connection is most apparent in the ritual invocation of "Ogoun," god of metalwork, hunting and warriors, in Part Two of *The Kingdom of This World*. For a useful discussion of Ogun in Africa and the Americas, see Sandra T. Barnes.

Works Cited

Primary Sources

Allende, Isabel. *The House of the Spirits*. 1982. Trans. Magda Bogin. London: Jonathan Cape, 1985.

Apuleius. *The Golden Ass or Metamorphoses: A New Translation*. Trans. E.J. Kenney. Harmondsworth: Penguin, 1998.

——. *The Apologia and Florida of Apuleius of Madaura*. Trans. H.E. Butler. Oxford: Clarendon Press, 1909.

Asturias, Miguel Ángel. *Hombres de maíz*. Paris: Klincksieck, 1981.

——. *Men of Maize*. 1949. Trans. and Coordinator, Gerald Martin. Pittsburgh and London: University of Pittsburgh Press/UNESCO Colección Archivos, 1993.

Blake, William. *The Marriage of Heaven and Hell*. 1793. Coral Gables, Fla: University of Miami Press, 1972. <http://www.bibliomania.com/0/2/81/197/frameset.html>.

Borges, Jorge Luis. "An Autobiographical Essay." *Critical Essays on Jorge Luis Borges*. Ed. Jaime Alazraki. Boston: G.K. Hall, 1987. 21–55.

——. "The Aleph." 1949. Borges, *Collected Fictions* 274–286.

——. "The Argentine Writer and Tradition." 1951. Borges, *Labyrinths* 211–220.

——. "Avatars of the Tortoise." 1939. Borges, *Labyrinths* 237–243.

——. "The Circular Ruins." 1941. Borges, *Collected Fictions* 96–100.

——. *Collected Fictions*. Trans. Andrew Hurley. Harmondsworth: Penguin, 1998.

——. "Death and the Compass." 1944. Borges, *Collected Fictions* 147–156.

——. "The Garden of Forking Paths." 1941. Borges, *Collected Fictions* 119–128.

——. "John Wilkins' Analytical Language." 1942. Borges, *The Total Library* 229–232.

——. *Labyrinths*. Ed. and trans. Donald A. Yates and James E. Irby. Harmondsworth: Penguin, 1970.

——. "The Mirror of Enigmas." 1952. *Labyrinths* 244–247.

——. "Narrative Art and Magic." 1932. Borges, *The Total Library* 75–82.

——. "A New Refutation of Time." 1944–1947. Borges, *Labyrinths* 252–270.

——. "The Secret Miracle." 1944. Borges, *Collected Fictions* 157–162.

——. "Tlön, Uqbar, Orbis Tertius." 1941. Borges, *Collected Fictions* 68–81.

——. *The Total Library: Non-Fiction 1922–1986*. Ed. Eliot Weinberger. Trans Esther Allen, Suzanne Jill Levine and Eliot Weinberger. Harmondsworth: Penguin, 2001.

Bronte, Emily. *Wuthering Heights*. 1847. Manchester: World International, 1990.

Bulgakov, Mikhail. *The Master and Margarita*. 1938. Trans. Michael Glenny. London: The Harvill Press, 1996.

Calinescu, Matei. Encomium in Zamora and Faris, dustcover.

Carpentier, Alejo. *¡Ecué-Yamba-O!* 1933. Buenos Aires: Editorial Xanandú, 1968.

———. *Explosion in a Cathedral.* 1963. Trans. John Sturrock. London: Minerva, 1991.

———. *The Kingdom of This World.* 1949. Trans. Harriet de Onís. Harmondsworth: Penguin, 1975.

———. *The Lost Steps.* 1953. Trans. Harriet de Onis. London: Gollancz, 1956.

———. *Los pasos perdidos.* 1953. México, D.F.: Compañia General de Ediciones, 1969.

———. *El reino de este mundo.* 1949. Barcelona: Editorial Seix Barral, 1969.

———. *El siglo de las luces.* La Habana: Ediciones Revolución, 1963.

Carroll, Lewis [Charles Dodgson]. *Alice in Wonderland.* 1865. Ed. Donald J. Gray. New York: Norton, 1973.

Carter, Angela. *Nights at the Circus.* London: Chatto & Windus, 1984.

Cervantes Saavedra, Miguel de. *The Adventures of Don Quixote.* 1605, 1615. Trans. J.M. Cohen. Harmondsworth: Penguin, 1954.

Cheney-Coker, Syl. *The Last Harmattan of Alusine Dunbar.* Oxford: Heinemann, 1990.

Chilam Balam of Chumayel, the Book of. Ed. and trans. Ralph L. Roys. Norman: University of Oklahoma Press, 1967.

Defoe, Daniel. *The True-Born Englishman.* 1701. Daniel Defoe. *The True-Born Englishman and Other Writings.* Ed. P.N. Furbank and W.R. Owens. London: Penguin Books, 1997.

Desani, G.V. *All about H. Hatterr.* London: Aldus Publications, 1948.

Eliot, T.S. *The Wasteland. Collected Poems: 1909–1962.* London: Faber and Faber, 1983.

Esquivel, Laura. *Like Water for Chocolate.* 1989. Trans. Carol Christensen and Thomas Christensen. London: Black Swan, 1993.

García Márquez, Gabriel. *Cien años de soledad.* Buenos Aires: Editorial Sudamericana, 1968.

———. *One Hundred Years of Solitude.* Trans. Gregory Rabassa. London: Picador, 1978.

———. "The Incredible and Sad Tale of Innocent Eréndira and her Heartless Grandmother." *Collected Stories* 283–342.

Goethe, Johann Wolfgang von. *Faust.* 1832. Trans. Abraham Hayward. Oxford and New York: Woodstock Books, 1993.

Hernández, José. *Martín Fierro: Edición Crítica.* 1872. Coord. Elida Lois and Angel Núñez. Paris: Ediciones UNESCO, 2001.

Lamming, George. *The Emigrants.* 1954. London: Allison and Busby, 1980.

Laye, Camara. *The Dark Child.* 1953. Trans. James Kirkup. London: Collins, 1955.

Milton, John. *Paradise Lost: A Poem in Twelve Books.* 1667. London: Folio Society, 2003.

Morrison, Toni. *Beloved.* London: Chatto & Windus, 1987.

Okri, Ben. *The Famished Road*. 1991. London: Vintage, 1992.
——. *Flowers and Shadows*. London: Longman, 1980.
——. *Incidents at the Shrine*. London: Heinemann, 1986.
——. *Infinite Riches*. London: Phoenix House, 1998.
——. *Mental Fight*. London: Phoenix, 1999.
——. *The Landscapes Within*. Harlow: Longman, 1981.
——. *Songs of Enchantment*. 1993. London: Vintage, 1994.
——. *Stars of the New Curfew*. London: Secker and Warburg, 1988.
Ovid. *Metamorphoses*. Trans. A.D. Melville. Oxford: Oxford UP, 1986.
Popol Vuh: The Sacred Book of the Ancient Quiche Maya. Ed. D. Goetz and S.G.
  Morley. Norman: University of Oklahoma Press, 1961.
Rushdie, Salman. *In Good Faith*. London: Granta, 1990.
——. *Midnight's Children*. 1981. London: Vintage, 1995.
——. *The Moor's Last Sigh*. London: Vintage, 1995.
——. *The Satanic Verses*. 1988. London: Vintage, 1998.
——. *Shame*. 1983. London: Vintage, 1995.
Scott, Walter. *Waverley*. 1814. London: Penguin, 1985.
——. *The Bride of Lammermoor*. 1819. Oxford: Oxford World's Classics, 1998.
Selvon, Samuel. *The Lonely Londoners*. 1956. London: Longman, 1979.
Soyinka, Wole. *Collected Plays*. Vol. 1. Oxford: Oxford UP, 1973.
——. "Death in the Dawn." *Idanre and Other Poems*. London: Methuen, 1967.
  10–11.
Steyn, J.C. "Op pad na die grens." *Op pad na die grens*. Cape Town: Tafelberg,
  1976.
Tutuola, Amos. *My Life in the Bush of Ghosts*. 1954. London: Faber and Faber,
  1978.
——. *The Witch Herbalist of the Remote Town*. 1981. London: Faber and Faber,
  1990.

Secondary Sources

Adorno, Theodor W. "Spengler after the Decline." *Prisms* by Theodor Adorno.
  Trans Samuel and Shierry Weber. Cambridge, MA: The MIT Press, 1983.
  53–72.
Ahmad, Aijaz. *In Theory: Classes, Nations, Literatures*. London and New York:
  Verso, 1992.
Aizenberg, Edna. "*The Famished Road*: Magical Realism and the Search for
  Social Equity." *Yearbook of Comparative and General Literature* 43 (1995):
  25–30.
Appiah, Kwame Anthony. *In My Father's House: Africa in the Philosophy of
  Culture*. London: Methuen, 1992.
——. "Spiritual Realism." Rev. of *The Famished Road*, by Ben Okri. *The Nation*
  255.4 (August 1992): 146–148.
Aravamudan, Srinivas. "'Being God's postman is no fun, yaar': Salman
  Rushdie's *The Satanic Verses*." *Diacritics* 19.2 (1989): 3–20.

Aristotle. *Poetics*. Ed. and trans. Stephen Halliwell. Cambridge, Mass.: Harvard UP, 1995.

Balasubramanian, Radha. "The Similarities between Mikhail Bulgakov's *The Master and Margarita* and Salman Rushdie's *The Satanic Verses*." *International Fiction Review* 22 (1995): 37–46.

Ball, John Clement. "An Interview with Salman Rushdie." Reder 101–119.

Barber, Karin. *I Could Speak Until Tomorrow: Oríkì, Women and the Past in a Yoruba Town*. Edinburgh: Edinburgh UP, 1991.

Barker, Francis, Peter Hulme, and Maragaret Iversen, eds. *Colonial discourse/ postcolonial theory*. Manchester: Manchester UP, 1994.

Barnes, Sandra T. *Africa's Ogun: Old World and New*. Bloomington and Indianapolis: Indiana UP, 1989.

Bassi, Shaul. "Salman Rushdie's Special Effects." Linguanti, Casotti and Concilio 47–60.

Beiser, Fredrick C. *German Idealism: The Struggle Against Subjectivism 1781–1801*. Cambridge, MA: Harvard University Press, 2002.

Bhabha, Homi K. "The Commitment to Theory." Bhabha, *Location of Culture* 19–39.

——. "DissemiNation: Time, Narrative and the Margins of the Modern Nation." Bhabha, *Nation and Narration* 291–320.

——. "Introduction." Bhabha, *Nation and Narration* 1–7.

——. *The Location of Culture*. London, Routledge: 1994.

——. *Nation and Narration*. London, Routledge: 1990.

——. "How Newness Enters the World: Postmodern Space, Postcolonial Times and the Trials of Cultural Translation." Bhabha, *Location of Culture* 212–235.

Bontempelli, Massimo. *L'avventura novecentista*. Florencia: Vallecchi, 1974.

Bowers, Maggie Ann. *Magic(al) Realism*. London : Routledge, 2004.

Brennan, Timothy. *At Home in the World: Cosmopolitanism Now*. Cambridge, Mass., London: Harvard UP, 1997.

——. *Salman Rushdie and the Third World: Myths of the Nation*. London: Macmillan, 1989.

Brians, Paul. *Notes on Salman Rushdie's The Satanic Verses* <http://www.wsu.edu/~brians/anglophone/satanic_verses>. Accessed 31 October 2008.

Brooks, David. "Salman Rushdie." (Interview) Reder 57–71.

Browning, Robert. *The Pied Piper of Hamelin*. 1842. Kingswood: World's Work, 1981.

Buck-Morss, Susan. "Hegel and Haiti." *Critical Inquiry* 26.4 (2000): 821–865.

Camayd-Freixas, Erik, *Realismo mágico y primitivismo: Relecturas de Carpentier, Asturias, Rulfo y García Márquez*. Lanham, MD: University Press of America, 1998.

Carpentier, Alejo. "The Baroque and the Marvellous Real." 1975. Trans. Tanya Huntington and Lois Parkinson Zamora. Zamora and Faris 89–108.

——. *Music in Cuba*. 1946. Ed. Timothy Brennan, trans. Alan West-Durán. Minneapolis and London: University of Minnesota Press, 2001.

——. "On the Marvellous Real in America." 1949/1964. Trans. Wendy B. Faris. Zamora and Faris 75–88.

——. *Tientos y differencias*. Mexico City: Universidad Nacional Autónoma de México, 1964.

Cezair-Thomson, Margaret. "Beyond the Postcolonial Novel: Ben Okri's *The Famished Road* and it's '*Abiku*' Traveller." *Journal of Commonwealth Literature* 31.2 (1996): 33–45.

Chanady, Amaryll. *Magical Realism and the Fantastic: Resolved Versus Unresolved Antinomy*. New York: Garland, 1985.

——. "The Territorialization of the Imaginary in Latin America: Self-affirmation and Resistance to Metropolitan Paradigms." Zamora and Faris 125–144.

Chatman, Seymour. "Story and Narrative." *Literature in the Modern World*. Ed. Dennis Walder. Oxford: Oxford UP, 1990. 105–114.

Chaudhuri, Una. "Imaginative Maps: Excerpts from a Conversation with Salman Rushdie." <http://www.subir.com/rushdie/uc_maps.html>. Accessed 22 September 2008.

Chiampi, Irlemar. *O realismo maravilhoso: Forma e ideologia no romance hispano-americano*. São Paulo: Editora Perspectiva, 1980.

——. *El realismo maravilloso: forma e ideología en la novela hispanoamericana* Trans. (from Portuguese) by Agustin Martiniez and Márgara Russotto. Caracas: Monte Avila, 1983.

Christ, Ronald. "The Text as Translation." 1975. Asturias, *Men of Maize* 435–444.

Connell, Liam. "Discarding Magic Realism: Modernism, Anthropology, and Critical Practice." *ARIEL* 29.2 (1998): 95–110.

Cooper, Brenda. *Magical Realism in West African Fiction: Seeing with a Third Eye*. London and New York: Routledge, 1998.

Defoe, Daniel. *A Brief History of the Poor Palatine Refugees*. 1709. Los Angeles: University of California, 1964.

——. *The History of the Devil Ancient and Modern in Two Parts*. 1726. London, EP Publishing, 1972.

Derrida, Jacques. *Dissemination*. Trans. Barbara Johnson. London: Athlone Press, 1993.

——. *Specters of Marx*. Trans. Peggy Kamuf. New York and London: Routledge, 1994.

Díaz del Castillo, Bernal. *The Conquest of New Spain*. Trans. J.M. Cohen. London: The Folio Society, 1973.

Dorfman, Ariel. "Myth as Time and Language." Asturias, *Men of Maize* 389–412.

Douglas, Mary. *Purity and Danger: An Analysis of Concepts of Pollution and Taboo*. Harmondsworth: Penguin, 1970.

Durix, Jean-Pierre. *Mimesis, Genres, and Post-Colonial Discourse: Deconstructing Magic Realism*. Houndmills: Macmillan, 1998.

Durkheim, Emile. *The Elementary Forms of Religious Life*. Trans. Joseph Ward Swain. London: George Allen and Unwin, 1976.

Dutheil, Martine Hennard. "The Epigraph to *The Satanic Verses*: Defoe's Devil and Rushdie's Migrant." *Southern Review: Literary and Interdisciplinary Essays* 30.1 (1997): 51–69.

Eco, Umberto. "In Praise of St. Thomas." *Faith in Fakes*. Trans. William Weaver. London: Vintage, 1998. 257–268.

Eliade, Mircea. *The Sacred and the Profane*. Trans. Willard R. Trask. New York: Harcourt Brace Jovanovich, 1959.

Evans-Pritchard, E.E. *Witchraft, Oracles and Magic among the Azande*. Oxford: Clarendon Press, 1937.

Faris, Wendy B. *Ordinary Enchantments: Magical Realism and the Remystification of Narrative*. Nashville: Vanderbilt University Press, 2004.

Fernández, Horacio. "The Double String: Franz Roh as Theorist and Photographer." *Franz Roh: teórico y fotógrafo*. Valencia: IVAM Centro Julio González, 1997. 112–118.

Fiddian, Robin, ed. *García Márquez*. London: Longman, 1995.

Foucault, Michel. *Madness and Civilization: A History of Insanity in the Age of Reason*. Trans. Richard Howard. London: Tavistock, 1967.

———. "Order of Discourse." Trans. Ian McLeod. *Untying the Text: A Poststructuralist Reader*. Ed. Robert Young. Boston, London and Henley: Routledge and Kegan Paul, 1981.

———. *The Order of Things: An Archaeology of the Human Sciences*. London: Routledge, 2000.

Franco, Jean. "What's Left of the Intelligentsia." *Critical Passions: Selected Essays*. Ed. Mary Louise Pratt and Kathleen Newman. Durham and London: Duke UP, 1999.

Fraser, Robert. Ben Okri: *Towards the Invisible City*. Tavistock: Northcote House, 2002.

Frazer, James, Sir. *The Golden Bough*. London: Macmillan, 1990.

Frye, Northrop. *Anatomy of Criticism*. Princeton: Princeton UP, 1957.

García Márquez, Gabriel. "The Solitude of Latin America." Nobel Lecture, 8 December, 1982. < http://nobelprize.org/literature/laureates/1982/marquez-lecture-e.html?> Accessed 22 September 2008.

———. *Living to Tell the Tale*. Trans. Edith Grossman. London: Jonathan Cape, 2003.

Garibay, A.M. *Veinte himnos sacros de los nahuas*. Mexico City: UNAM, 1958.

———. *Poesía indígena de la altiplanicie*. Mexico City: UNAM, 1971.

Garuba, Harry: "Explorations in Animist Materialism: Notes on Reading/Writing African Literature, Culture, and Society." *Public Culture* 15.2 (2003): 261–285.

Gates, Henry Louis Jr. "Between the Living and the Unborn." Rev. of *The Famished Road* by Ben Okri. *New York Times Book Review*. 28 June 1992.

Gaylard, Gerald. *After Colonialism: African Postmodernism and Magical Realism* Johannesburg: Wits University Press, 2005.

Geertz, Clifford. *The Interpretation of Cultures*. London: Fontana Press, 1993.

Geggus, David. "The Haitian Revolution." *The Modern Caribbean*. Ed. Franklin W. Knight and Colin A. Palmer. Chapel Hill and London: University of North Carolina Press, 1989.

Genette, Gerard. *Narrative Discourse*. Trans. Jane E. Lewin. London: Blackwell, 1980.

Gimpelevich, Zina. "Skaldin, Bulgakov and Rushdie: Who Art Thou, Then? (Similarities in The Wanderings and Adventures of Nikodim the Elder, The Master and Margarita and The Satanic Verses)." *Canadian-American Slavic Studies* 30.1 (1996): 69–80.

Girouard, Mark. *The Return to Camelot: Chivalry and the English Gentleman.* New Haven: Yale University Press, 1981.

Gonzalez, Anibal. "Translation and Genealogy: *One Hundred Years of Solitude.*" McGuirk and Cardwell 65–79.

González Echevarría, Roberto. "Isla a su vuelo fugitiva: Carpentier y el realismo mágico." *Revista Iberoamericana* 40.86 (1974): 9–64.

——. *Alejo Carpentier: The Pilgrim at Home.* Ithaca: Cornell UP, 1977.

——. *Myth and Archive: A Theory of Latin American Narrative.* Cambridge: Cambridge UP, 1990.

——. "*One Hundred Years of Solitude*: The Novel as Myth and Archive." Fiddian 79–99.

Guenther, Irene. "Magic Realism, New Objectivity, and the Arts during the Weimar Republic." Zamora and Faris 33–73.

Guerra, Ramiro. 1927. *Sugar and Society in the Caribbean. An Economic History of Cuban Agriculture.* Trans. Marjorie M. Urquidi. New Haven and London: Yale UP, 1964.

Gyurko, Lanin A. "The Metaphysical World of Borges and Its Impact on the Novelists of the Boom Generation." *Ibero-Amerikanisches Archiv* 14.2 (1988): 215–261.

Haffenden, John. "Salman Rushdie." (Interview.) Reder 30–56.

Hallward, Peter. *Absolutely Postcolonial: Writing between the Singular and the Specific.* Manchester: Manchester University Press, 2001.

Harlow, Barbara. *Resistance Literature.* London: Methuen, 1987.

Harss, Luis and Barbara Dohmann. 1966. "Miguel Ángel Asturias, or the Land Where the Flowers Bloom." Asturias, *Men of Maize* 413–434.

Hart, Stephen M and Wen-chin Ouyang. *A Companion to Magical Realism.* Woodbridge: Tamesis, 2005.

Hegerfeldt, Anne C. *Lies that Tell the Truth: Magic Realism Seen through Contemporary Fiction from Britain.* Amsterdam: Rodopi, 2005.

Heng, Geraldine. *Empire of Magic: Medieval Romance and the Politics of Cultural Fantasy.* New York: Columbia University Press, 2003.

Herf, Jeffrey. *Reactionary Modernism: Technology, Culture, and Politics in Weimar and the Third Reich.* Cambridge: Cambridge UP, 1984.

Henighan, Stephen. 'Two Paths to the Boom: Carpentier, Asturias and the Performative Split', *Modern Language Review* 94 (1999): 1009–1024.

"Homeless Is Where the Art Is." (Anonymous interview with Salman Rushdie). Reder 162–166.

Hutcheon, Linda. "Circling the Downspout of Empire: Post-colonialism and Postmodernism." Bill Ashcroft, Gareth Griffiths and Helen Tiffin, eds. *The Post-colonial Studies Reader.* London and New York: Routledge, 1995.

——. *A Poetics of Postmodernism: History, Theory, Fiction.* New York: Routledge, 1988.

Hutcheon, Linda. *The Politics of Postmodernism*. London: Routledge, 1989.

Irvine, Dean J. "Fables of the Plague Years: Postcolonialism, Postmodernism, and Magic Realism in Cien anos de soledad." *ARIEL* 29.4 (1998): 53–80.

Jakobson, Roman. "The Metaphoric and Metonymic Poles." Lodge 57–61.

James, C.L.R. *The Black Jacobins*. London: Allison and Busby, 1980.

Jameson, Fredric. *The Political Unconscious: Narrative as a Socially Symbolic Act*. London: Routledge Classics, 2002.

——. "On Magic Realism in Film." *Critical Inquiry* 12.2 (1986): 301–325.

Jussawalla, Feroza. "Rushdie's Dastan-E-Dilruba: The Satanic Verses as Rushdie's Love Letter to Islam." *Diacritics* 26.1 (1996): 50–73.

Kenney, E.J. Introduction. *The Golden Ass* by Apuleius ix–xxxviii.

King, John. "Editor's Preface." *Jorge Luis Borges* by Sarlo vii–xviii.

Kuortti, Joel. *Index to The Satanic Verses*. Updated: 27 April 1999. <http://www.uta.fi/~f1joku/svindex2.htm>.

Landon, Richard G. Introduction. *The History of the Devil* by Daniel Defoe. East Ardsley, Wakefield: E.P. Publishing, 1972.

Lazarus, Neil. "The Politics of Postcolonial Modernism." Loomba and Kaul 423–438.

Lévy-Bruhl, Lucien. *How Natives Think*. London: George Allen Unwin, 1926.

Linguanti, Elsa, Francesco Casotti and Carmen Concilio, eds. *Coterminous Worlds: Magical Realism and Contemporary Post-Colonial Literature in English*. Amsterdam: Rodopi, 1999.

Little, Christopher "*Eréndira* in the Middle Ages: the Medievalness of García Márquez" in Robin Fiddian, ed. *García Márquez* 204–213.

Lodge, David. *20th Century Literary Criticism: A Reader*. London: Longman, 1972.

Loomba, Ania, Suvir Kaul, Matti Bunzl, Antoinette Burton, Jed Esty, eds. *Postcolonial Studies and Beyond*. Durham: Duke UP, 2005.

Lucretius Carus, Titus. *De Rerum Natura*. Trans. W.H.D. Rouse. Cambridge, Mass.: Harvard UP, 1975.

Luhrmann Tanya. *Persuasions of the Witch's Craft: Ritual Magic in Contemporary England*. Cambridge, Mass.: Harvard UP, 1991.

MacCabe, Colin et al "Salman Rushdie talks to the London Consortium about *The Satanic Verses*." (Interview.) *Critical Quarterly* 38.2 (1996): 51–70.

Mag-Well. Advertisement. <http://www.mtnhigh.com/mag_econ.html>.

——. *Halliburton To Offer Magnetic Fluid Conditioning Tool*. <http://www.mtnhigh.com/haliburt.html>. Accessed 23 June 2003.

Manoraj, Satiyesh, Greg Wilcox, Tosin Sulaiman, Verity Evans and Emma Pomfret. "Race in Britain: A 12 Page Special Report." *The Observer*. 25 November 2001.

Margolis, Mac. "Is Magical Realism Dead?" *Newsweek* 139.18. 6 May 2002: 52–55.

Martin, Gerald. Introduction. *Men of Maize* by Asturias. xi–xxxii.

——. *Journeys Through the Labyrinth: Latin American Fiction in the Twentieth Century*. London: Verso, 1989.

——. "On 'Magical' and Social Realism in García Márquez." Fiddian 100–120.

Martín, Marina. "Borges, the Apologist for Idealism." *Proceedings of the Twentieth World Congress of Philosophy*, Boston, Massachusetts, 10–15 August 1998. <http://www.bu.edu/wcp/Papers/Lati/LatiMart.htm>. Accessed 22 September 2008.

Marx, Karl and Friedrick Engels. *The Communist Manifesto*. London: Verso, 1998.

McCabe, Douglas: "'Higher Realities': New Age Spirituality in Ben Okri's The Famished Road." *Research in African Literatures* 36.4 (2005): 1–21.

McCarthy Brown, Karen. "Systematic Remembering, Systematic Forgetting: Ogou in Haiti." Barnes 65–89.

McClure, John. *Late Imperial Romance*. London: Verso, 1994.

McCrum, Robert. "Now You See It, Now You Don't. Has Magic Realism Run It's Course?" *The Observer Review* 12 May 2002: 18.

McGuirk, Bernard and Richard Cardwell. *Gabriel García Márquez: New Readings*. Cambridge: Cambridge University Press, 1987.

McHale, Brian. *Postmodernist Fiction*. New York and London: Methuen, 1987.

Meer, Ameena. "Salman Rushdie." (Interview). Reder 110–122.

Mendoza, Plinio Apuleyo. *The Fragrance of Guava: Conversations with Gabriel García Márquez*. London: Faber and Faber, 1988.

Menton, Seymour. *Magic Realism Rediscovered 1918–1981*. Philadelphia: Art Alliance Press, 1983.

——. *Historia verdadera del realismo mágico*. Mexico City: Fondo de Cultura Económica, 1998.

Minta, Stephen. *Gabriel García Márquez: Writer of Columbia*. London: Jonathan Cape, 1987.

Minzesheimer, Bob. "*Solitude* Gets Boost from Oprah Selection." *USA Today*. 28 January 2004. <http://www.usatoday.com/life/books/news/2004–01-28-solitude-oprah_x.htm>. Accessed 22 September 2008.

Mitchell, Jerome. *Scott, Chaucer, and Medieval Romance: A Study in Sir Walter Scott's Indebtedness to the Literature of the Middle Ages*. Lexington: University Press of Kentucky, 1987.

Neubauer, John. *Novalis*. Boston: Twayne, 1980

——. "Novalis." *Encyclopedia of Aesthetics*. Ed. Michael Kelly. Oxford: OUP, 1998. 379–382.

Novalis (Friedrich Freiherr von Hardenberg). "Allgemeine Brouillon." 1798–1799. Ed. G. Schultz. *Werke*. Munich: C.H. Beck, 1969.

——. *Schriften*. 4 Vols. Stuttgart: Kohlhammer, 1960.

Ogunsanwo, Olatubosun. "Intertextuality and Post-Colonial Literature in Ben Okri's *The Famished Road*." *Research in African Literatures* 26.1 (1995): 40–52.

——. Rev. of *Magical Realism in West African Fiction: Seeing with a Third Eye*, by Brenda Cooper. *Research in African Literatures* 31.2 (2000) 226–228.

Oliva, Renato. "Re-Dreaming the World: Ben Okri's Shamanic Realism." Linguanti, Casotti and Concilio 171–194.

Palencia-Roth, Michael. "Prisms of consciousness in the 'new worlds' of Columbus and García Márquez." Fiddian 144–160.

Paravisini-Gebert, Lizabeth. "The Haitian Revolution in Interstices and Shadows: A Re-Reading of Alejo Carpentier's *The Kingdom of This World*." *Research in African Literatures* 35.2 (2004): 114–127.

Pasztory, Esther. "Aztec Poetry." *The Nahua Newsletter* 35 (2003). <http://www. nahuanewsletter.org/nnarchive/newsletters/Nahua35.html#anchor333603>. Accessed 22 September 2008.

Pattanayak, Chandrabhanu. "Interview with Salman Rushdie." Reder 17–19.

Pinkard, Terry. *German Philosophy 1760–1860: The Legacy of Idealism*. Cambridge, Cambridge UP, 2002.

Plato. *Phaedo. Great Dialogues of Plato*. Ed Eric Warmington and Philip G. Rouse. Trans W.H.D. Rouse. Markham, Ontario: Penguin, 1984.

Prieto, Rene. *Miguel Ángel Asturias's Archeology of Return*. Cambridge: Cambridge UP, 1993.

Quayson, Ato. "Fecundities of the Unexpected: Magical Realism, Narrative and History." *The Encyclopedia of the Novel*. Vol. 1. Ed. Franco Moretti. Princeton: Princeton UP, 2006. 726–756.

——. *Postcolonialism: Theory, Practice or Process*. Cambridge: Polity Press, 2000.

——. *Strategic Transformations in Nigerian Writing*. Oxford: James Currey, 1997.

Radcliffe-Brown, A.R. *Structure and Function in Primitive Society*. London: Cohen and West, 1968.

Reder, Michael, ed. *Conversations with Salman Rushdie*. Jackson: University of Mississippi Press, 2000.

Rincón, Carlos: "The Peripheral Center of Postmodernism: On Borges, García Márquez, and Alterity." *Boundary 2: An International Journal of Literature and Culture* 20.3 (1993): 162–179.

Robinson, Lorna: "Latin America and Magical Realism: The Insomnia Plague in *Cien años de soledad*." *Neophilologus* 90.2 (2006): 249–269.

Roh, Franz. "Magic Realism: Post-Expressionism." Zamora and Faris 15–31.

——. *Nach Expressionismus, Magischer Realismus: Probleme der Neuesten Europäischen Europäischen Mallerei*. Leipzig: Klinkhardt und Biermann, 1925.

Ross, Jean. "*Contemporary Authors* Interview with Ben Okri." *Contemporary Authors* Vol. 138. Ed. Donna Olendorf. Detroit: Gale Research, 1993. 337–341.

Rushdie, Salman. "Gabriel García Márquez." *Imaginary Homelands*. London: Granta, 1992. 299–307.

——. *Step Across this Line: Collected Non-Fiction, 1992–2002*. London: Jonathan Cape, 2002.

Sahagún, B. de. *Historia general de las cosas de Nueva España*. Ed. A.M. Garibay. 4 Vols. Mexico City: Porrúa, 1969.

Sala-Molins, Louis. *Dark Side of the Light: Slavery and the French Enlightenment*. Translated by John Conteh-Morgan. Minneapolis: University of Minnesota Press, 2006.

Saldívar, José David: "Ideology and Deconstruction in Macondo." *Latin American Literary Review* 13.25 (1985): 29–43.

Sarlo, Beatriz. *Jorge Luis Borges: A Writer on the Edge*. 1993. Ed. John King. London: Verso, 2006.

Schroeder, Shannin. *Rediscovering Magical Realism in the Americas*. Westport; London: Praeger, 2004.

Shaw, Donald L. Review of Camayd-Freixas, Erik, *"Realismo mágico y primitivismo* and Menton, Seymour. *Historia verdadera del realismo mágico."* *Hispanic Review* 67.4 (1999): 577–579.

Shklovsky, Viktor. "Art As Technique." *Russian Formalist Criticism: Four Essays*. Ed. and trans. L. T. Lemon & M. J. Reis. Lincoln, NE: University of Nebraska Press, 1965.

Slemon, Stephen. "Magic Realism as Postcolonial Discourse." Zamora and Faris 407–426.

Smale, David, Ed. *Salman Rushdie: Midnight's Children and The Satanic Verses: A Reader's Guide to Essential Criticism*. Cambridge: Icon Books, 2001.

Soyinka, Wole. *Myth, Literature and the African World*. Cambridge: Cambridge UP, 1976.

Spengler, Oswald. *Decline of the West*. Trans. Charles Francis Atkinson. London: G. Allen and Unwin, 1926.

Sturrock, John. *Paper Tigers: The Ideal Fictions of Jorge Luis Borges*. Oxford: Clarendon Press, 1977.

Suleri, Sara. *The Rhetoric of English India*. Chicago: Chicago UP, 1992.

Tambiah, Stanley. "Form and Meaning of Magical Acts." *Culture, Thought and Social Action: An Anthropological Perspective*. Cambridge, Mass.: Harvard UP, 1985. 60–86.

——. *Magic, Science, Religion and the Scope of Rationality*. Cambridge: Cambridge UP, 1990.

Ten Kortenaar, Neil. "Midnight's Children and the Allegory of History." *ARIEL* 26.2 (1995): 41–62.

Thomas, Keith. *Religion and the Decline of Magic: Studies in Popular Beliefs in Sixteenth and Seventeenth Century England*. London: Weidenfeld and Nicolson, 1971.

Thornhill, John. "Magic Realist Economy." *Financial Times* 1 August 1998: 1.

Tobin, Patricia: "The Autumn of the Signifier: The Deconstructionist Moment of García Márquez." *Latin American Literary Review* 13.25 (1985): 65–78.

Todorov, Tzvetan. *The Fantastic: A Structural Approach to a Literary Genre*. Trans. Richard Howard. Ithaca: Cornell UP, 1975.

Tylor, E.B. *Primitive Culture: Researches into the Development of Mythology, Philosophy, Religion, Langauge, Art and Custom*. Vol. 1. London: John Murray, 1873.

Valdez Moses, Michael. "Magical Realism at World's End." *Literary Imagination: The Review of the Association of Literary Scholars and Critics*. 3.1 (2001): 105–133.

Vargas Llosa, Mario. "Amadís in America." *Fiddian* 56–57.

Waisman, Sergio. *Borges and Translation: the Irrverence of the Periphery.* Lewisburg: Bucknell University Press, 2005.

Warnes, Christopher. "Magical Realism and the Legacy of German Idealism." *Modern Language Review* 101.2 (2006): 488–498.

——. "Avatars of Amadis: Magical Realism as Postcolonial Romance." *Journal of Commonwealth Literature* 40.3 (2005): 7–20.

——. "Naturalizing the Supernatural: Faith, Irreverence and Magical Realism." *Literature Compass* 2.1 (2005): 1–16.

——. "The Hermeneutics of Vagueness: Magical Realism in Current Literary Critical Discourse." *Journal of Postcolonial Writing* 41.1 (2005): 1–13.

——. "Ben Okri." *World Writers in English.* Ed. Jay Parini. New York: Charles Scribner's Sons, 2003. 459–476.

Watt, Ian. *The Rise of the Novel: Studies in Defoe, Richardson and Fielding.* London: Chatto & Windus, 1957.

Watt, Nicholas and Martin Wainright. "New Race Speech Blow to Hague." *The Guardian.* 28 March 2001: 10.

Weiner, Adam. *By Authors Possessed: The Demonic Novel in Russia.* Evanston: Northwestern UP, 1998.

Wheeler, Kathleen, ed. *German Aesthetic and Literary Criticism: The Romantic Ironists and Goethe.* Cambridge: Cambridge UP, 1984.

Wilkinson, Jane. *Talking with African Writers.* London: James Currey, 1992. 77–110.

Williamson, Edwin. "Magical Realism and the Theme of Incest in *One Hundred Years of Solitude.*" McGuirk and Cardwell 45–63.

——. *Borges: A Life.* London: Penguin, 2004.

Winfrey, Oprah. "Novel: One Hundred Years of Solitude." <http://www.oprah.com/obc_classic/featbook/oyos/novel/oyos_novel_synopsis.jhtml>. Accessed 22 September 2008.

Wolin, Richard. *The Seduction of Unreason: The Intellectual Romance with Fascism from Nietzsche to Postmodernism.* Princeton: Princeton University Press, 2004.

Wright, Derek. "Interpreting the Interspace: Ben Okri's *The Famished Road.*" *CRNLE Review* 1–2 (1995): 18–30.

——. "Postmodernism as Realism: Magic History in Recent West African Fiction." *Contemporary African Fiction.* Ed. Derek Wright. Bayreuth: Bayreuth African Studies, 1997. 181–207.

——. "Pre- and Post-Modernity in Recent West African Fiction." *Commonwealth Essays and Studies* 21.2 (1999): 5–12.

Young, Richard. *Carpentier: El reino de este mundo.* London: Grant and Cutler, 1983.

Young, Robert. *Colonial Desire: Colonial Desire: Hybridity in Theory, Culture, and Race.* London: Routledge, 1995.

——. *White Mythologies: Writing History and the West. London and New York*: London: Routledge, 1990.

Zamora, Lois Parkinson and Wendy B. Faris, eds. *Magical Realism: Theory, History, Community.* Durham and London: Duke UP, 1995.

Zamora, Lois Parkinson. "Swords and Silver Rings: Magical Object in the Work of Jorge Luis Borges and Gabriel García Márquez." Hart and Ouyang 28–45.

——. "Magical Romance/Magical Realism: Ghosts in U.S. and Latin American Fiction." Zamora and Faris 497–550.

Index

Achebe, Chinua, 134, 147
Adorno, Theodor, 60, 63
Aeschylus, 97, 162n1
aesthetics, 5, 10–11, 18–19, 21, 24,
    69, 85, 99, 102, 114, 124, 135–6,
    147, 153, 165n6
Ahmad, Aijaz, 100, 157n7
Aizenberg, Edna, 133
Akira, Kurosawa, 162n1
Alain-Fournier, 31
alchemy, 86–7
Algeria, 151
Allende, Isabel, 2, 44, 99
Althusser, Louis, 150
Amadís of Gaul, 32, 35, 37–8
animism, 89, 128, 148
anthropology, 8, 10, 49, 93,
    130, 153
Appiah, Kwame Anthony, 128–9,
    166n10
Apuleius, 102, 109, 110–11, 115,
    116–17, 122, 164n10
Arabian Nights, 162n1
Aravamudan, Srinivas, 102
Argentina, 13, 46–7, 77, 92
Aristotle, 45
Asimov, Isaac, 97, 162n1
Asturias, Miguel Ángel, 48–61 and
    passim
  and Borges, 48, 158n9
  and Carpentier, 28, 41, 69, 72, 78
  and ecology, 51
  and faith-based magical realism,
      11–12, 45, 152
  and García Márquez, 5, 29, 76, 78,
      80, 82, 90–1, 96
  and idealism, 58–60
  and identity, 5, 42, 46, 151
  and Jungian elements, 54
  and language, 53

  and Latin American literature, 29,
      41, 158n5
  Mayan and Aztec sources, 49–50,
      158n6
  and myth, 15, 55–7, 71–2
  and Okri, 133, 146–8
  in Paris, 28
  and representation of women,
      158nn4,11
  and Rushdie, 15, 118
  and stereotype in, 59
  and structure, 54–5
  and surrealism, 49
  Los ojos de los enterrados, 58
  Men of Maize, 48–61 and *passim*
Aztecs, 49–50, 52, 148, 158

Balasubramanian, Radha, 163n6
Bandele-Thomas, Biyi, 124
Baranczak, Stanislaw, 162n1
Barber, Karin, 158
Barker, Francis, Peter Hulme and
    Margaret Iversen, 1
Barnes, Sandra T., 160n19
Barrie, J.M., 162n1
Bassi, Shaul, 98
Bataille, George, 60
Bay of Pigs invasion, 92
Beiser, Fredric, 21–3, 44
Bentham, Jeremy, 162n1
Berkeley, George, 42, 44–5, 48
Bhabha, Homi K., 1, 99–100, 113,
    120–2, 133, 164n9
binaries, 6–7, 39, 48, 94, 97
Blake, William, 102, 105, 108,
    162n1
Boccaccio, Giovanni, 115
Bollywood, 97
Bonaparte, Pauline, 66
Bontempelli, Massimo, 20, 27–9, 62